MONSTER ISLAND

A Zombie Novel

David Wellington

snowbooks

Proudly Published in 2007 by
Snowbooks Ltd.

1

Snowbooks Ltd.
120 Pentonville Road
London
N1 9JN
Tel: 0207 837 6482
Fax: 0207 837 6348
email: info@snowbooks.com
www.snowbooks.com

British Library Cataloguing in Publication Data
A catalogue record for this book is available from the
British Library.

ISBN13 978-1-905005-48-2

Printed in Great Britain by J. H. Haynes & Co. Ltd.

MONSTER ISLAND

A Zombie Novel

Part
One

Chapter One

Osman leaned over the rail and spat into the grey sea before turning again to shout orders at his first mate Yusuf. The GPS had died two weeks out to sea, and in the fog we would be lucky not to crash into the side of Manhattan at full speed. With no harbor lights to follow and nothing at all on the radio he could only rely on dead reckoning and intuition. He shot me an anxious look. "*Naga amus*, Dekalb," he said, *shut up*, though I hadn't said a word.

He ran from one side of the deck to the other, pushing girls out of his way. I could barely see him through the mist when he reached the starboard rail, ropy coils of vapor wrapping around his feet, splattering the wood and glass of the foredeck with tiny beads of dew. The girls chattered and shrieked like they always did but in the claustrophobic fog they sounded like carrion birds squabbling over some prize giblets.

Yusuf shouted something from the wheelhouse, something Osman clearly didn't want to hear. "*Hooyaa da was!*" the captain screamed back. Then, in English, "Quarter steam! Bring her down to quarter steam!" He must have sensed something out in the murk.

For whatever reason I turned then to look ahead and to

port. The only thing over that way was a trio of the girls. In their uniforms they looked like a girl band gone horribly wrong. Grey head scarves, navy school blazers, plaid skirts, combat boots. AK-47s slung over their shoulders. Sixteen years old and armed to the teeth, the Glorious Girl Army of the Free Women's Republic of Somaliland. One of the girls raised her arm, pointed at something. She looked back at me as if for validation, but I couldn't see anything out there. Then I did and I nodded agreeably. A hand rising from high above the sea. A bloated, enormous green hand holding a giant torch, the gold at the top dull in the fog.

"This is New York, yes, Mr. Dekalb? That is the famous Statue of Liberty." Ayaan didn't look me in the eye, but she wasn't looking at the statue, either. She had the most English of any of the girls so she'd acted as my interpreter on the voyage but we weren't exactly what you'd call close. Ayaan wasn't close with anybody, unless you counted her weapon. She was supposed to be a crack shot with that AK and a ruthless killer. She still couldn't help but remind me of my daughter Sarah and the maniacs I'd left her with back in Mogadishu. At least Sarah would only have to worry about human dangers. I had a personal guarantee from Mama Halima, the warlord in charge of the FWRS, that she would be protected from the supernatural. Ayaan ignored my stare. "They showed us the picture of the statue in the *madrassa*. They made us spit on the picture."

I ignored her as best I could and watched as the statue materialized out of the fog. Lady Liberty looked alright, about the way I'd left her five years before, the last time I'd come to New York. Long before the Epidemic began.

I guess I'd been expecting to see something, some sign of damage or decay but she had already gone green with verdigris long before I was born. In the distance through the mist I could make out the pediment, the star-shaped base of the statue. It seemed impossibly real, hallucinatorily perfect and unblemished. In Africa I'd seen so much horror I think I'd forgotten what the West could be like with its sheen of normalcy and health.

"*Fiir*!" one of the girls at the rail shouted. Ayaan and I pushed forward and stared into the mist. We could make out most of Liberty Island now and the shadow of Ellis Island beyond. The girls were pointing with agitation at the walkway that ringed Liberty, at the people there. American clothes, American hair exposed to the elements. Tourists, perhaps. Perhaps not.

"Osman," I shouted, "Osman, we're getting too close," but the captain just yelled for me to shut up again. On the island I saw hundreds of them, hundreds of people. They waved at us, their arms moving stiffly like something from a silent movie. They pushed toward the railing, to get closer to us. As the trawler rolled closer I could see them crawling over one another in their desperation to touch us, to swarm onboard.

I thought maybe, just maybe they were alright, maybe they'd run to Liberty Island for refuge and been safe there and were just waiting for us, waiting for rescue but then I smelled them and I knew. I knew they weren't alright at all. Give me your tired, your poor, your wretched refuse, my brain repeated over and over, a mantra. My brain wouldn't stop. Give me your huddled masses. Huddled masses yearning to breathe. "Osman! Turn away!"

One of them toppled over the side of the railing,

maybe pushed by the straining crowd behind. A woman in a bright red windbreaker, her hair a matted lump on one side of her head. She tried desperately to dog-paddle toward the trawler but she was hindered by the fact that she kept reaching up, reaching up one bluish hand to try to grab at us. She wanted us so badly. Wanted to reach us, to touch us.

Give me your tired, your so very, very tired. I couldn't take this, didn't know what I had thought I could accomplish coming here. I couldn't look at another one. Another dead person clawing for my face.

One of the girls opened up with her rifle, a controlled burst, three shots. *Chut chut chut* chopping up the grey water. *Chut chut chut* and the bullets tore through the red windbreaker, tore open the woman's neck. *Chut chut chut* and her head popped open like an overripe melon and she sank, slipping beneath the water without so much as a splash or a bubble and still, pressed up against the railing on Liberty Island, a hundred more reached for us. Reached with pleading skeletal hands to clutch at us, to take what was theirs.

Your huddled masses. Give me your dead, I thought. The ship heeled hard over to one side as Osman finally brought her around, nosed around the edge of Liberty Island and kept us from running up on the rocks. Give me your wretched dead, yearning to devour, your shambling masses. Give me. That was what they were thinking, wasn't it? The living dead over there on the island. If there was any spark left in their brains, any thought possible to decayed neurons it was this: give me. Give me. Give me your life, your warmth, your flesh. Give me.

Chapter Two

Shattered light and pale shadows swirled before Gary's eyes. He couldn't remember opening them, could barely remember a time when they weren't open. Slowly he was able to resolve the image. He could see that he was looking up from underneath at a molten drift of ice cubes. Something hard and intrusive was pushing air into his lungs in a rhythmic pumping that was not so much painful. No, his body was half-frozen and he didn't feel any pain at all. But it was incredibly uncomfortable.

He reared up so fast that spots swam before his eyes and with cold-numbed fingers tore at the mask taped across his face, tore it away and then pulled, pulled at an impossibly long length of tubing that came out of his chest, from somewhere deep down with a tugging sensation then a tearing but still there was no pain.

He looked around at the bathroom tiles, at the tub full of ice and yellowish water. At the tubes attached to his left arm. He tore those away, too, leaving a deep gouge in his arm when the shunt there tore open his rubbery wet skin. No blood seeped from the wound.

No. No, of course not.

Gary began a careful self-check of his faculties. The

spots that danced in front of his eyes to the tune of tinnitus weren't going away. There was a buzzing at the back of his head. It made him want to reach for the telephone. Not a sign of brain damage, that impulse, just simple Pavlovian response, of course. You heard a ringing tone in that particular frequency and you rushed to answer it, the way you'd been doing all your life. There weren't any telephones anymore, of course. He would never hear a ringing telephone again. He would have to unlearn the behavior.

His legs felt a bit weak. Nothing to panic about. His brain. . . had survived, had come through almost unscathed. It had worked! Before he could celebrate, though, he had to assuage his vanity. He stumped over to the sink, held onto the porcelain with both hands. Looked up and into the mirror.

A trifle cyanotic, maybe. Blueness in his jaw, at his temples. Very pale. His eyes were shot with red where capillaries had burst open. . . perhaps that would heal, in time. If he could heal anymore. A vein under his left cheek lay dead and swollen so blue it was almost black. Peering, prodding, stretching the skin of his face with his fingers he found other clots and occlusions, weblike traceries of dead veins. Like the veins in a piece of marble, he thought, or a nice piece of Stilton. Without the veins a piece of marble is just granite. Without the blue veins a piece of Stilton is just plain cheese. The dead veins gave his face a certain character, maybe, a certain gravitas.

It was better than he'd hoped for.

He pushed against his wrist with two fingers, found no pulse. He closed his eyes and listened and realized for the first time that he wasn't breathing. Primordial urges swelled up in his reptilian cortex, inbred terrors of drowning and suffocation and his chest spasmed, flexed, tried to suck in air but couldn't.

Panicking—knowing it was panic, unable to stop— he knocked over the stolen dialysis machine and heard it smash on the floor as he pushed his way out of the enclosed bathroom, pushed his way out toward light and air. His legs twisted beneath him, threatening to topple him at any second, his arms stretched out, the muscles straining, stretching taut as steel cables beneath his cold skin.

He stumbled forward until his legs gave way, until he smashed down onto the white shag carpet. His body heaved and shuddered trying to catch a breath, any puff of air at all. Just instinct, he screamed in his mind, it's just reflex and it'll stop, it'll stop soon. His cheek rubbed back and forth across the shag and he felt the heat of friction as his body moved spasmodically.

Eventually his system quieted, his body gave in. His lungs stopped moving and he lay still, energy gone. Kind of hungry. He looked up, looked at the bluest sky beyond his windows. The white fleecy clouds, passing by.

It was all going to work out.

Chapter Three

Six weeks earlier:

Sarah slept, finally, under the threadbare blanket they'd given her when I bitched long enough. She was learning to sleep through anything. Good kid. I kept an arm around her, shielding her whether or not there was any immediate threat. It had become an instinct, to keep as much of my body between her and the world as I could. Even before the Epidemic I'd done that. We'd seen things in Africa nobody was supposed to, discovered in ourselves resources that just shouldn't have been there. I had done things. . . it didn't matter. I'd gotten us out of Nairobi. I'd gotten us across the border to Somalia. There had been three of us and now there were two. But we made it. Sarah's mother was not around anymore but we made it. We made it to Somalia, only to be picked up by a bunch of mercenaries at a roadblock and dumped in this cell with a bunch of other Westerners. Thrown here to await the pleasure of the local warlord.

Fuck it. I wouldn't blame myself for what I'd done. We were alive. We were still among the living. We were in the happy minority.

"I can't understand it," Toshiro said. One sleeve of his

suit was ripped at the shoulder, revealing a good quarter-inch of fluffy padding underneath but he kept his tie perfectly knotted at his neck. Even in the heat of the cell he was a salaryman. He waved his cell phone around the room. "I'm getting a perfect signal. Four bars! Why can I not raise Yokohama? No one in the office is answering. In the old economy we never let this occur!"

In the far corner the German backpackers clutched one another and tried not to look at him. They knew where Yokohama had gone as well as I did, but in those first bad days of the Epidemic you didn't talk about that. It wasn't so much a matter of denial as of scale. As far as we knew, all of Europe was gone. It might as well not be there anymore. Russia was gone. By the time you got to wondering where America went there just wasn't any more room for it in your brain. A world without an America just couldn't happen—the global economy would collapse. Every twopenny warlord and dictator in the Third World would have a field day. It just wasn't possible. It would mean global chaos. It would mean the end of history as we knew it.

Which was exactly what had happened.

The civilized countries, the ones with bicameral parliaments and honest police forces and good infrastructure and the rule of law and wealth and privilege, the entire West—when the dead came home they couldn't hold out. It was only the pisspots of the world that made it. The most dangerous places. The unstable countries, the feudal states, the anarchic backwaters, places you wouldn't dare walk out the door without a gun, where bodyguards were fashion accessories—those places did a lot better in the end.

From what we'd heard the last refuge of humanity was the Middle East. Afghanistan and Pakistan were getting along just fine. Somalia didn't even have a government. There were more mercenaries in the country than farmhands. Somalia was pretty much okay. I used to be a weapons inspector, with the UN. We used to have a map of the world in my office in Nairobi. It showed the countries of the world shaded various colors to depict how many firearms there were per capita there. You could take the legend off that map now and put a new one in its place: World Population Density.

"Four bars!" Toshiro whined. "I helped build this network, it is all digital! Dekalb—you must have some news for me, yes? You must know what is happening? I must be reconnected. You will help me with that. You have to help me. You are UN. You have to help anyone who asks!"

I shook my head but not with much conviction. So tired, so hot. So dehydrated in that little cell. We'd never wanted for water in Kenya before the Epidemic, the three of us. When the dead started coming back to life. In Nairobi with our valet and our chauffeur and our gardener there had been a fountain in our enclosed little world and we kept it splashing all year round. Although she knew it was for the best, Sarah hadn't wanted to leave to go to the International Boarding School in Geneva next year, she'd liked Africa so much.

Jesus. Geneva. I had a lot of friends there, colleagues at the UN field office there. What must it have been like? Switzerland had some guns. Not enough. Geneva had to be gone.

The door opened and hot light spilled across all of us.

A silhouette of a girl gestured at me. For a second I didn't understand—I had thought I was going to be in the cell for good. Then I stumbled to my feet and picked up Sarah in my arms.

"Dekalb! You ask them about my connection! Damn you if you don't!"

I nodded, a sort of farewell, a sort of assent. I followed the girl soldier out of the cell and into the sun-colored courtyard beyond. The smell of burning bodies was thick but better than the smell of the latrine bucket in the cell. Sarah pushed her face against my chest and I held her close. I didn't know what was going to happen next. It could be our turn to get some food, the first we'd had in two days. The girl soldier might be leading me to a torture chamber or a refugee center with hot showers and clean bedding and some kind of promise for the future. This could be a summons to an execution.

If Geneva was gone, so was the Geneva Convention.

"Come!" the soldier said.

I went.

Chapter Four

Six weeks earlier, continued:

A Chinese-built helicopter stirred up the dust in the courtyard with its lazily turning rotor. Whoever had just arrived must be important—I hadn't seen an aircraft of any kind in weeks. In the shade of the barracks building a group of huddled women in khimars and modest dresses held their hands over the mortars where they'd been grinding grain.

The girl soldier led me past a pair of "technicals"—commercial pickup trucks with heavy machine guns mounted in their beds. A particularly Somali brand of nastiness. Normally technicals were crewed by mercenaries, but these had been hastily emblazoned with Mama Halima's colors: light blue and yellow like an Easter egg. The vehicles belonged to the Free Women's Republic now. Girl soldiers loitered around the trucks, their rifles slung loosely in their arms, chewing distractedly on *qat* and waiting for the order to shoot somebody.

Past the technicals we walked around a corpsefire. It was a lot bigger than it had been when Sarah and I were first brought to the compound. The soldiers had wrapped the bodies in white sheets and then packed them with camel dung as an accelerant. Gasoline was too valuable to waste. The fumes coming off the fire were terrible and I could feel Sarah clench against my chest but our guide didn't even flinch.

I tried to summon up my identity, tried to draw some strength from my professional outrage. Jesus. Child soldiers. Kids as young as ten—babies—dragged out of school and given guns, given drugs to keep them happy and made to fight in wars they couldn't begin to understand. I'd worked so hard to outlaw that obscenity and now I depended on them for my daughter's safety.

We entered a low brick building that had taken a bad artillery hit and never been repaired. The dust billowed in the sunlight streaming through the collapsed roof. At the far end of a dark hallway we came to a kind of command post. Weapons lay in carefully sorted piles on the floor while a heap of cell phones and transistor radios littered a wooden table where a woman in military fatigues sat, staring listlessly at a piece of paper. She was perhaps twenty-five, a little younger than me, and she wore no covering on her head at all. In the Islamic world that was a message I was expected to get immediately. She didn't look up as she spoke to me. "You're Dekalb. With the United Nations," she said, reading off a list. "And daughter." She gestured and our guide went and sat down beside her.

I didn't bother assenting. "You have foreign nationals in that cell who are being treated in an inhumane fashion. I have a list of demands."

"I'm not interested," she began.

I cut her off. "We need food, first of all. Clean food. Better sanitation. There's more."

She fixed me with a glance at my midsection that I felt like a stabbing knife. This was not a woman to be trifled with.

"If it's still possible we need to be afforded communication with our various consulates. We need–"

"Your daughter is black." She hadn't been looking at me at all. She'd been looking at Sarah. My mouth filled with a bitter taste. "But you're white. Her mother?"

I breathed hard through my nose for a minute. "Kenyan. Dead." She looked me in the eyes then and it just came out. "We found her—I mean, I found her rooting in our garbage one night, she'd had a fever but we thought she would make it, I brought her inside but I didn't let her out of my sight, I couldn't—"

"You knew she was one of the dead."

"Yes."

"Did you dispose of her properly?"

My whole body twitched at the thought. "We—I locked her in the bathroom. We left, then. The servants had already gone, the block was half-deserted. The police were nowhere to be found. Even the army couldn't hold out much longer."

"They didn't. Nairobi was overrun two days after you left, according to my intelligence." The woman sighed, a horribly human sound. I could understand this woman as a deadly bureaucrat. I could understand her as a soldier. I couldn't handle it if she expressed any sympathy. I begged her silently not to pity me.

Lucky me.

"We can't feed you and this installation isn't defensible so we can't let you stay here, either," she said. "And I don't have time to argue about your list of demands. The unit is decamping tonight as part of a tactical withdrawal. If you want to come with us you have five minutes to justify your keep. You're with the UN. A relief worker? We need food and medical supplies, more than anything."

"No. I was a weapons inspector. What about Sarah?"

"Your daughter? We'll take her. Mama Halima loves all the orphan girls of Africa." It sounded like a political slogan. The fact that Sarah wasn't an orphan didn't need to be clarified—if I failed now she would be. It was at that moment I realized what being one of the living meant. It meant doing whatever it took not to be one of the dead.

"There's a cache of weapons—small arms, mostly, some light antitank weapons—just over the border—I can take you there, show you where to dig." We'd lacked the money and equipment to destroy the cache when we found it. We'd put the guns in a sealed bunker undergound in hopes of destroying them one day. Stupid us.

"Weapons," she said. She glanced at the pile of rifles on the floor by my feet. "Weapons we have. We are in no danger of running short on ammunition."

I clutched Sarah hard enough to wake her, then. She wiped her nose on my shirt and looked up at me but she kept quiet. Good kid.

The officer met my gaze. "Your daughter will be protected. Fed, educated."

"In a *madrassa*?" She nodded. As far as I knew that was the current limit of the Somali educational system. Daily recitation of the Koran and endless prayers. At least she would learn to read. There was something impacted in my heart just then, something so tight I couldn't relax it ever. The knowledge that this was the best Sarah could hope for, that any protests I made, any suggestion that maybe this wasn't enough was unrealistic and counterproductive.

In a couple of years when she was old enough to hold a gun my daughter was going to become a child soldier and that was the best I could give her.

"The prisoners," I said, done with that train of thought. I had to be hard now. "You have to leave us some weapons when you go. Give us a fighting chance."

"Yes. But I'm not done with you." She glanced at her sheet of paper again. "You worked for the United Nations. You were part of the international relief community."

"I guess," I said.

"Perhaps you can help me find something. Something we need most desperately." She kept talking then but for a while I couldn't hear anything, I was too busy imagining my own death. When I realized she wasn't going to kill me I snapped back to attention. "It's Mama Halima, you see." She put down her paper and looked at me, really looked at me. Not like I was an unpleasant task she had to deal with but like I was a human being. "She has succumbed to a condition all too prevalent in Africa. She has become dependent on certain chemicals. Chemicals we are dangerously short of."

Drugs. The local warlord had a habit, and she needed a mule to go pick up her supply of dope. Somebody desperate enough to go and pick up her fix for her. I would do it, of course. No question.

"What kind of 'chemicals' are we talking about? Heroin? Cocaine?"

She pursed her lips like she was wondering whether she'd made a mistake in picking me for this mission. "No. More like AZT."

Chapter Five

Five weeks earlier:

Mama Halima had AIDS—a condition far too prevalent in Africa, indeed. It was up to me to find the drugs she needed, the combination of pills that could keep her viral load down and keep her from showing weakness. It meant a new life for Sarah, and maybe even for me. They asked me to identify hospitals and supply dumps, the headquarters of international medical aid organizations and clinics set up by the World Health Organization. I did what I could, of course. I drew crosses on maps and then they took me where I had indicated and kept me alive while I looted.

In Egypt, in the darkness rifles cracked, one by one. Out past the wire bodies spun and fell. I didn't have to get close enough to see their faces. I was glad for that.

In the stiff breeze coming off the desert the tents shook on their aluminum poles and ripples passed over them. On top of each tent a red cross had been painted so it would be visible from the air. Inside, by the light of kerosene lamps, girls no older than Sarah overturned crate after crate, pouring their contents out onto the packed earth floor. Plastic bags full of antibiotics, painkillers in foil pouches, insulin in preloaded hypodermics. I sorted through the treasures one by one, reading the inscriptions printed in boldface type on each label. The Red Cross had deserted this place and they'd left a treasure trove behind. How many people out there in the African night were dying in that very second for lack of a few tablets of erythromycin?

An eighteen-year-old girl in a military uniform stepped through the flap of the tent and studied my face. I crouched among the spilled drugs and shook my head. "Not yet," I told her.

Four weeks earlier:

Two days outside of *Dar es Salaam* we found a field hospital set up by *Médecins Sans Frontières* in the remains of a fortified camp. The relief station sat underneath an overgrown hill. Trees screened the narrow bunker-style entrance. Machine-gun nests stood guard, now abandoned to the rain. Inside the station, underneath the earth, we shone flashlights into every corner, lit up every surgery, every examination room. In the spooky dimness my light kept catching on things, shadows in the shape of human bodies, glints, reflections of my own face in bedpans, in scrub sinks.

There was nothing there. Not a pill, not a pinch of medicinal powders. Professionals had taken the place apart, stripped it down and left nothing behind but fear and shadows. We emerged back into the sunlight and suddenly the girl soldiers around me had their weapons out. Something was wrong—they felt it.

I couldn't sense anything at all. Then I could—a noise, a crack of twigs broken under the weight of a human foot.

A moment later I caught the smell.

I was beginning to learn a little Somali. I knew what the commander of the girls called for them to protect me at all costs. I wasn't too flattered. It had been pointed out to me more than once that I was the only one who knew where the drugs were.

We headed back down to the water in a loose formation with me at its center. From time to time somebody discharged a weapon. I couldn't see anything through the trees. We made it.

Three weeks earlier:

"How many millions of people in Africa suffer from AIDS?" I demanded. "How many of them had the same idea we did?"

"For your sake, Dekalb, I should hope not all." Ifiyah, the commander of the teenage soldiers, made a complex gesture. Behind her the troops lined up. Behind us the Oxfam headquarters at Maputo stood dark and deserted. Like every other fucking building in Africa. We had seen some survivors in Kenya, six days earlier. There were none in Mozambique, as far as we could tell. We'd come down by helicopter and as we flew over the jungle we had seen nothing moving, nothing at all.

The dead were out there. They were probably closer than I would like. Our plan—my plan—had been to hit the Oxfam center hard and fast, and get out before any undead bastard could smell us and wander over to get a snack. One look inside the facilities at Maputo, however, had convinced us all we were wasting our time. The place had been gutted by fire. Nothing remained of the supplies inside but cold ash and the occasional warm ember.

"There are no AIDS drugs left," I shouted at Ifiyah's back as she stepped away from me. Her rifle swayed on her shoulder but she didn't turn to face me. "Not here. Not now." I was too tired to have this fight. I'd been sleeping maybe three hours a night. Not from lack of opportunity. From pure terror.

"So what is it then that you might suggest?" she asked me. Her voice was dangerously soft.

"I don't know. I don't know any place else to look, not in Africa." Even the Oxfam site had been a stretch. Oxfam was a development organization—they had never stockpiled drugs. "There's only one place that I know that has what you're looking for."

"A place you are sure of? Why are you not saying it sooner?" She did turn to look at me then.

"Because it's about half a world away," I told her. It was a sick joke, I knew. It was cold comfort I had to offer, the surety that what she wanted existed, even if it was in a place impossible to reach.

I never thought she would take me up on it. "The UN building," I told her.

"Which UN building now? We have seen so many of these, you and I, in one fortnight." She squinted at me like she knew I was joking but she didn't get it.

"No, no, the UN Headquarters building. The Secretariat Building, in New York, in America. There's a whole medical suite on the fifth floor. I used to go there every year for a flu shot. It's like a whole miniature hospital in there. They have drugs for every condition you could possibly name, anything a delegate might contract. There's a whole chronic-care ward. HIV medication like you wouldn't believe."

She showed me her teeth and looked confused, but only for a second. "Very well," she said.

"Come on, I was just kidding," I told her an hour later when we were loaded back into the helicopters and headed back for Mogadishu. "We can't go to New York City for these drugs. That's crazy."

"I will gladly do some crazy thing, to save her," Ifiyah told me. Her eyes were set, calm. "I will go around the world, yes. And I will touch the face of death, yes."

"But think for a second! You can't just fly to New York anymore. There's no safe way to land a plane over there."

"Then we must take boats."

I shook my head. "Even then, even then—how many dead people are there in Manhattan right now?"

"We can fight them," she told me. Just like that.

"You've fought dozens of them before. Maybe a hundred at one time. There will be ten million of them in New York." I was hoping that would scare her. It scared me plenty. She just shrugged.

"Have you ever been hearing of what infibulation is?" she asked me. "Yes? It is a common practice in Somalia. Or it was."

I shook my head, not wanting to get distracted. I knew where this was headed and I couldn't let the conversation derail. "I know what it is, it's a kind of female circumcision—"

Ifiyah interrupted me. "Circumcision of the clitoris is but one first part. Then the men take the vagina and they sew it shut. They leave one small hole for urine and menses to pass. When the girl is married some stitches are torn out, so she can be fucked as the husband pleases.

Many girls gain infections from this lovely process. We have many more women die in their childbirth here than most places. Many more who die upon receiving their first period."

"That's horrible. I've spent my life working against barbarities like that," I assured her, trying to get some ground back under my feet.

She didn't want to hear it. "Mama Halima kills any man who tries to do this. She made it illegal. It was too late for me, but not for my kumayo sisters." She gestured broadly at the girls strapped into the crew seats. "They did not get your barbarity. So if you are asking me, will I do the mad thing and go to America to get these pills to save Mama Halima, I think you now have an answer."

What could I do after that but hang my head in shame?

Chapter Six

Now:

Gary sat on the floor of his kitchenette, surrounded by wrappers and boxes—all of them empty. He licked the inside of a wrapper that used to hold a granola bar, dug out the tiny crumbs with his tongue. All gone.

He was hungrier than ever.

He could feel his stomach distend. He knew he was full, fuller than he'd ever been in life. It didn't seem to matter. Being among the dead meant always being hungry, obviously. It meant this gnawing inside of you that you could never quench. It explained so much. He had wondered—in his old life—why they had attacked people, even people they knew, people they loved. Maybe they had tried to stop themselves. The hunger was just too great. The need to eat, to consume, was awesome and frightening. Was this what he had consigned himself to?

Even as he considered this he was rising to his feet, his hands reaching for the cupboards. His fingers were clumsy now. That worried him. Had he damaged his nervous system too much? His fingers obeyed him enough to get the door open. The cupboards were almost empty and he felt a gulf open inside him, a desperate dark place that needed to be filled. Food. He needed food.

He'd thought he was done with the things of life. That had been the point. The age of humanity was over and the time of Homo mortis had come. The hospital had been in chaos, dying patients rising to grab at the healthy, policemen discharging their weapons in the halls, the power fluctuating wildly. He had walked out the emergency-room doors with a laundry cart full of expensive equipment and nobody had even tried to stop him.

He found a box of rigatoni, took it down from the shelf. The gas stove didn't work. How was he going to cook it? His thumbnail dug into the carton's flap anyway. Wishful thinking.

There had been no other option. You either joined them or you fed them—and they didn't stop coming, you could run and hide but they were everywhere. There were more of them every day and less places to turn to, fewer sections of the city that the National Guard could claim were safely quarantined. Even after they initiated proper disposal protocol for the dead. The mayor had given up, they said. Certainly he had left the public eye. The only thing on television was a public-service announcement from the CDC about the proper way to trepan your loved ones. Fires burning everywhere outside the police lines. Smoke and screaming. Like September 11, but in every neighborhood of the city at once.

Gary pried a noodle out of the box and stuffed it between his lips. Maybe he'd suck on it until it got soft, he thought.

Maybe it didn't have to be so bad, Gary had thought. If you were going to die anyway, die and come back. . .

the worst part was losing your intellect, your brainpower. Everything else he could do without but he couldn't handle being a mindless corpse wandering the earth forever. But maybe it didn't have to be that way. The stupidity of the dead had to come from organic brain damage—right?— brought on by anoxia. The critical moment came between when you stopped breathing and you woke up again, that was when it must happen, the juncture between thinking rational human and dumb dead animal. If you could keep yourself oxygenated, have yourself ventilated, hooked up to a dialysis machine to keep your blood moving, carrying that critical oxygen to your head, yeah. With everything on battery power in case the grid went down.

His teeth bit down hard, his stomach unwilling to wait for saliva to break the noodle down. He chewed hard, crunching the rigatoni into fragments as hard and sharp as little knives. Put another noodle in his mouth. Another.

One day he'd watched a government helicopter, the first one he'd seen in a week, come down with a noise like a car crash somewhere in the park. For hours he watched the black smoke rise from the site, watched the tips of orange flames dancing above the skyline. Nobody went to the rescue. Nobody went to put out the fire. He knew the time had come. A piece of noodle dug deep into his lower lip, neatly puncturing his skin.

With a start he realized what he was doing and spat the noodle fragments in the dry sink. With probing fingers he dug around inside his lips, feeling a hundred tiny lacerations there. He could have really injured himself— but he'd barely felt anything. The pain had been so distant, just a faint glow on the horizon.

He was going nuts cooped up inside. He needed to get

out of his apartment. He needed to find more food. Real food.

Meat.

Chapter Seven

"Epivir. Ziagen. Retrovir." Osman went down the list, shaking his head. "These are anti-AIDS drugs."

I nodded but I was barely listening. Yusuf brought the good ship Arawelo around a few points and Manhattan appeared out of the clearing fog. It looked like a cubist mountain range hovering over the water. Like a crumbling fortress. But then it had always looked like that. I expected to see some kind of obvious damage, some scar left by the Epidemic. There was nothing. Only the silence, the perfect quiet on the water told you something bad had happened here.

Osman laughed. "But Mama Halima doesn't have AIDS. You must be mistaken."

I'd figured that as we approached the city I owed it to Osman to explain why we'd crossed half the planet to reach a haunted city. He and Yusuf—and of course the girl soldiers—were about to risk their lives for my mission. They deserved to know. "These are my orders. Read them however you want." Mama Halima was the only thing standing between Osman's family and a horde of the undead. If he wanted to think she was beyond the reach of HIV I was ready to let him. I wished I could just ignore the facts myself—Sarah was counting on Halima as well. Somalia was held together by nothing but one woman's vicious charisma. If Halima died now rival factions would claim her legacy. Tempers would flare, old feuds would come to the foreground. Somalia would tear itself apart. How long could a country in the middle of a civil war resist the dead?

Yusuf brought us up alongside Battery Park, past the Staten Island Ferry docks. All the boats were gone now—most likely they'd been commandeered by refugees. We cruised by a hundred yards out from the docks and headed northeast, up into the East River, passing Governors Island on our right. Brooklyn was a brown shadow to the east.

"This is madness, though. These drugs can be found anywhere. Let me take you somewhere else," Osman suggested, sounding infinitely reasonable.

"I've heard that before," I sighed. "By the time they picked me they'd already combed every city in Africa, sent suicide squads into Nairobi and Brazzaville and Jo'burg. I suggested half a dozen more places—refugee camps, UN medical stations they might not have heard of. All of them were overrun or demolished. Then I hit upon this bright idea. I didn't think it would actually happen." Mama Halima's agents had presumed you could get AIDS drugs over the counter in any Duane Reade in New York. As far as I knew, though, there was only one place in the world I could be guaranteed of finding everything on the list. The fifth floor of the UN Secretariat Building, in the medical offices. And the Secretariat was right on the water, accessible by boat.

Mama Halima's troops had wasted no time. They had commandeered Osman's ship, painted a new name on its prow, and we were on our way. If Osman didn't like the mission—and he didn't—he was too smart to voice that opinion.

Yusuf poured on a little steam as we turned northward and entered the main channel of the East River. He steered right for the dark solid mass of the Brooklyn Bridge, still wrapped in mist. Osman rubbed at his clean-shaven face and looked like he was about to have a great idea any time now.

"I think I know," he said, finally. "I think I know it now."

I stared at him, expectantly.

"She wants the drugs to give them to other people. People who are infected with AIDS. She is a very generous woman, Mama Halima."

I just shrugged and moved to the bow of the trawler where some of the girls were clustered, pointing out the buildings we passed as if they were tourists looking for the Empire State and the Chrysler building. I kept my eye on the shore, on the masses of pilings and docks that made up the South Street Seaport. They were abandoned, stripped clean of anything that might float. Here and there I could see people moving on the piers. Dead people, I knew, but in the mist I could pretend. Otherwise I would jump every time one of them moved.

This would all be over in a couple of hours, I told myself. Get in, get the drugs, get out. Then I could go back and see Sarah again. Start my life over somehow, I guess. Survival was the first order of the day. Then we could start thinking about how to fix things. The hardest and the longest part would be rebuilding.

My abdomen kept hitching up, like I was sucking in my

gut but I couldn't relax the muscles.

The girls started chattering excitedly and I followed their eyes as they leaned out over the bow. It was nothing, just a yellow buoy. Someone had painted something on it black, a crude design I knew I recognized. Oh. Yeah. The international biohazard symbol. Osman came up behind me and grabbed my bicep. He saw it too and yelled back for Yusuf to ease up on the throttle.

"It's nothing," I told him. "Just a warning. We already know this place is dangerous."

He shook his head but didn't say anything. I supposed he knew more about maritime signage than I did. He pointed at a shadow out on the water and told Yusuf to stop the propellers altogether.

"It's nothing," I said again. Maybe I was susceptible to denial myself. The trawler rolled north, quiet now, so quiet we could hear the water slapping against the hull. The shadow on the water started to resolve itself. It formed a line across the estuary, a dark smudge edged with tiny white breakers. There was some kind of big building on a pier that stuck way out and beyond that the water just changed texture. We drew steadily closer on momentum alone until Osman had to order the engines thrown into reverse. We were getting too close if it was some kind of obstruction. The smudge took shape as we coasted, turning into piles, heaps of something dumped in the water, lots of little things dumped in heaps.

Bodies.

I couldn't see them very well. I didn't want to. Osman pushed a pair of binoculars at me and I took a look anyway. The East River was clogged with human corpses. My mouth was dry but I forced myself to swallow and look again. On the forehead of each corpse (I checked a dozen or so to make sure) was a puckered red wound. Not a bullet wound. More like something you would make with an ice pick.

They had known—the authorities in New York had known what was happening to their dead. They must have known and they tried to stop it—or at least slow it down. You destroy the brain and the corpse stays down, that was the lesson we'd all learned at so much cost. In Somalia they burned the bodies afterward and buried the remains in pits but here, in a city of millions, there just wouldn't have been anywhere to put them. The authorities must have just dumped the bodies in the river hoping the current would wash them away but there had been too many dead for even the sea to accept.

Thousands of bodies. Tens of thousands and it hadn't been enough, the work couldn't be done fast enough maybe. It would have been arduous, nasty work. I could feel it in my arms, as if I'd done it myself. Punching through bone and grey matter with a spike, over and over again. And it would have been dangerous, too, a body you went to dispose of could sit up and grab for your arm, your face and next thing you knew you would be on the pile yourself. Who had done it? The National Guard? The firemen?

"Dekalb," Osman said softly. "Dekalb. We can't go through. There's no way through."

I stared north past the raft of corpses. It stretched as far as I could see, well past the Brooklyn Bridge. He was right. I couldn't quite see the UN from there but it was so close. My chest started to heave, with sobbing tears maybe, or maybe I wanted to throw up, I couldn't tell. The drugs, my only chance to see Sarah again, were right there but they might as well be a million miles away.

Yusuf got the Arawelo turned around and headed back toward the bay while Osman and I tried to figure out what to do next. You could go up, up the Hudson and around, through the Harlem River, circumnavigating Manhattan, and then back down the East-River. Osman threw away that plan immediately. "The Harlem River," he said, pointing at a narrow ribbon of blue on his charts, "it is too shallow. Too much danger of running on the ground."

"It's the best chance we have," I said, my arms tight around my stomach as I stared at the maps.

"I am sorry," he said, "but this is not possible. Maybe there is something else. Some other place, a hospital. Or a drugstore."

I stared and stared at the maps. I knew this place. I knew it better than anyone else on the boat. Why couldn't I think of anything?

Chapter Eight

Back in the freezer section of the little bodega, back in the dark Gary finally found what he'd been looking for behind smooth clear glass. He took the box of hamburger patties up to the front and laid them out on the plastic counter by the display of disposable lighters and the lotto machine. They'd been cool to the touch in the freezer— completely thawed out and with a little fuzzy white mold on top but still good, he thought. They looked good to him, anyway. He was starving. He contemplated different ways to cook them until he got up the nerve to just bite into one raw and take his chances.

His mouth flooded with saliva and he forced himself to chew, to savor the meat even though his eyes were watering up. The tension in his stomach, the crawling hunger, began to subside and he leaned on the counter with both hands. It had taken him all of the morning to find any scrap of meat at all. He'd wandered far afield from his apartment, north into the West Village. But at every butcher's shop and grocery store he'd found only empty walk-in freezers and vacant meat hooks swaying on their chains. Clearly he wasn't the first one to be drawn to where the meat used to be. For the last hour he'd been combing all the little neighborhood convenience stores and the back pantries of shoebox-sized diners and this was all he'd found. Judging by the way his stomach was relaxing and his hands had stopped shaking the walk had been worth it.

He was devouring his second burger patty when he heard a noise behind him and he turned around to find he wasn't alone. A big guy in a trucker cap and sideburns had stumbled into the store and knocked over a rack of SlimJims. It was the first of the walking dead that Gary had ever seen up close. The intruder's head rolled on his thick neck and drool slid from his slack lower lip as he stared at Gary with eyes that couldn't quite seem to focus. He had the same dead veins and bluish pallor Gary had seen in his bathroom mirror but this guy's face was slack and loose, the skin hanging in folds at his jowls and neck. He was missing a big chunk out of his left thigh. His jeans were caked with clotted blood and as he slouched forward the leg bent underneath him all wrong, threatening to tumble him right into Gary's chest.

Slowly, painfully, Trucker Cap got his leg back underneath him and lurched across the counter. Without a word the dead man lurched forward and his hands went out, grabbing at the remaining burgers. Before Gary could stop him the big guy shoved one of the patties into his mouth and started reaching for another, the last of the four.

Gary said, "Hey, come on, that's mine" and grabbed the back of the guy's flannel shirt to pull him away from the food but it was like trying to move a refrigerator. He tried to grab the guy's arm and got swatted backward, knocking him into a display of clattering cans of StarKist tuna. Slowly the big guy turned to face Gary with those dull glassy eyes. Gary looked down and saw he still had part of the hamburger patty in his left hand.

The big guy's jaw stretched wider as if he would swallow Gary like a snake swallowing an egg. Still no sound came out of him, no sound at all. He took a wobbling step forward on his bad leg, nearly fell. Corrected himself. His hands came up in fists.

"No,"—Gary scrabbled to get to his feet but slipped in the spill of cans—"get away from me." The big guy kept coming. "Don't you dare!" Gary shrieked, sounding absurd even to his own ears but it just came out. "Stop!"

The big guy stopped in mid-stride. The expression on his face changed from hungry anger to just plain confusion. He looked around for a minute and Gary could feel the guy's cold form looming over him, a dead shadow in the air ready to come down like a ton of bricks, to smash him, to pummel him into mush.

He just stood there, coming no closer.

"Fuck off and die!" Gary screamed, terrified.

Without a sound the big guy turned on his good heel and walked out of the bodega. He didn't look back.

Gary watched him go then pulled himself back up to his feet. He was feeling shaky again. Almost nauseous. He finished the patty in his hand but it didn't help as much as his first one had. The fight with the big guy had taken something out of him. He ran a hand through his hair, looked back at the freezer section. It was empty now. He bent down and gathered up all the SlimJims the big guy had knocked over. Those were meat too, he thought. Maybe they would help.

As Gary shambled out of the bodega the ringing in his

ears came back with no warning and louder than ever. He knew he had to move—to get away from the area before the big guy came back for-more—but he could barely stand upright. He clutched his head as the world reeled around him and leaned against the cool plate glass of the store window. A burst of white noise shot through his head like an icy jet of water and he staggered out into the street—what the hell was happening? He felt his legs moving under him, felt himself propelled through space but he couldn't see anything, couldn't make his eyes focus.

What was going on? His medical training was useless in describing what was happening to him. Aneurysm? Ischemic event? His brain felt as if it was drying out and shrinking—was this all he got for his hard work, half a day's worth of intellect? Was he going to lose it now?

He felt something hard and metallic collide with his thighs and he forced himself to stop moving. He reached down and felt a railing, a metal railing that he clutched to as he sank down to his knees. With great effort he forced his eyes open and knelt there staring, staring with a desperate intensity at the Hudson River in front of him. If he had taken another three steps he would have fallen in.

Everything was so vivid, clearer than it had ever been in life. Gary looked up at New Jersey across the water, at the hills there and saw the ground shake. He clutched hard at the railing as the earth rolled beneath him and cracks ran through the rock, cracks spouting noxious black fumes that filled the whole world with their smoke.

Behind him at the bodega the big guy's trucker cap rolled off his head as he collapsed to the pavement. His hands spasmed as the spark of animation flowed out of him and his eyes fluttered closed.

Chapter Nine

"That one is too active," Ayaan said, scanning the wharf with her binoculars. The dead man in question wore nothing but a pair of tight jeans that overflowed with his bloated flesh. He clutched to a wooden piling with one arm while the other snatched at the air. His hungry face followed the boat as we steamed past.

On top of the wheelhouse Mariam called down for her Dragunov and one of the other girls passed it up. Mariam steadied herself against the Arawelo's radar dome and peered through the scope of the sniper rifle. I put my fingers in my ears a moment before she fired. The dead man on the pier spun around in a cloud of exploding brain matter and fell into the water.

Sixteen years old and Mariam was already an expert sniper. When did the girl soldiers have time to train? I suppose there hadn't been anything else to do in Somalia. No cable TV, no shopping malls.

Osman cleared his throat and I looked back at the map. "Here," I said, pointing at a blue letter H on the map, just a few blocks in from the Hudson. I looked up at the line of buildings on the shore and pointed at a spot between two of them. "St. Vincent Medical Center. They have—or rather, they had—an HIV care center." I shrugged. "It's dangerous. We'll be out of sight of the ship for at least an hour. But it's the best option, if we can't get to the UN."

The captain rubbed his face and nodded. He yelled at Yusuf to bring the ship in at an empty pier and the girls surged across the deck, shouldering their weapons and checking their actions. Osman and I struggled with a piece of corrugated tin ten feet long and just as wide that served the trawler in the place of a gangplank.

The engines whined and water churned as Yusuf brought us in to a bumping stop. The girls started jumping across even before we had the plank down—Commander Ifiyah at the fore, calling all her kumayo sisters to join her. They roared like lions as they raced to take up their assigned positions in two ranks of twelve on the wooden pier (Mariam was still up on the wheelhouse with her Dragunov). I shouldered my pack, shook Osman's hand, and picked my way carefully across the plank as if afraid I was going to fall in the water. I felt calm, far calmer than when we'd tried the East River. Ayaan had taught me a trick, to force myself to vomit before the battle so I wouldn't feel the need afterward. It hadn't been hard. The smell of death and decay rolling off Manhattan added to my general seasickness and left me feeling queasy ever since we'd spotted the Statue of Liberty.

The sounds of my footsteps on the pier echoed in the stillness. I moved to crouch behind Ayaan, who paid no attention to me whatsoever. She was so focused, so completely at peace in this madness. I lifted my own AK-47 and tried to copy her firing stance, but I knew by the way the stock felt on my shoulder that I had it wrong.

"Xaaraan," she said softly, but not to me. The word

meant "ritually unclean," or more literally "improperly butchered meat." I'd never heard a more apropos description of the men and women who came at us then up the pier. Grotesque twisted faces on top of swollen bloody bodies that bent at unnatural angles—the hands reaching for us with fingers crooked like talons—the broken teeth—the rolling eyes—their silence—the silence was the worst. People, real people made noise. These were the dead.

"Diyaar!" Ifiyah screamed and the girls let loose, one rifle after another jumping upward with a cracking noise that left another corpse spinning down to smack the pier. I saw one get caught right in the teeth. Enamel danced in the air. Another with shoulder-length hair clutched at his stomach but kept moving toward us, not running so much as flopping on uncertain feet, flopping toward us with an inexorability that terrified me. A woman in a jeans jacket and high black boots pushed past him and came right for me, the wind ruffling back her hair to show that both of her cheeks had been eaten away. Her exposed jaws snapped in anticipation as she raised her arms to grapple me. A puff of smoke burst from her stomach and she fell back but others pushed to take her place.

"Madaxa!" Ifiyah ordered—shoot for the head. I saw a few of the younger girls shift their stance nervously and raise the barrels of their rifles a hair. They fired again and the dead fell away, dropping to the pier with a thud or spinning down to the water or falling backward into the crowd which just surged around them and came faster. Had they been waiting for us? There were so many— even with the noise we were making I couldn't imagine us drawing so many of them without warning. Unless maybe New York, the perennially crowded city, just had that many walking dead in it. If so we were doomed. It would be impossible to complete our mission.

"Iminka," Ifiyah breathed. Now. In my horror I had barely noticed the most horrifying thing of all—that the dead were gaining on us. Only a few meters separated us from their oncoming tide. The girls didn't panic but I know I did, hyperventilating and coming very close to shitting my pants. As one they adjusted their rifles with a ringing clack and opened up in full automatic.

If I had thought the carnage was bad before, well, I had no idea. I had seen assault rifles fired in full automatic before. In my job as a weapon inspector there had been plenty of times when some local chieftain or hetman wanted to impress me with the sight of his firepower. I'd never seen automatic assault weapons turned against Americans though. It didn't seem to matter if they were already dead. The line of them in front of me just exploded, their heads pulped, their necks and torsos torn to fibrous shreds. The ones behind them just shook and shook as if they were succumbing to violent seizures as the bullets rattled around inside of them.

The noise of twenty-four Kalashnikovs burning on full automatic cannot be described, so I won't try. It shakes you up, literally—the vibration makes your heart feel like it's going to stop and the sheer volume of noise can damage your internal organs with prolonged exposure. It went on, and on and on.

When it was done we were standing before a pile of unmoving bodies. One woman in an I Love New York shirt with the sleeves ripped off struggled out from under the heap and came clawing at us but one of the girls—

Fathia—just stepped forward and stabbed her in the head with the bayonet at the end of her rifle. The corpse went down. After that we all listened to the ringing in our ears for a while, we studied the shore end of the pier waiting for another wave but it didn't come.

"*Nadiif*," Ifiyah announced. The pier was clean. The girls visibly relaxed and shouldered their rifles. A few laughed boisterously and kicked at the slaughtered bodies on the wooden pier. Fathia and Ifiyah traded a high-five. All of the girls smiled—except Ayaan.

Her face was as hard as a mask as she reached up and grabbed the muzzle break of my Kalashnikov. I winced, thinking she was intentionally burning herself for some reason—the AK-47 was notorious for overheating after prolonged firing—but then she pulled her hand away and showed me her unblemished palm.

"You did not discharge it," Ayaan said. The disgust in her face was withering.

I suddenly realized I hadn't fired my weapon at all. I had been too busy watching the girls. "I'm not a killer," I protested.

She shook her head bitterly. "If you will not fight, then you are already one of the *xaaraan*."

The girls spread out down the pier, Commander Ifiyah taking the van as they swept the shore for any sign of movement. Ayaan ran to her position in the front of the wedge. I turned and looked back at the Arawelo. Osman flashed me an "okay" sign with one hand. "You go after them now, Dekalb," he said, smiling broadly. "We'll stay here and guard the ship."

Chapter Ten

Fanning out across the street the girls threw hand signals at one another. The barrels of their Kalashnikovs swept the street corners, the recessed doorways, the hundreds of cars abandoned on the cobblestones. I had expected—well, I guess I had hoped—that the roads would be clear. We could have commandeered some transport and driven to the hospital.

Not a chance. In the panic of the Epidemic the usual Manhattan gridlock must have turned into a death trap. There were cars everywhere, many of them dented or damaged. They lined every side-street we passed, crowded every intersection. I saw a Hummer 2 up on the sidewalk, its shiny front bumper wedged permanently between a mailbox and the broken wood front of a deserted bistro. On the other side of the street Fathia clambered up on top of a taxi with four flat tires and scanned the road ahead with her rifle at her eye.

"This way," I told Ifiyah and she gestured for her troops to follow us. I led her down a short block of Horatio Street, past a gas station with shuttered windows. Paper signs had been wrapped around the pumps and secured with duct tape: NO GAS, NO MONEY, NO BATHROOM. GOD

BLESS YOU. Around the corner was a storefront psychic (the garish neon tubes visible in the window were dead now) and a little boutique that must have sold women's clothing. The front window showed three cheerily dressed mannequins and a bunch of billowing green cloth.

Ayaan stopped in front of the window and peered inside.

"Thinking of a new look for summer?" I asked, wanting her to hurry up. It was understandable, of course—Ayaan had probably never seen real women's fashions before. She had spent most of her life in a uniform and the lure of Western dress must—

"I saw movement in there," she insisted.

Oh.

The soldiers pressed in, some of them walking backwards with their rifles facing out as others led them with a hand on their shoulders. Their discipline was heartening. In another life I might have found the way these girls worked together creepy, but now it meant I might just survive this ludicrous mission.

Without warning a dead woman pushed through the folds of green in the window and slammed up against the glass from the inside. She was a willowy blonde with thin refined features. Her face was pockmarked only here and there with tiny sores that looked almost like sequins. She wore a flowing maroon sleeveless dress and for a heartbeat we were all transfixed by the sight of her elegance.

Then her thin arms came up and her tiny fists started bashing at the glass. Her face thrust forward and her jaw opened against the window as if she were trying to chew her way through it with her yellow teeth. The black hole of her mouth made a perfect seal on the glass as she hungered for us.

Fathia raised her rifle but I shook my head. "That's tempered glass—shatterproof. She'll never get through it. If you shoot now the noise might draw others, though."

The soldier looked to her commander. Ifiyah nodded once and we moved on, leaving the dead woman behind us. After we turned the block we couldn't even hear the muffled thuds of her fists on the window.

In the broader expanse of Greenwich Avenue we found a water truck still dripping from a splatter of gunshot holes. Tied to its hitch an incredibly long streamer of yellow police tape flapped in the breeze. I grabbed a handful and read QUARANTINE AREA: TRESPASSERS WILL BE MET WITH LETHAL FORCE before letting it flutter away. We made a left on Twelfth and the girls spread out rapidly. We had arrived. Ifiyah called for her troops to establish fire zones and to designate a CCP—a Casualty Collection Point—where they would meet up if they got separated. I led Ayaan up to the closed emergency-room doors of St. Vincent and peered inside.

"It's dark in there," I said. Well, of course it was. Did I expect the power to be on six weeks after the end of the world? "I don't like it."

"It is not for you to decide," Ayaan said but there was less anger in her voice than usual. She slipped her thin fingers into the crack between the two automatic doors and tugged. They moved an inch and then slipped back. Looking over at Ifiyah she held up three fingers and we were joined quickly by a trio of sixteen-year-olds. Between the five of us we pried the doors open wide enough for me to fit through.

Ayaan handed me a flashlight from her *dambiil* bag

and checked her own by switching it on and off rapidly. The three girls who had joined us ran through the same procedure. I glanced at Ifiyah for authorization to begin and then stepped inside. The lobby of the emergency room was a mess of overturned chairs and blank-screened television sets but at least a little light came in the glass doors and cut through the gloom.

The admissions desk was half buried under a slurry of glossy pamphlets about heart disease and secondhand smoke. I stepped on them being careful not to slip and found a photocopied directory taped to the wall. "This way," I said, pointing at a pair of swinging doors leading off the main lobby. The HIV clinic was deep inside the building. It might take us ten minutes to get there in the dark and just as long to get back. Ifiyah had given us ninety minutes to complete the mission and exfiltrate back to the boat.

I had to do this only once, I told myself. Just once and then I can go see Sarah. The thought of my seven-year-old daughter languishing in a Somalian religious school made my heart rattle in my suddenly airless chest.

I kicked open the double doors and flashed my light down the pitch darkness of the corridor beyond. The cone of illumination caught a couple of hospital beds pushed up against the wall. A heap of stained linen on the floor. Two rows of doors, dozens of them, that could be hiding anything.

"Let's get this over with," I said. Ayaan pursed her lips as if rankled at being given an order by a civilian. But she lifted her rifle to her shoulder and stepped into the hallway.

Chapter Eleven

Gary shook his head hard and slowly rose to his feet. Looking across at Hoboken he saw nothing but empty buildings and quiet streets. The geysers of poisonous gas he'd seen erupt there were gone. They had never been there. Just a hallucination.

He flexed his hands, observed himself for a second. Everything intact and in working order. In fact he felt better than ever—the buzzing had left his head and his hands didn't shake like they had before. Most importantly his hunger was gone. Not entirely—he could feel it looming at the horizon of his awareness, knew it would come back stronger than ever soon enough, but for now at least, his stomach felt at peace.

He turned around slowly, uncertain how long this newfound sense of health might last or how fragile it might be. Behind him he saw that nothing else had changed—New York was the same as ever. Just as quiet. He saw a body lying beside the bodega where he'd fought with the trucker cap and decided to investigate.

What he found didn't answer any questions. Trucker Cap was dead. Not undead, not walking dead—just dead, lying there decomposing in the sun. That wasn't supposed to happen. The dead kept coming until you destroyed their brains—everyone knew that, the vice president had announced as much on live television. Gary could find no damage to the guy's head, no signs of trauma at all but for some reason he had just stopped. Fallen down and stopped—permanently, by the look of it.

Gary picked up the hat and turned it around in his hands. Then he dropped it with a start and scrabbled backwards on all fours away from the corpse. He had forgotten—he was one of the dead, himself. Whatever had done this to the big guy might still be around—and he would be vulnerable to it as well. What if a sniper waited on the rooftops? What if the apocalypse was finally over and the dead had stopped coming back to life? What if some new and pernicious virus had adapted to attack the dead?

No. It couldn't be a virus—a virus needed living cells to replicate itself. A bacterium might have done it or even more likely some kind of fungal infection, sure, a fungus spread by airborne spores—

But spores that just happened along at the exact second of Gary's dark epiphany? It made no sense. Gary had told the guy to fuck off and die. To think that some fungus that just happened to counteract the effects of the Epidemic had wafted by at that exact moment was ludicrous. Something had struck down Trucker Cap, though, something had happened right after Gary told him to—

Gary might have contemplated this more if he hadn't heard gunfire. Guns—which meant a survivor was near. The dead lacked the muscular coordination to use firearms. Some desperate lone survivor must have been making his last stand somewhere to the-north. Up in the Meatpacking District by the sound of it. It wouldn't last. Gary should just ignore it, go home to his apartment and start making plans for the future, now that he actually had one-again.

He'd never been able to resist his own curiosity, though. It was what got him into med school in the first place, his desire to know what made things tick.

Despite his best interests he found himself running northward toward the noise of the shots. They stopped abruptly when he was halfway there but he'd figured out by then they were coming from near the river, maybe on one of the piers.

Advancing carefully, he nearly got himself shot. A black girl in a schoolgirl uniform and a scarf around her head was pointing a rifle right in his direction. He slid down behind an abandoned car and screwed his eyes shut, his arms clutched around his knees, trying hard to make himself small and insignificant. She'd looked pretty serious about her weapon. Like a soldier or a policeman or something. Absurd. . . but this was a day for absurdities, it seemed.

There were others with her. A whole team of them, it sounded like. Their weapons jangled as they moved. He heard one of them talking—a hard, cold voice with an accent to it. She must be from Brooklyn. "I saw movement in there," she said.

No. No no no no no.

"If you shoot now the noise might draw others," another of them said—a man.

Thank you, whoever you are, Gary thought.

He waited in desperate stillness for a long while, long after he heard them moving off. It sounded like they were headed over toward Gary's old work. So much for curiosity. He would definitely leave them alone. When he was certain they were all out of sight he got up and moved as fast as he could toward the river—away from them. He tried to run but the best he could pull off was a loping walk. But when he got to the river he found another surprise.

A ship stood out in the Hudson, maybe a hundred yards off the embankment. Just an old tub with visible rust on its hull and a jury-rigged wooden superstructure. The ship's registration on its nose was illegible, written in an alphabet Gary didn't recognize—a little like Hebrew, maybe, and a lot like medieval calligraphy. He peered closer and saw people on board. Two black men leaning on the rail, studying the wharves while a girl in that same costume of school uniform and head wrap stood on top of the wooden structure with an exceedingly long rifle in her hands.

He knew enough to keep his head down this time.

There were. . . survivors, he thought. Organized survivors with a way to get out of Manhattan. He had no idea what they were doing in New York but their presence meant at least one inescapable, dreadful thing. His decision to transform himself into one of the walking dead—to become this unliving creature—had been based on the fact that New York was done, extinct, over. That there was no hope for the human race.

It looked like if he'd waited a couple of more days he might have been rescued.

Chapter Twelve

I took a step forward and my hip connected with something hard and square that shot away from me. I heard Ayaan's rifle swing around with a clatter and I brought my light up fast but the thing I'd collided with in the dark was just a rolling cabinet. A plastic cart full of medical supplies. The halls were full of them. It drifted for a few more feet and then stopped in the middle of the hall. Sheepishly I pushed it out of the way. I could sense the girls behind me—Ayaan and her three squad-mates— uncoil as they came down from a tense alert.

For myself I just couldn't relax. I'd never liked hospitals—well, who does? The chemical stink of the disinfectant they use. The desolate utilitarianism of their furnishings. The lingering sense of decay and dissolution. I felt like something was crawling around on my shoulders, one of those long, wet-looking millipedes covered in hairs as fine and curved as eyelashes.

I kicked over a pile of bloody linens half-expecting something underneath to jump up and bite my leg. Nothing. Ayaan gave me a look and we pressed on. We were making lousy time, by necessity. The hallways of the deserted dark hospital were full of things to trip over, as I had just proved, and every few dozens yards the corridor was broken by a pair of swinging doors. Each of these could hide a crowd of the dead so the girls had developed a strategy for opening them. Two of the girls would kneel down on either side of the doors, their rifles at the ready, their flashlight beams converging on the doors. Ayaan would stand back a few yards ready for a frontal attack. Then I would push on the doors and step back hurriedly as they swung open. Theoretically, I could roll out of the way before the shooting started if we found anything. I was pretty sure this was my punishment for not discharging my weapon back on the docks.

We covered a whole floor of the hospital this way. By the time we reached an elevator lobby sweat had soaked through my shirt even though it was cool in the dark corridors. The muscles in my face kept twitching. Every time we passed a side door that was even slightly ajar I could literally feel my skin trying to crawl off my back. Every time the corridor branched off to the sides I felt like I'd entered an abyss of cyclopean proportions where something horrible and huge might have been lying in wait for years, hoping for just this opportunity to strike.

In the elevator lobby I looked at the signs on the walls, whited out by the fierce bright wash of my flashlight, and tried to figure out what had happened. I knew we were lost, that was perfectly clear. I also knew I couldn't say as much out loud. This was supposed to be my role in the mission, to act as a native guide. Admitting failure at this point might have inspired the girls to head back outside and leave me here alone. Alone and lost, unable to find my way back.

I really didn't want that.

Ayaan cleared her throat. I ran my flashlight over her face, making her eyes glow like glass marbles lit from within. She didn't look scared, which I irrationally took as a sign of contempt for me. How dare she be so calm when I was ready to throw up from sheer terror?

I played the light over the color-coded signs again and then pointed it at the emergency stairwell. "This way," I told them, and the girls stormed the fire door as if they were assaulting an enemy fortress. Was I just a coward? I wondered. In my career I had purposefully gone into some of the worst places on Earth (at least they had been before the dead came back to life—now every place was alike in its badness), actively looking for war criminals and heavily armed psychopaths so I could ask them to pretty please turn over their guns for disposal and destruction. I had never felt particularly afraid back then, though I had known when to duck and when to leave with or without what I'd come for. One time in Sudan I'd been in a convoy full of food and sanitary supplies heading to a village in the extreme south of the country. That just happened to be the day the rebels decided to seize that particular road. A hundred men wearing green hospital gowns (they couldn't afford uniforms—they could afford plenty of guns, though) had stopped us and demanded that we just hand over the contents of our trucks. There was some discussion as to whether they should shoot us as well. Eventually they left us with one truck and all of our lives intact and we sped all the way back to Khartoum. I remember my heart beating a little faster then. It was nothing like this, this horripilating dread, this crawling fear.

Back then, no matter how bad things got, there was still some possibility of safety. There would always be a United

Nations, and a Red Cross, and an Amnesty International. There were people somewhere who would work night and day to get you released from captivity or transferred to a clean well-run medical facility or airlifted out of harm's way. Since the Epidemic all that was gone. My American citizenship got me nothing here—no help, no relief. Even in the middle of New York City I was helpless.

Ayaan and her squad could have sympathized—that was the only kind of life they'd ever known, even before the world died. As we entered the emergency stairwell and started up the stairs I considered how much I had to learn from them, how much I was going to have to change to survive. I tried not to hate them so much for having a head start.

Clang, clang. Clang, clang. Every step on the stairs rattled and banged with noise. The echoes rolled up and down the seemingly limitless vertical shaft of the stairwell, the sound shivering the cold air that we climbed through. It was loud enough to wake the dead, you know, if they hadn't already been. . . damn. Even dumb jokes couldn't help.

I was scared shitless.

It was some kind of help to me, then, when we rushed the doorway to the second floor and I pointed my flashlight right at a sign that pointed us towards the HIV Center. We'd made it. We had nearly reached our destination. Now we just had to grab the drugs and get back out the way we came.

We attacked another door and just like all the others there was nothing beyond it but more darkness and nasty-smelling hospital. More carts on casters and more piles of soiled linen. Nothing moving, nothing voicelessly lusting for our flesh. No sound at all. I took a step into the hallway and saw the reception desk for the HIV Center right ahead of me in the yellow stab of my flashlight. I took another step but I could tell the girls hadn't followed. I spun around to demand why.

"*Amus!*" Ayaan hissed. I shut my mouth.

Nothing. Silence. An absolute lack of sound so distinct I could hear my own breath moving in and out of my chest. And underneath that something dull and atonal, and very, very distant. It was getting louder, though. Louder and more insistent.

Clang. Clang. Clang clang clang. Clang. Just like the sound our feet had made on the metal stairs—but without the rhythm of footsteps. The sound a fist makes when it hits a piece of metal but without any organization or purpose behind it. Clang. Clang clang. We heard something snap and clatter, a latch breaking off a door perhaps. An image came to me, why I don't know, of fists pounding on the inside of a closed metal cabinet door and the door finally giving way. Sure, I thought. Like the metal door on a refrigerator or a meat storage locker. Or the heavy insulated door that might seal off a hospital's morgue from the warmer air outside.

That was the other thing I hated about hospitals—people died there. Other people got taken there for storage. Dead people.

We heard silence for a while. None of us moved. Then we heard the noise come back. Slow, painfully slow but loud. Very loud. Clang, clang. Pause. Clang, clang. Clang, clang.

Something was coming up the stairs behind us.

Chapter Thirteen

"First we find the drugs," Ayaan said, pointing her rifle at me. "Then we can run." I tried to grab the muzzle and push it away, certain she wouldn't shoot me but she took a deft step backward that left me lunging at air. "They are slow. We have the time, still."

In the light of just a couple of flashlights I couldn't read her face very well. I could hear the dead men coming up the stairs behind us perfectly, though.

I pushed past the girls and into the clinic lobby, my light stabbing through the swirling dust in the corridor. A ward of double rooms stretched to the right—I had no time for this!—to where a nurse's station connected two hallways. Move, I told myself, move, and I broke into a dash. I splashed light across every door I saw. Tub room. Patients' Lounge. Linen Services. Dispensary. Okay. Okay. Yes.

The door had a hefty lock on it, the kind you would need a key card to enter. With the power out it probably sealed automatically. I ran my hand along the jamb hoping there was some kind of emergency-release mechanism and nearly yelped when the door fell open at my touch.

No, I began to howl in my head but I shelved the

thought—it didn't necessarily mean anything. Maybe the door opened automatically when the power failed. I stepped inside the closet-sized room and something crunched under my foot. I pointed my flashlight down and saw a couple of dozen pills in bright orange and dull yellow and-that powdery pink so beloved of pharmaceutical companies. Looking up again I saw bare cabinets with their doors hanging morosely open.

To be sure I searched every cabinet with fingers made clumsy by stress. I found a bottle of Tylenol in one of them. Tylenol.

"Looters," I told Ayaan as I raced back around the corner, tossing the bottle at her. She caught it without looking away from my face. "It makes sense—there were patients here, living patients. They couldn't survive for long without their medicine. When they were evacuated they must have taken everything with them." She didn't move. "There are no drugs here," I shouted at her, trying to grab her arm. She shied away from me again.

The sound of the dead coming up the stairwell had grown deafening, their heavy feet smashing down on the metal risers. They would be here any second.

"Is there another room here where drugs will be kept?" Ayaan asked me. "A main dispensary?" But I was busy playing my flashlight along the walls of the north-south corridor that led away from the nurses' station. According to the directory I'd seen downstairs there was another stairwell at the far end of the building and maybe it was clear. Otherwise we were going to have to jump out a window.

"Don't worry, American," one of the girls said. She adjusted the selector lever of her AK-47 and smiled sweetly for me. "We fight them for you."

I pointed my light at her face. Her sixteen-year-old complexion was marred only at her chin where she had a bad pimple.

It happened like something seen underwater. With the kind of slow, liquid grace of a nightmare where you are falling and you never hit the ground.

As I watched in horror a hand trailing strips of torn skin reached around her mouth and pulled her backwards into the darkness outside my cone of light. I heard her muffled scream as the stairwell door swung shut and a noise like a bedsheet being torn to ribbons. I ran.

Panic surged through me, bubbles of adrenaline fizzing away in my blood as I raced down the hallway. In the dancing light of my flashlight I saw wheeled carts and piles of dirty linen everywhere—I dodged around the former and jumped over the latter and knew for a certainty I was going to break my leg like this but the option, the only option, was to stop and let them catch up with me.

Behind me I heard shots—the rapid buzz of automatic fire. The discipline the girls had shown on the piers had evaporated in the face of a dark hallway full of death. Was it Ayaan I heard shooting, I wondered, or had they already got her? I dashed forward into the dark and pushed open a set of swinging doors to find myself in the other elevator lobby, facing the other emergency stairway.

I looked back. I pushed open the doors and ran my flashlight over the corridor beyond, searched for any signs of pursuit. "Girls?" I called, knowing it would attract the dead but also knowing I couldn't just leave them behind, not if there was a chance of regrouping with them. "Ayaan?"

In the very far distance I heard someone shouting in Somali. She was yelling too rapidly for me to make out any of the words in my limited vocabulary. I listened, craning my head forward as if I could hear better if I could get closer to the sound, but no gunfire or screams followed. Just silence.

"Ayaan," I called, knowing I was alone.

I gave her the time it took me to breathe ten long breaths and then I tried to push open the stairwell door. It resisted so I put my shoulder into it and finally it budged, opening maybe two or three inches. It must have been blocked from the other side. I kicked furiously at it which didn't seem to help at all.

Halfway down the corridor to my right I heard something rolling toward me. I stabbed out with my flashlight and saw a rolling cart spinning slowly until it collided with a wall. Farther up the passage my light speared a pile of bedclothes, thick with dried blood.

No. Not bedclothes. A woman in a blue paper hospital gown. Dead, of course. Her hair was so fine and sparse it looked like silken threads tied to her mottled scalp. In the yellow flare of my flashlight her skin showed up as a pale green. She didn't have any eyes. I realized in a second what had happened. Coming down the hallway toward me she had stumbled against the rolling cart and fallen to the floor. Even if she couldn't see me she knew I was there. Maybe she could smell me.

Slowly, achingly she began to rise to her feet, bracing herself against the wall with one unfeeling arm.

I pushed again at the unyielding door to the fire stairs but it just wouldn't move. I pushed my AK-47 into the gap I'd made and tried to pry open the door. I felt it give a little. . . and then a little more. The woman was on her feet at this point and walking toward me. She was stooped and she walked with a pronounced stiffness in her leg. I kept my flashlight on her all the time as I heaved and heaved against the stock of the rifle. Finally the door sprang open and I saw what had been blocking it—a heavy metal bookshelf. Judging by the bloodstains on the floor of the landing someone had barricaded themselves in the stairwell. Unsuccessfully.

I didn't worry about that. I pushed past it and raced down the stairs and into the hallways of the ground floor.

Chapter Fourteen

A bullet pranged off the passenger-side door and the car rocked on its tires. The Volkswagen's windshield had a long silver crack running across its width but it hadn't broken yet. Gary assumed a fetal position in the leg well of the driver's seat and tried not to make a sound.

The demented Girl Scouts—or whatever they were—had spotted him and opened fire before he could say a word. He'd tried to run away but he was pinned between two hazards: the boat on the river with its sniper ready to shoot anything that moved, and these heavily armed schoolgirls who had taken over half of the West Village. It was inevitable that he would be spotted. He'd barely had time to take cover in the abandoned car before they started spraying the neighborhood with lead. He was pretty sure they didn't have a fix on him, though, that they were just firing blind. He was pretty sure they would eventually leave, if he could stay perfectly still and not give himself away. Which, considering his current state of health (undead), seemed entirely doable.

If it wasn't for the damned fly.

His fellow passenger buzzed angrily every time the car moved. It would climb along the dashboard for a while then take to the air with a sudden leap and make a circuit of the enclosed space before settling down again on a headrest. Gary felt truly sorry for implicating it in his peril—clearly the fly had a good thing going here. The backseat of the car was full of rotten groceries. Much of the former food had long since turned to white fuzzy mold but maybe the fly ate that, too. Either way the fly looked plump and contented. Bursting with life—real life, not the sham kind that animated Gary. A kind of golden aura shimmered around it, inside of it, as if it glowed with pure captured sunlight. It was the first living thing (other than the gun-toting girls) that Gary had seen since his reanimation. It was beautiful—exquisite. Priceless in its immunity to death, in its continued breathing existence.

There was a deep-seated, urgent, and entirely unbearable need in Gary's soul to get this fly, somehow, into his mouth.

A bullet hit one of the VW's tires and the car sagged to one side with a sharp popping noise that echoed off the brick facades of the surrounding townhouses. Gary, whose hand had been creeping toward the fly, pulled himself into an even tighter ball on the floor of the car and tried not to think about anything at all. It didn't work.

The fly landed on a seat-belt latch and fanned its prismatic wings briefly in the sunlight. Its whole body seemed to glow with the light of its health. It rubbed its hands together like a cartoon character about to sit down to a satisfying hamburger—all it needed was a tiny little bib. How cute would that be? Oh God, Gary wanted so much to eat the fly. His fly, he had decided. It was his.

The fly leapt into the air again with a flourish of wings and Gary's hand shot out for it. The fly evaded him and he lunged upward, catching it between two cupped palms. In a moment he had shoveled it into his maw and he felt its wings brush frantically against the roof of his mouth. He bit down and felt its juices burst across his dry tongue. Energy surged through him even before he'd swallowed the morsel, an electric jolt of well-being that burned in him like a white flame that nourished him instead of consuming him. If the hamburger patties he'd eaten earlier had calmed his hunger the fly instead sated him fully, suffusing him with a euphoria the insect's tiny mass could not possibly account for. He felt good, he felt warm and dry and satisfied, he felt so good.

The feeling had barely begun to recede when he realized with a start that he was sitting up, perched on the front seats of the car and clearly visible through the windows. He heard gunshots and knew he'd been discovered. Desperate but feeling safe and potent now Gary pushed open the driver's-side door and rolled out of the car. He got his feet on the asphalt and started loping away from the Volkswagen, certain he could reach safety if he just hurried up a little, if his legs would just move a little faster—

A bayonet blade slid through his back and right into his heart.

Good thing he wasn't using it.

He tried to turn but found himself transfixed—literally—by the bayonet. He raised his hands in the air, the universal signal of surrender. "Don't shoot," he shouted, "I'm not one of them!"

"*Kumaad tahay*?" One of the girls came around into his field of vision and raised her rifle. She panted with exertion or fear perhaps, her weapon bobbing up and down. He could see the dark O of its muzzle waggling at him, the gap between a bullet and his brain. She yanked on a latch on the side of the weapon and flexed her trigger finger.

"Please!" Gary shouted. "Please! I'm not like them!"

"*Joojin*!" someone shouted. He heard booted footsteps running up behind him. "*Joojin*!" The rifle in front of him steadied in the girl's hands. Was she receiving the order to fire or to not fire? Gary's forehead began to feel hot, anticipating the bullet.

Another girl came up in front of him. She barked orders at the others and Gary felt the bayonet yank backwards out of his body. The girls argued amongst themselves—he kept hearing the word "*xaaraan*"—but clearly their orders were to stand down.

"You talks," the girl who'd given the orders said. She studied his face, obviously confused by the dead veins in his cheeks.

"I talk," Gary confirmed.

"You *fekar*?"

"I don't know what that means."

She nodded and threw a complicated hand gesture at her soldiers. Gary gathered by the gold epaulets on the shoulders of her navy jacket that she must be an officer of some kind, though that made no sense. What army in the world had officers who were teenage girls? Gary couldn't shake the idea that he had been captured by a school field trip gone horribly, horribly awry.

"We kills you, if you says any wrong thing," the officer suggested. She shook her rifle at him. "We kills you, if you dos any wrong thing. You do only right thing, maybe we kills you anyway because of the smell of you."

"Fair enough," Gary said, slowly lowering his hands.

Chapter Fifteen

I wedged myself through the spring-loaded emergency-room doors and ran down the wheelchair ramp to the sidewalk, half-expecting to find myself alone. Commander Ifiyah and her company were there waiting for me—with a prisoner, it looked like. They had somebody kneeling on the ground with a rope around his neck.

It didn't matter—I had to tell Ifiyah what had happened. It had been stupid of us to think we could actually find the medical supplies we needed in this haunted city. We had to leave—and now—before anyone else died.

"Ifiyah," I shouted, waving her over. I leaned forward with my hands on my thighs and tried to get my wind back. "Ifiyah! At least one of your soldiers is dead. The enemy is in there, and they are coming for us!"

The commander turned to face me with a look of passionately studied disinterest. "Three, is dead," she said. I saw then that Ayaan stood next to her. Oh, thank God, I thought, at least one of the girls survived. "Ayaan kept her head on and made slaughter with your enemies, Dekalb. They are no more."

I headed over to where they stood looking down at the prisoner. "Great—but still, there's no reason for us to stay here. There were no drugs in there. The place had been looted," I told Ifiyah. She just nodded distractedly—of course Ayaan would have told her as much. A cold pang went through me as I thought of what else Ayaan might have told her commanding officer. How I ran at the first sign of trouble, for one thing (although surely they would understand—we were talking about the living dead here), abandoning my teammates.

It was while pondering the fact that not only would Ayaan be within her rights to give such a report she would be duty bound to do so and that I was, in fact, pretty derelict in my duty back in that hospital that I finally spared the time to glance down at the prisoner and see he was one of the dead.

Jesus fucking Christ, they've got one of those things on a leash—

My brain sputtered to a stop even as my feet danced backward, carrying me away from the animated corpse. For one of his kind he didn't look so bad—you could see the dark veins under his pasty white face and his eyes looked kind of yellow but otherwise his flesh was intact. He showed me his teeth though and I gave out a startled yelp until I realized he was smiling at me.

"Thank God, you're an American," he said.

That just made my brain hurt. The dead didn't talk. They didn't moan or howl or whimper. They certainly weren't capable of distinguishing between people of different nationalities—true believers in diversity, the dead were equal-opportunity devourers.

"You have to help me," the thing started, but then we heard a thumping sound and looked back to see two of the dead—including the eyeless one who nearly got me in the hospital—slamming up against the emergency-room doors. There might have been more of them inside. It was too dark to tell.

"Ifiyah, we need to head back to the boat now," I said, but the commander had got there before me. She threw hand signals to her squads and with only a couple of barked words we got moving. Ayaan fell in beside me. "I thought you said you got them all," I told her, not feeling very generous at that moment.

"I thought I had," she countered. She squinted back at the hospital but the doors held—the dead lacked the mental power to figure out they needed to pry the doors open instead of just pushing at them. "The two that ate my *kumayo* sisters are no more. I did not hear you firing in our defense. You are not a man, Dekalb, are you? At least we know that much."

My face burned with something that was a little bit anger, a little bit guilt, and a lot of annoyance that she didn't get it, that she just didn't understand what I'd been through. I knew better than to say anything, though. Even to myself I would sound like a spoiled brat. I grimaced and stepped up my pace to get away from her. I guessed correctly that she was too disciplined to break ranks. Moving ahead I caught up with the captive dead man and the girl soldier who held his leash—it was Fathia, the bayonet expert.

"Listen, just talk to them for me," the dead man pleaded when he saw me.

As we turned onto Fourteenth Street I shook my head sadly. "What the hell are you? You're not one of them, not really—"

"Yes, really," he admitted, hanging his head. "I know

what I am; you don't need to humor me. That's not all I am, though. I was a doctor, originally." He couldn't meet my eyes. "Okay, to be honest, a med student. But I could help you guys—every army needs some doctors, right? Yeah, like on M*A*S*H! I can be your Hawkeye Pierce!"

The massacre in the hospital had left my imagination stoked up. "A doctor. Did you—did one of your patients attack you? Somebody you thought was still alive?"

"My name's Gary, by the way," he answered, looking away from me. He held out his hand but I couldn't bring myself to shake it. "Fair enough," he said. "No, it wasn't one of my patients. I did it to myself."

I must have blanched at that.

"Look—there didn't seem to be any choice. The city was burning. New York was burning to the ground. Everybody else was dead. It was either join them or be their dinner. Okay?" When I didn't answer he raised his voice. "Okay?"

"Sure," I mumbled. This didn't make any sense. . . except that it did. I had done terrible things to survive the Epidemic. I had entrusted my seven-year-old daughter to a fundamentalist warlord. I had locked up my dead wife and just abandoned her. All because it seemed like the logical choice at the time.

"I'm a physician, like I said, so I knew what was going to happen to me. I knew my brain would start to die the second I stopped breathing. That's why the dead are so stupid—in the time between when they die and when they stand back up there's no oxygen in their brains and the cells just die. But it didn't have to happen like that. I could protect my brain. I had the equipment. Christ, I bet I'm the smartest one on the planet right now."

"The smartest of the undead," I clarified.

"If you don't mind, I prefer the term unliving." He shot me a grin to show he'd been joking. He seemed so desperate and lonely—I wanted to reach out to him but, well, come on. Even for a bleeding heart like me this was a stretch.

"I put myself on a ventilator and then submerged myself in a bathtub full of ice," Gary explained. "It stopped my heart instantly but oxygen kept flowing to my brain. When I woke up I could still think for myself. I can still control myself. You can trust me, man, okay? Okay?"

I didn't answer. The soldiers had stopped and Ifiyah was yelling orders I couldn't understand. I looked up the street, trying to figure out what was going on. We were in front of Western Beef, the meat market. You couldn't have got me to go in there for a million dollars. Two doors down was another kind of meat market—a swank nightclub called Lotus. That's the Meatpacking District for you. You could cut the irony with a spork.

Ayaan dropped to one knee and brought up her gun. Had somebody heard something? I couldn't see any movement amongst the piles of cardboard crates in front of Western Beef. The smell was god-awful but what did you expect of a warehouse full of meat when the power goes down?

The door of Lotus opened first. A short, squat man in a fashionably cut black suit stumbled out into the street. At this range he might just have been drunk, not dead. Ayaan lined up a shot with perfect slowness and precision and caved in his left temple. He fell to the street in an ungainly heap of black cloth like a dead crow.

"There may be more of them," I said out loud. One of the more superfluous comments I've ever made. The shot made the air around us vibrate like a bell, the noise of it echoing off concrete storefronts and brick buildings long after the dead man fell. Summoned by the sound, others came.

Dozens of them, big burly guys in white aprons stumbling out of Western Beef, Eurotrash out of the club, not even stopping to acknowledge one another, sometimes crawling over each other in their frenzy to get at us. Dozens turned into scores.

When you added the dead who came staggering out of the buildings on every side, well.

Scores turned into hundreds.

Chapter Sixteen

They filled the street ahead of us, a shambling horde with gaping jaws and rolling eyes. Some looked pristine, nearly as healthy as they must have looked while they lived. Others lacked limbs or skin or even faces. Their clothes hung in tatters or in perfectly creased folds and all of them—all of them—were coming for us. They wouldn't stop until we were torn to pieces.

"We've got to go," I shouted at Ifiyah. I tried to grab her arm but she shrugged me off. With short clipped words she ordered her girl soldiers into a firing formation—the same one she'd used back on the docks.

There were a lot more of them this time and their movements were less constrained. I just didn't know if we could survive this.

"We can outrun them, head down a side street," I suggested. The dead took another step toward us. And another. They would never slow down. "Ifiyah—"

"They have no guns, Dekalb," the commander said as if she were brushing off an insect. "They are so stupid, to lie for us in wait here and they even have no guns."

"This isn't an ambush—they're not capable of that level of planning," I insisted. I looked at Gary, the smartest dead man in the world, and he nodded a confirmation.

But Ayaan ignored me studiously. Unlike the others she had to know what was about to happen. She'd been there, in the hospital, when the girls died. I could see her breathing hard through her nose, her jaw clamped shut but she didn't move from her firing crouch. Orders are orders, I guess. The girls opened up with their rifles, going for head shots only. Maybe, I thought, maybe it was true. Maybe I was just a coward. The girls were trained soldiers and they weren't panicking. Maybe making a stand here was exactly the right thing to do.

"We're fucked," Gary moaned, tugging at his leash. The other end had been tied securely to a fire hydrant.

The dead fell without a sound one by one but others merely crawled over the inert bodies and continued with the advance. Ayaan and Fathia knelt together and spotted for one another, thinning out the ranks of those closest to us but even as their rifles snapped and spat, more of the dead spilled out into the street. I could remember this place in happier times and just how crowded and noisy it had been then but it was nothing like this. The noise we made must have been drawing every animated corpse in the Village.

"It is too dangerous to run now," Ifiyah shouted. "We will not leave here until every one of them is dead! Then, *inshallah*, it will be safe." I don't know who she was talking to—she certainly wasn't looking at me.

I moved back just to scout the side streets and saw that they were blocked as well—not with the solid wall of the dead that stood between us and the river but with dozens of straggling corpses moving toward us from every direction. To the west—away from the river and therefore farther from safety—the street looked relatively clear but who could know what we would find even if we ran now?

Right next to me one of the girl soldiers—a skinny one with scrapes on her kneecaps—switched her rifle over to full auto and sprayed bullets at the oncoming horde. Panic had gripped her—firing so quickly, at this range she couldn't hope for accurate head shots—and Ifiyah moved quickly to smack at her hands and make her stop. She was wasting bullets if nothing else.

I could see the girl's eyes as she felt the cold intensity of her commanding officer's anger suffuse her. I had expected to see fear there but instead I found only shame. The soldiers were ready to die here if Ifiyah ordered it, certain that to die for a noble cause is better than to live without honor.

Personally I'd rather live even if it meant having the word COWARD tattooed on my forehead. When the dead emerged from the side streets and began to flank us I snatched at Ayaan's arm and howled into her ear our need to retreat. I figured if anyone could talk some sense into Ifiyah it would be her.

The air went out of me as the stock of her AK-47 slammed into my stomach. "You don't give me my orders!" she shrieked over the noise of the company's rifles. "You give no orders at all, *gaal we'el! Sedex goor* I tell you this, and still you chirp like a baby bird at me! *Waad walantahay!*"

The dead came at us thick and fast while I tried to get my wind back. They came right for us, never deviating, never turning aside. The bullets weren't even slowing them down. Ifiyah ran back and forth shouting encouragement or abuse at one or another of her *kumayo* sisters. A dead man in a green cardigan and wingtip shoes came up on her left, having slipped through the cracks in the girls' defense. He reached for her trying to get a handful of her jacket, her head scarf, her flesh, and she cut him in half with automatic fire, literally separating his torso from his legs in a roiling haze of torn skin and bone fragments. "*Sharmutaada ayaa ku dhashay was*!" she howled, her face lit up with exultation.

The dead man in the cardigan didn't even pause. The second his top half hit the ground, he began crawling toward Ifiyah again. The commander emptied the rest of her cartridge into the body but completely missed the head. Before she had a chance to reload two skeletal hands were clutching her knee and broken teeth sank deep into her thigh.

Two of the girl soldiers pulled the corpse free from Ifiyah's leg. They stomped on the dead man's head with the heels of their combat boots until there was nothing left but grease and bone fragments. But it was too late. Ifiyah clutched at her wound, her rifle forgotten, and gazed up at her charges as if looking for ideas.

"We need to find a secure CCP," Ayaan said to me, "and you're our regional specialist." I was so engrossed with what had happened to Ifiyah, I didn't see her come up and I yelped with startlement. "Get us out of here, Dekalb!"

I nodded and stared west on Fourteenth. Only a few of the dead staggered toward us from that direction. "Somebody untie him," I said, pointing at Gary. "He's a doctor. A *takhtar*. We need him." They did as I said. The dead man claimed he couldn't run so I detailed two of the girls to carry him. If they disliked this duty they were too well trained to say so. I picked up Ifiyah myself—a little disturbed to find she weighed only a little more than my seven-year-old daughter Sarah—and then we were running, tearing down Fourteenth, our weapons clattering against our backs. We dodged around the dead there as they clawed at us. One of the girls got snared by a particularly dextrous corpse but she kicked him in the face and got free again.

Out of breath before we'd covered one avenue block I didn't let myself slow down until we ran past a building covered in scaffolding and the street opened up into the tree-lined expanse of Union Square. I realized then I had no idea where I was going. We were headed away from the river and the safety of the ship. What kind of shelter could we possibly find from the dead?

Chapter Seventeen

I called for a stop and we clustered around the statue of Gandhi at the edge of Union Square. I looked up at the smiling bronze face and issued a silent apology for surrounding him with heavily armed child soldiers. I could remember when hippie kids would put garlands of flowers around the pacifist's neck but all I saw there now were loops of wire.

"They ate the flowers," Gary pointed out. I looked back down at him.

"Flowers?" I demanded.

"Anything living. Meat is better and living meat is the best but they'll gnaw the bark off a tree if they have to." He stepped over to a big bowed oak and laid a hand on one of its thick branches. Strips of bark were indeed missing, leaving big parallel gouges in the wood.

"Why, damn it? Why do they do this?"

Gary shrugged and sat down at the base of the tree. "It's a compulsion. You can't fight it for long—the hunger just takes over. I have a theory. . . I mean, they should have all rotted away by now. Human bodies decompose fast. They should be piles of bone and goo by now but they look pretty healthy to me."

I glared at him.

"Okay, okay, that was a brain fart. By 'healthy' I mean 'in one piece.' I think when they eat living meat they get some kind of life force or whatever out of it. Some energy that helps hold them together."

"Horseshit," I breathed. I looked at the girls to see if they agreed with me but they might have been statues themselves. They had shut down, unable to contemplate just how bad things had gotten. They needed someone to tell them what to do and now, with Commander Ifiyah out of action, they didn't know where to look.

I was out of ideas. Where were we going to go? Our only escape route was cut off. We could take shelter in one of the buildings—maybe the Barnes & Noble on the north side of Union Square. At least then we would have plenty of reading material to distract us while we slowly starved to death. I had gotten this far on adrenaline but now. . .

We didn't hear the dead coming for us. They made no sound. Through the trees in the park we could hardly see them either but somehow we knew we were being surrounded. Call it battlefield paranoia if you want. Maybe we were developing a sixth sense for the dead. I ordered the girls up the stone steps and into Union Square proper where maybe we could see things a little better. When we got to one of the pavilions over the subway entrances the girls raised their rifles out of sheer habit.

"*Wacan. . . kurta. . .* " Ifiyah said softly. Something about head shots. She seemed to lack the strength to issue a real order. I looked at her leg and saw it was still bleeding badly. I called Gary over and told him to tend to it. He'd been a doctor, once. A med student, anyway and that would have to be good enough. I put a hand up to shield my eyes from the sun and scanned the far, western side of the park, looking for any movement.

I found it quickly enough. There was plenty to be seen—dozens, maybe fifty corpses converging on us while we just waited for them to show up. But what could we do? We were about to be pinned down. We had a horde of the undead coming up behind us. They weren't moving much faster than we could walk but they didn't need to rest and eventually they would catch up. There were a lot fewer of them in front of us. We would just have to fight our way through.

"Fathia," I said, summoning the soldier to stand next to me. "There, do you see them? Are they in range? Every shot has to count."

She nodded and raised her rifle to her eye. Her shot echoed around the park and a branch fell out of a tree in the distance. She took another shot and I could see one of the dead men flinch. He kept coming, though. Ayaan took her turn next but had no better results. I would have given a lot for a pair of binoculars just then.

They came out into the open near the statue of Lafayette. Big guys with bald heads—no, helmets, they were wearing helmets of some kind. Motorcyclists? One of them had either a big stick or a rifle in his hand and for a bad second I considered the possibility of dead men with guns. Whatever it was, he dropped it to free his hand so that he could reach for us even if he was a hundred yards away. These things were like meat-seeking missiles, incapable of guile or subterfuge. They just wanted us so badly they could do nothing else but want.

"That one." I pointed at the foremost and three shots rang out in quick succession. One of them must have connected—I saw sparks leap up from his helmet. He barely flinched, though. With a start I realized what we were looking at. Riot police.

Sure. There had been fairly widespread looting in the early days of the Epidemic. Lots of public panic. Of course they would have called out the riot cops to keep order. And of course some of them would have succumbed. "Try again," I said, and they both fired at once. The ex-policeman spun around in a circle as the bullets pelted his head. He collapsed to the ground and I breathed a sigh of relief.

Then he slowly got back up.

"The helmet—it must be armored," Ayaan said. Jesus, she had to be right. Only a head shot could destroy the walking dead and these particular corpses had bulletproof helmets on.

What the hell could we do? The girls kept firing. I knew they were wasting ammunition but what else could we do? They were trying for face shots now but the helmets had visors to protect against that.

"Give the orders," one of the girls said, looking up at me. "You in commander now. So give the orders."

I rubbed my cheek furiously as I looked around. There was a Virgin Megastore on the southern side of the park. I remembered going there when I was last in New York and I seemed to recall it had only a couple of entrances. It would take time, though, to get inside and barricade the place. Time we didn't have if we couldn't stop these xaaraan. "Shoot for the legs," I suggested, "if they can't walk. . . " But of course riot cops would be wearing body armor too.

The horde of the dead coming up Fourteenth were still

getting closer. The former riot cops were maybe fifty yards away.

"Give the orders," the girl insisted. I stood there as still as a block of stone without a single idea in my head.

Chapter Eighteen

The dead riot police were only forty yards away. We could see them clearly now—their padded armor, their helmets with their clear plastic visors showing the cyanotic skin underneath. They moved haltingly as if their muscles had stiffened until they had all the pliability of dry wood. Their feet slipped along the ground, looking for equilibrium that seemed in short supply.

"They won't stop," Gary told me. "They won't ever stop."

I hardly needed the information. Ifiyah, the wounded commander of the child soldiers who surrounded me had made the mistake of treating the walking dead like any other enemy force. She had tried to rout them with sustained gunfire from a defensible point. She had thought you could kill them all. But there just weren't enough bullets.

Ayaan fired again and split open a cop's boot. He stumbled and nearly fell but it didn't take him down. The one vulnerable part of his body—his head—was covered by a helmet that the relatively slow round of an AK-47 couldn't penetrate.

I knew that better than anyone. It might as well have

been one of the problems I'd had to solve back when I was getting my training from the UN. At 710 meters per second—roughly twice the speed of sound at sea level on a sunny day—the bullets could impose a great deal of force on those helmets but it would be dispersed by the mesh of Kevlar ballistic fibers lining the inside. The kind of thing a UN weapon inspector would be expected to know. Whether the target was alive or undead had not been one of the variables we'd ever needed to take into account.

At the east side of the park—our exposed flank, as it were—I heard a shout and looked over to see one of the girls waving at me. I'd sent her there to scout the opposition and the signal meant that we had a horde—a veritable army of the undead—crossing Sixth Avenue, no more than two avenue blocks away from our position. At their standard walking speed of three miles per hour (standard living human walking speed is four miles per hour but the dead tend to dawdle) that gave us at most ten minutes before we were overrun. Maybe—maybe—we could fight off the ex-riot cops when we engaged them at close quarters but doing so would take time, time we didn't have.

I had nothing to fall back on at that point except my training and so I kept doing the numbers in my head. It didn't matter how pointless my calculations might be.

The ex-police were only thirty yards away when I finally snapped out of it. The girls kept shooting—pointlessly. They weren't prepared for this, not mentally. They were still fighting a guerrilla war. Guerrilla tactics assume your opponent will make logical choices in response to your actions. The dead knew nothing of logic. I had to do something crazy, truly insane.

The girls had dumped their excess weaponry in a heap at the base of the statue of Gandhi—an irony I ignored for the moment. I'm not sure what if anything I was thinking except that I had better arm myself. The AK-47 I'd been issued back on the boat had a bent barrel, the result of my desperate use of the weapon as a pry bar back in the hospital. I needed a new weapon if I was going to fight.

I had never fired a gun before with the intent of harming anyone. I knew their specs and schematics and statistics by heart but I'd never fired so much as a pistol in a combat situation. I wasn't even looking at the weapon I picked up. I knew in an abstract way that it was a Russian-made antiarmor piece, an RPG-7V. I knew that I'd read its user manual before. I knew how to load a grenade in the front end of the barrel and how to rest the tube on my shoulder. I knew enough to take the lens cap off the sighting mechanism and how to close one eye and look through the sight with the other. I lined up the crosshairs with the helmet of the nearest undead cop. Then I lowered my aim until I was shooting at his feet. I pulled the trigger. I knew how to do that, even if I'd never fired that particular weapon before.

The dead men were twenty yards away.

A three-foot cone of sparks and fire jumped out the back of the tube. Fathia leapt back screaming—the exhaust had scorched her cheek. The grenade leapt away from me. There was no recoil at all. I let the now-empty tube fall away from my eye and watched the rocket-propelled grenade disappear at the tip of a column of white smoke. It moved so slowly, seeming to hang in the air. I watched fins pop out of its tail, saw it visibly stabilize itself in midair and correct its tumbling spin. I saw it touch the ground right in front of the leading dead man.

The briefest flash of searing white light got swallowed up instantly by a puff of grey mist that swelled up into an angry squid of billowing smoke. Debris was everywhere, falling from the sky—broken chips of concrete, divots of grass, a severed hand. A lot less noise than I would have predicted. A hot breeze washed over us, ruffling the girls' head scarves, making me blink away grit and dust.

The smoke cleared and I saw a three-foot crater in the ground surrounded by mangled bodies, limbs torn away, exposed bones pointing accusingly up at the air. A couple of the former cops were still moving, twitching mostly but still hauling themselves toward us with fingers that bent all wrong. More of them lay motionless on the sidewalk, victims of shrapnel and hydrostatic shock.

"*Xariif*," Ayaan muttered. It meant "clever" and it was the nicest thing she'd ever said to me.

I slung the empty tube, still dribbling smoke from both ends, over my shoulder and waved for our scout to come join us. Time was still very much an issue. Once we had regrouped I led the girls in a desperate run down Fourteenth Street to the east—toward the Virgin Megastore there. The main entrance, a triangular shaped lobby of glass doors was locked up tight but that was a good thing. A second entrance near the store's café opened when I yanked on the chrome handle of the door. I ushered the girls inside, telling them to fan out and secure the place. Gary brought up the end of the line. I held my arm across the opening before he could go in. We were spooked, tired, and still in a lot of danger. It wasn't going to do much for morale if the girls had to watch Ifiyah die. I wanted to talk to Gary about what could be done and what our options might be.

"She's going to die," I tried, but he was ready for me.

"Let me look at her. Maybe I can save her."

We both knew the likelihood of that. Nobody ever survived being bitten by the undead. The mouth of the dead man who attacked Ifiyah would have been swimming with microbes—gangrene, septicemia, typhus would have been injected right into her wound. Add shock and the massive loss of blood and Ifiyah barely stood more of a chance inside with us than outside with the dead.

Still. She was alive, for now. I may have just fired a rocket-propelled grenade into a crowd but it hadn't completely changed who I was. If there was a chance for Ifiyah to make it I had to give her that much.

I sighed but I held the door open for him. He mumbled thanks as he stepped into the gloomy megastore. I followed right on his heels and pulled the door shut behind me.

Chapter Nineteen

We spread out to cover the first floor of the megastore, moving quietly through the rows of display racks, pointing rifles behind counters and into closets. The store was comprised of two floors, a main level fronted with plate glass where we could look out across the Square and a basement full of DVDs. The afternoon daylight lit up the main floor pretty well but the lower level was lost in darkness. I sent Ayaan and a squad of girls down there with flashlights to scope it out. They returned in a few minutes looking scared but with nothing to report. Good.

The first order of business was to secure the café door. We found the keys to the store in a manager's office and locked it, then pushed tables and chairs up against it to form a barricade. Some of the girls did likewise with the front doors. By this point the dead had already arrived. They pressed up against the windows. They shoved and jostled each other trying to walk through the glass. They beat their hands against it, crushed their faces up against it. For a bad ten minutes or so I thought the glass might break just from the pressure of their bodies. It held. They were terrible to look at—their faces covered in white and pink sores, their hands cut and broken as they impotently pummeled the glass. I told the girls to move away from the windows, into the shadowy back of the store, just for morale's sake.

We got Ifiyah propped up in the manager's leather chair and Gary used a first-aid kit from the café to bandage her wound. The skin around the bite looked bloodless and swollen. I didn't hold out a lot of hope. Commander Ifiyah could still talk at that point and Fathia, her bayonet expert, held her hand and asked her a series of quiet questions I didn't fully understand.

"*See tahay*?" Fathia asked.

"*Waan xanuunsanahay*," was the reply. "*Biyo*?"

Fathia handed her commander a canteen and the wounded girl drank greedily, spilling water all down the front of her blazer. I turned away and saw Ayaan coming toward me down the display aisles. "Dekalb. We are safe for now, yes? Some of the girls would like to pray. It has been too long already."

I nodded, surprised she would even ask. It seemed that in the power vacuum left by Ifiyah's debilitation I had become the absolute authority of the team. I wasn't sure how I felt about that. I didn't think I really wanted that kind of responsibility though as a Westerner it was a relief to not have anyone else barking orders at me.

More than half of the girls wanted to pray. They laid down handwoven *derin* mats on the floor of the megastore and pointed them toward the east, my best guess for the direction of Mecca. They chanted in Arabic while I watched the other girls—the less-devout ones, I suppose. Mostly they stared out the windows at the dead outside. Were they wondering what we were going to do next? I know I was.

One girl—one of the youngest, her name was Leyla, I think—wandered along the merchandise racks, one hand holding the strap of her AK-47, the other flipping through the various CDs on display. Her lower lip curled down or up as she read the titles. When she found one that really appealed to her she would bend at the waist as if desperately trying to contain the urge to jump up and down. Watching her made me think of Sarah. Leyla might be a good deal older and much more dangerous but she still possessed the thrumming spirit, the barely controlled energy I had come to adore in my daughter.

God, Sarah had never been so far away as then.

"There's nothing more that I can do for her," Gary told me, peeling off a pair of latex gloves. I looked over at Ifiyah and saw that she was sleeping or at least passed out. Ragged strips of cloth had been tied tight around her leg until her foot turned purple. A tourniquet. Even if she survived she was probably going to lose the leg.

Gary sat down on the floor and peeled open a piece of beef jerky. Chewing idly on it he stared at me until I began to feel the silence between us turn into something that had to be tamed. But Gary spoke first. "Why did you come to New York?" he asked. "Did you have family here?"

I shook my head. "A long time ago, yeah. But my parents died before. . . this. My Mom died in a plane crash and my Dad couldn't live without her. He just faded away. It's funny—at my Mom's funeral I remember thinking how badly I wanted her to come back." I glanced toward the windows. "I guess you should be careful what you wish for, huh?"

"Christ, you're so hard-core," Gary said, rolling his eyes. "Relax a little."

I nodded and squatted down next to him. I realized I was hungry and gratefully took one of his plastic-wrapped foodlike snacks. "Sorry. I guess I'm scared. No, we came to Manhattan looking for medical supplies. The President-for-Life of Somaliland has AIDS, but anti-retrovirals just aren't available in Africa right now."

"What's in it for you?"

I took Sarah's picture from my wallet but I didn't let him touch it, not with those dead hands. I showed it to him and then stared at it for a while myself. "She and I get full citizenship in one of the last safe places on Earth." In the picture Sarah, aged five, petted the nose of a camel that had been unaccountably docile at the time. The picture didn't show what came next—the camel's wet sneeze, little Sarah's shrieks as she ran all over a camp full of nomads who smiled and clapped their hands for her and offered her pieces of fruit. That had been a good day. I always tended to think of Africa as one long horror story—an occupational hazard, I guess—but there had been so many good days.

"I'd like to rest a while, if you don't mind," I told him. I wasn't tired so much as so introspective it was becoming difficult to focus on anyone else. He obliged by scuttling off to a dusty corner of the store where he could chew on his SlimJims in peace.

For my part I turned to look out the window—not at the dead people there, I was barely aware of them—but instead at the Empire State Building, clearly visible above the trees at the north end of Union Square. The iconic skyscraper seemed to just hover there, detached from the world. I wondered what, if anything, you would find in its uppermost stories now. A hell of a walk, since the elevator wouldn't be running, but worth it, maybe. What kind of safety, what manner of serenity might still exist up there? I'd visited the observation deck plenty of times when I was a kid and I knew you could see the entire city from up there but in my musing nothing was visible but long icy sweeps of cloud, a veil between me and the filth on the surface.

I'm told this kind of detachment is common among veteran soldiers. In the aftermath of a perilous fight the mind shuts down its faculties one by one and drifts— perhaps endlessly reliving the moment when a squad mate caught a bullet, perhaps trying to remember all the details of the chaos once it was past, perhaps just—as mine was doing here—wandering without thought or feeling at all. There's even a name for this phenomenon, the "Thousand-Yard Stare," this kind of temporary mindlessness. Modern medicine sometimes refers to it as "Combat Stress Reaction." It's a lot less zen than it sounds. More like the opposite of mindless enlightenment. It's like being trapped inside your own worst memory. Usually a victim snaps right out of it as soon as a new task or duty presents itself. Sometimes soldiers never come out of it, and sometimes they drift in and out of it for the rest of their lives—that's called "Post Traumatic Stress Disorder," which everyone knows about.

There was no stimulus to bring me out, not just then. For me there was nothing to do but wait—wait for the dead people outside to rot away. Wait for one of the girls to have a brilliant idea. Wait for all of us to starve to death. I watched the light change, the Empire State changing from a grey eminence to a ruddy obelisk to a stroke of black paint across the starry blue sky as afternoon gave way to evening gave way to night.

In time, I slept, and I dreamed.

Chapter Twenty

"Baryo," the girl—the commander of the girls—moaned, stirring in her sleep. Gary had secured her to a padded office chair with his own belt so that she wouldn't fall out if she went into convulsions.

He didn't look at her. He couldn't—not quite yet. He knew she was dying and he knew what he would see if he turned around and looked at her and he didn't want to see it. Instead he looked out through the glass at the crowd of the dead there. They pressed up just as tightly against the windows as before but over the last few hours their desperation had slackened a bit. Not that they would be any less hungry, of course—but night, and darkness, seemed to mellow them a little. They didn't need to sleep. Gary knew that firsthand. He couldn't sleep, himself—the old remembered feeling, the drooping eyes, the leaden limbs. No. That was over for him, and for them. Yet some kind of ingrained memory of their lives must be telling them that when the sun went down it was time to rest. It would be fascinating to study their behavior firsthand, Gary thought. What an opportunity to do science!

"Daawo," she said, behind him. He started to glance over his shoulder. Stopped himself in time.

He would have plenty of time to live among the dead and learn their ways. It had become clear to him in the last few hours that the Somalis wouldn't take him with them when they left. Of course they wouldn't—he was undead. Unclean in their eyes. Yet some sort of bizarre vestigial hope of rescue had been swelling in him every since he saw their boat out on the Hudson. In the heat of his capture and then the battle that followed he hadn't been able to think clearly but now, now. . . there was no escaping it. No matter how much he helped them, sucked up to them, wheedled his way into their hearts, they would never take him away from New York. He would be lucky to get a pat on the back. More likely a bullet to the forehead would be his recompense for all his good service.

"*Maxaa? Madaya ayaa i xanuunaya. . . gaajo.*"

Gary wished he understood what she was saying. She was in such distress he couldn't help it. He turned around and looked. The girl's face had turned the color of cigarette ash and her eyes were protruding from her head. He bent down and lifted the blanket off her legs. They had swollen up so much he could barely tell where her knees used to be. Not just the injured leg, either. The infection had spread throughout her lower body. She was doomed.

"*Canjeero,*" she said plaintively. "*Soor. Maya, Hilib. Hilib. Xalaal hilib. Baryo.*"

He could feel the heat radiating from her face. No, not heat. Something else. A sort of energy, but not anything truly palpable. Like the vibration you feel when you're sitting inside a building and a heavy truck rumbles by outside. Or the way your skin crawls when you know someone is walking right behind you but you can't see them. A phantom sensation, barely liminal but there if you reached for it.

Gary reached.

"*Fadlan maya*," the girl moaned, as if she could sense what he was doing. Then, angrier: "*Ka tegid*!" He didn't know the words but he could guess the meaning. She wanted to be left alone. Just give me a second, he thought, knowing he could use some work on his bedside manner. Still, he had to know.

He didn't so much study her with his eyes or nose or ears but with something else—the hairs on the back of his arms, the skin behind his earlobes. Some part of his body was responding to this weird energy she was putting off. It made his toes curl. Energy. Like the vibrations of a tuning fork. It coiled around her and spun off into the air like smoke, like embers exploding out of a bonfire. It warmed his skin where it touched him, irritated him a little in a good way. Like a lover's breath on the back of his neck. Gary had never had many girlfriends, but he knew what it felt like to be touched. To be caressed. What was happening to him?

To understand a little better he stepped over to where Dekalb and the other, healthy girls were sleeping, wrapped in their colorful woven mats. He stilled himself and tried to make himself as absorbent as possible. The energy was there, in all of them, but it was very different—a compact mass of it, pulsing on a low register, vibrating like a drum. Dekalb had a little more of it—he was bigger than the girls—but the energy contained in the girls felt more vibrant, more exciting somehow.

"*Waan xanuunsanahay*," the wounded girl muttered.

Gary returned to her, squatted before her. Whatever this energy was—and Gary knew, knew with a certainty that it was her life—it was leaking from her. Draining away. She would be dead within the hour, judging by how little of it was left in her. She would go to waste. What a strange thing to think, but there it was. She would die and she would go to waste.

Gary backed off and tore open the plastic wrapping of another SlimJim. Chewed on it pensively. He couldn't— he shouldn't look at her anymore, it was giving him bad ideas. He could control himself. It was one of the first things he'd said to Dekalb. He could think for himself. He didn't have to obey every passing whim.

He pressed one hand against the glass of the windows. The dead outside glanced at his hand for a moment, then went back to pressing their faces against the glass, staring at the people inside. Back to wanting, to needing. He was like them, in so many ways, but he had this one difference. His willpower. His will. He could resist any urge if he tried hard enough.

"*Waan xanuunsanahay. Hilib.*"

He considered leaving, going out into the throng out there—they wouldn't hurt him, he didn't think. He was useless to them. Nothing that could concern them. He didn't know how he could open the door, however, without letting hundreds of them push their way inside before he could get out and close the door behind him.

There was just no way out. He was stuck in here— trapped, with the rest of them.

"*Biyo,*" the girl begged. "*Biyo!*"

Maybe, he thought, maybe her cries would wake the others. Maybe Dekalb would wake up and realize he'd forgotten to post a guard. Maybe the girls would wake up and take care of their commander, give her what she needed. Maybe they would put her out of her misery. But they didn't even stir.

He ate another SlimJim with shaking hands but it wasn't hunger that had him so agitated—not the kind of hunger that the snack food could quench, anyway.

"*Takhtar*! *Kaalay dhaqsi*!" The girl sounded almost lucid. Gary rushed to the far side of the store, to the manager's office. He found a closet and stepped inside and shut the door behind him. Sitting on the floor with his head between his knees he pressed his hands against his ears.

It would be alright. He could control himself. It would be alright.

Chapter Twenty-One

In my dream I was driving.

Big car, eight cylinders probably. Leather interior, chrome on the wheels. Hell, let's give it tail fins. A big-voiced throaty roar whenever I stepped on the gas and one of those radios with a luminous needle that rolled back and forth across the airwaves, scratching for hits. My hands on the scalloped steering wheel were huge and strong and brown.

It was night, and I was driving through the desert. Moonlight picked out the brush and the weeds and the rolling hills of sand and the dead. It was dark inside the car except for that luminous needle and the reflections it made in Sarah's eyes. Inside, in the dark Sarah looked just like Ayaan but it was Sarah. It was Sarah. Outside the dead were running alongside the car, keeping up pretty well even though the car was pushing ninety. I poured on a little more speed and saw Helen smiling at me from the left, her legs pumping madly so she could match velocities with us. Her teeth fell out. Her skin peeled away, she was running so fast and soon she was nothing but bones but still running. She waved and I nodded back, one big round elbow hanging out my open window. My body rocked as the car just rumbled along.

"Dekalb," Sarah said, "*iga raali noqo*, but what's that?" She was staring at my hand on the wheel.

I switched on the dome light and saw my hands were covered in blood. "Hell, girl, that's nothing," I drawled. "Just a little fluid. I—"

I woke before I could finish the thought. I opened my eyes but there was nothing to see—without power Manhattan was as dark at night as the depths of the country. Darker since the skyscrapers blocked out even the starlight. I lay on my side, stiff and uncomfortable and chilled to the bone. Something wet and sticky had pooled under my hand—dew, perhaps.

I sat up slowly with a groan and flexed my knees to try to get some circulation back in my legs. I thought I could hear something moving nearby but I presumed it was just the dead outside, waiting for us to come out and be eaten. Ignoring it I rose to my feet. There had been a bathroom next to the manager's office and I went there, careful not to step on any of the sleeping girls. It wasn't easy—my eyes had adjusted to the darkness but there was still barely enough light for me to discern individual shadows in the gloom. I urinated noisily into the dry toilet and then, despite the obvious fact that the water shouldn't work, I reached out for the lever in the murky darkness and flushed. Strangely enough it worked. Water rushed into the bowl and carried away my waste. I don't know what kind of water system Manhattan has but it must be a marvel—months after the last living person was around to maintain it, the plumbing in the Virgin Megastore was functioning perfectly. Such a small thing, a stupid thing but it made up for so much. Something that still worked.

Something from the old world, the old life and it still worked.

Impressed and relieved I went back out onto the floor and wondered if there was any food left in the café's pantry. I kind of doubted it but I was hungry enough to make a cursory search, at least. Halfway there I heard the noise again, the movement I'd heard immediately after waking. This time I was certain that it was inside the store.

Fear, of course, clears the mind. Adrenaline pumped out from my kidneys and spread through my body in a rush. My back prickled and the skin beneath my earlobes started to sweat. It could have been a rat, or one of the girls stirring in her sleep. It could have been an animated corpse that had somehow found its way into the building at a time when we couldn't see to defend ourselves.

I took my flashlight out of my pocket and clicked it on.

"Dekalb." It was Gary, the world's smartest dead man. I began to turn and point my light in his direction but he said, "No, please, don't look yet." I stopped and switched my light off.

I heard him come closer. Maybe he could see in the dark—he wasn't stumbling around like me. "Dekalb," he said, "I need your help. I need you to explain to them. They have to understand."

"I don't know what you're talking about," I said.

"I can be a great asset to you," he said. His voice was soothing, almost hypnotic in the darkness. "You need to find those AIDS drugs before you can leave, right? I can walk anywhere in the city and be safe. I can get the drugs you need and bring them to your boat. You can sit on the boat and be safe and just wait for me to come to you."

"Gary," I tried, "did you do something—"

"Let's not go there yet. I have something else—an idea about how you can get out of here in one piece. Right now you're screwed, right? You can't walk out that door without getting pulled to pieces. You have no food, no radio. There's nobody coming to save you. You need this. You need this solution I've come up with."

He was right about that. "Tell me," I said.

"Not until you speak to the girls on my behalf. You have to keep them away from me, Dekalb. That's what you do, right? You used to work for the UN. You mediate disputes. You have to mediate for me, you have to help me, come on. Just say you will."

I might as well have just eaten twenty snow cones. My belly was full of ice. "I'm going to turn my light on, Gary," I started.

He moved so quickly he could have snapped my neck if he wanted to. Instead he merely grabbed my hand and forced me to drop my flashlight. I could feel his body very close to mine, smell the decay of his flesh—and something else, something fresher but no less gruesome. "You help me, Dekalb. Damn you, you're going to help me," he whispered in my face and I smelled salami. "She was going to die anyway."

CLISH-CLACK! The sound of the selector lever on an AK-47 being switched from SAFE to SINGLE FIRE. It was Ayaan. "Dekalb, what is this? Why are you making so much noise?" Her light speared through the darkness and showed me Gary's face. There was blood on his chin, red, wet blood.

Unh-uh. No, I thought, that wasn't in the plan. No, I didn't plan for this.

"I can get the drugs for you, Dekalb. I can get you out of here!"

I could feel Ayaan staring at the back of my head. Waiting for an order. In a second she would make a decision for herself and lift her flashlight to point it in the corner, where we'd left Ifiyah unconscious in an office chair.

I could feel Gary's body convulsing in dread, only inches away. "You can't do it without me! Dekalb!"

The cone of light drifted up and over. The three of us must all have seen the trail of blood on the floor. I remembered the pool of sticky liquid I'd woken up in and my throat squirmed. I had blood on my hands in my dream.

"Dekalb! Save me!"

As revealed by the flashlight Ifiyah's body had undergone a sea change. Her jacket and shirt had been removed. As had most of her torso. I could see yellow ribs glinting in the dim light. I couldn't see her face or her left arm—they might have been lost in the shadows. They might have been.

"Ayaan," I said, softly, "let's think about our next move here before—"

I heard the bullet snap through the air, as loud as thunder. I heard it splinter Gary's skull. I felt something dry and powdery splatter across my face and chest as Gary's body slumped away from me, spinning down to collapse on its side.

I tried to breathe but breath wouldn't come. Then with a spasm it burst from my throat. A kind of whimper.

I reached down and picked up my own flashlight. Switched it on and pointed it at him.

The smartest dead man in the world had a finger-wide hole in his right temple. There was no blood but something grey oozed from the wound—brains, I would imagine. His body flexed and twisted spasmodically for a while. Then it stopped.

Part
Two

Chapter One

*fingers digging, twisting pressing open wound smell of
cinnamon laughing dark dark dark cold hungry fingers
digging, grabbing, tearing—*

Gary was losing. Dying. His spark, his animating force
was draining out of him, out of the hole in his head.

Start again.

(There was someone else there. Someone strong and so
determined, so determined not to let Gary give up. There
was someone else there.)

Falling, free and weightless for just a moment in the
darkness, even the yellow cones of the flashlights lost to
him now in this comfortable quiet blindness he tumbled
as he fell, tossed from the railing, ejected from paradise
into the depths of the megastore. Colliding, his back
striking the soft rubber handrail of an escalator but at
this speed everything was hard, so hard and brittle and
he could feel his vertebrae snapping, T6, then T7, T8 all
gone, pulverized as his body folded like a spring-loaded
pocketknife across the handrail, never walk again, ha ha
ha.

In the darkness, the darkness of blindness, there was
this shape, see, this white tree shape like something

burned into Gary's retinas, the flash, the muzzle flash of an assault rifle the last thing he saw the last thing he would ever see, it looked kind of like a tree, maybe the branches were the veins in his eyes lit up as they exploded from the hydrostatic shock of the gunshot, maybe they weren't branches, though, maybe—

Gary slid to the floor in an ungainly pile.

fingers fingers fingers in the pie, dig around, wiggle it around

Oozing out of him this unlife, this half light was flickering away.

Start again.

White and fat, fleshy almost, the tree rose out of fertile ground to stretch bright leaves smeared across the sky, its fat fleshy trunk pulsing with life but no, shattered, the tree had been shattered by lightning or by rain, just a trunk now, Gary could see it, its limbs broken and scattered around its base, just a trunk sticking up out of the ground, fractured, a big knot right in the middle of the stump like a surprised mouth open in an eternal O as if frozen in the moment of surprise, the moment when the coyote has not yet realized he's standing on air, the tree is just a stump.

All of this splattered across his vision. The only thing he could see. His muscles—his body, this rubbery doll kept moving underneath him. Spasms dragged his head across the floor, just die already, he could feel the bullet in his head so hot, so hot and solid as it floated in the liquid, in the jelly of his brains. That was it, of course, the end, finito. The dead die but twice and this is it, this is, of course, it. Bullet to the head. The end.

(Not the end. The someone—the benefactor—who was there in the darkness—the strong one—the determined

one said this is not the end said you still have a chance but
you have to take it.)

The tree was just a stump. Still. Pulsing with life.
Goddamn well throbbing with it.

He still had a little control. A trembling frail energy
that was his, his to use even as it frittered away. Feeling
weightless, lighter than air, his hand went up to his temple
and found the wound, the entry hole. Dampness on his
fingers.

God. Disgusting. The hole was wide enough to stick
a finger inside.

the sound a mop makes when it hits the floor

. . . but that was a memory, not a real sound. Gary
probed again with his finger and heard the same sound.
Almost like pressing a key on a piano. He pressed again
and this time. . . this time he felt something real. Hard
metal that resisted his finger.

The bullet.

*sucking life from somewhere, jesus you could see it
move as it throbbed as the fluids flowed as the life moved
under the fleshy white bark, inside the wet fibrous wood
just a stump but taking life from somewhere*

Almost over now. Why keep striving, when there was
no hope?

START AGAIN.

(the benefactor insisted.)

maybe they weren't branches maybe they were roots

Thought became mercurial, slippery as a fish in
a stream as your fingers reach for it, silver and bright
under the splashing water, silvery and hard in your head
reaching for it, going to take two fingers have to open up
just a little wider come on say ah, aaahhh very good, you

are easily the most well-behaved little boy it has ever been my pleasure to perform open brain surgery on tee hee two fingers in, does it hurt? Does it hurt? Nothing hurts right now, man, I am comfortably numb like the song goes and now I've got two fingers in but the visuals, man, like this tree, this TREE—

Its roots go down forever. Up above in the sunlight there may be golden apples, tight little bundles of life force the color of. . . of. . . just such a lovely color nothing you could see with your eyes, though. None of the seven colors they teach you about in school. Was it two dozen? Dekalb and the girls, sure, two dozen of them waiting, hunkering down in the dark so afraid and cold and hungry and alone but they didn't know, they couldn't know just how beautifully alive-they were. Up there in the sunlight, metaphorical of course because certainly it's still night up there it must be pitch dark in the megastore but in this metaphorical space, this place you've fled to because you've passed out—yeah, good one, dead man fainting— passed out because you're literally trying to dig a bullet out of your head with your fingers, in this metaphorical space Dekalb etc. are up there, up there in a summer day compared to what's down here, down deep deep-sixed eighty-sixed down in davy jones' locker, down among the dead men, the dead men, the dead men

YES.

(nodding, the benefactor agreed.)

Because they, the dead men, were there too, if only dimly perceptible. Down underneath in the soil in the dirt where the roots dug endlessly like blind worms searching, scratching, like fingers digging for the bullet because oh, yes, just because you passed out Gary doesn't mean you stopped trying to grab for that brass ring, that lead sinker in the muddle, stop that, in the middle of your gelatin head.

But, Gary thought, I digress. I was speaking of the dead men who feed the tree. Stinking little buggers, stinking of the life force because it was positively dripping from them, fuming up like steam off their backs as it evaporated away not the golden shiny life of Dekalb and friends, no, this was the shadow of that energy—lacking dimension, cold instead of hot, dark, dark purple instead of bright—but it was still energy of a kind. Enough to feed the tree. Enough to feed anybody if you could tap it and yes, Gary could. Gary could. Because unlike the discrete packets of energy inside of Dekalb's Angels, those ripe bursting fruits of life force, the dead men were all connected, interconnected, tied together in a web of fuming darkness. There were what, six, seven billion people before the Epidemic but now there was only one dead man, in a sense. The thing, the Epidemic, the disaster that brought the dead back joined them together, made them as one, like a cloud of locusts so thick they darken the sky like clouds, an infinite number of tiny droplets of water but where does one end and one begin there is no answer it's a zen koan there is only one of us with many bodies and I am its will. I am its commander.

YES.

(there is a connection, the benefactor said, a web that joins us.)

Remember Trucker Cap? Remember him, because Gary sure did remember how Trucker Cap had attacked him and Gary had told him to stop and he did. And Gary had told him to fuck off and die and lo and behold so it had come to pass because Gary, alone among the dead, could still think. He could still reach out. He alone had the willpower. He was connected to them all, he was one of them, but he alone could exploit that.

He sucked dark energy from the crowd that surrounded the megastore, sucked it out from a distance and felt it surge up through his arm, thrilling into his fingers and yes and yes and yes there it was god fucking damn you, there he had it eureka he had it and he pulled, so much power in his hand he had to make a conscious act of will to keep from yanking the fucking thing out and then it was in his hand wet and hot and he clutched it, squeezed it, the goddamn bullet was out of his head. It was out of his head. The damage was done, brain tissue torn up like a wet wad of toilet paper skin bone and muscle pierced vertebrae broken, shattered but you know what? None of it mattered.

The tree pulsed with life as it would forever. Fucking forever man I'm going to live forever and you cannot stop me, Gary thought, he wanted to scream it at fucking Ayaan and fucking Dekalb you cannot stop me I am billions strong.

He dropped the bullet and it made a sound like a tiny bell ringing. From above he heard a tense whisper. "What was that?"

He heard it. He could hear again.

When dawn came and with it the light, he could see again. He was standing, standing in the shadows, looking at an Olsen Twins DVD in his hand and he could read the smallest text on the back of the jewel case. He could see. He could stand and walk. Life (of a sort, the dark sort) pulsed through him so furiously, so strongly he was surprised he wasn't glowing.

YES.

(yes, the benefactor said. yes.)

Chapter Two

The gunshot woke the girls, of course. Ayaan rushed to throw her blazer over Ifiyah's ravaged form so the others wouldn't see what Gary had done to her. Together she and I lifted Gary's lifeless body and threw it over the edge, threw it down into the darkness of the lower level. The girls would have torn him to pieces for what he did to Ifiyah, and I couldn't stomach that. As it was the girls had a million questions. I tried to explain as calmly as I could that she was gone, and Gary too. There was some wailing and crying and a few of the girls offered up prayers for Ifiyah. None of us slept after that.

Whatever Gary had done to Ifiyah, she didn't reanimate. Either he ate her brain or. . . hell. I didn't understand how the Epidemic worked. All I knew was that she didn't get up again.

In the first light of day I heard a tiny sound, a tinny sound like a bell ringing somewhere. "What was that?" I whispered, thinking of the bells that rang when you walked into a bodega in this city. This was the Virgin Megastore, though, and the doors were locked up tight—we checked. The sound was not repeated.

I couldn't relax, couldn't get comfortable, though

fatigue softened my head and made my thoughts slow and cold as glaciers moving through an ice age, growing a few inches a year it felt like. I stood and watched the dead outside pressing up against the windows and didn't have the mental energy to plan or consider options. I barely noticed when one of the dead men slumped to the ground and others surged in to take his place.

A woman with a long open wound on her arm and an Yves Saint Laurent bag still dangling from the crook of her elbow slapped the glass with a greasy palm and then fell, her body held up for a moment by the crowd behind her. She slid down the glass, her flabby cheek rippling where it pressed up against the window until she landed on the sidewalk outside. A teenage boy in a white T-shirt climbed on top of her but then he too collapsed.

Here and there others fell—singly at first, then in great clumps that rolled backwards like waves receding from a shoreline. I grabbed my rifle, thinking this must be some trick. But that had been Ifiyah's mistake, of course, to think the dead were capable of subterfuge. As far as I could tell they just were with no art or thought required. As they fell away from the megastore sunlight streaked in through the windows and lit up the faces of the girls.

"They *dhimasha*, Commander," Fathia said, as if she were giving me a report from the front. They are dying, is what I think she meant to say.

I could see that for myself. Of the hundreds, maybe thousands of dead people who had mobbed the megastore trying to get at us only a few were still standing and they were clutching their heads and wandering aimlessly around Union Square. They seemed less interested in us than in whatever had claimed their fellows. Almost certainly that was giving them too much credit but that's what it looked like.

Leadership, I was once told by a Regional Field Head for the Disarmament Project in Sudan, has less to do with making the best decision than making a decision. "Get your things, we're leaving," I told the girls.

They snapped to it. Prayer mats were rolled up, weapons were checked and thrown over shoulders. Fathia and Leyla, the youngest girl, moved to collect Ifiyah's body, but I shook my head. We were going to move fast and couldn't afford to be slowed down by carrying the dead commander.

I unlocked the door but Ayaan was the first one out, her weapon swinging wildly as she tried to cover each of the stragglers in turn. They didn't react to her presence at all. I shuffled the rest of the girls out the door and then took up the rear. I caught myself about to yell out an order—the noise might have broken the dead out of their spell—and instead jogged forward to tap Ayaan's shoulder. I pointed in the direction of the river.

It was all she needed. She threw three quick hand signals at the girls and we broke into a run, not so much a sprint (we were each carrying twenty pounds of gear at the least) as a loping jog but there was urgency there, believe me. At first we had to leap over piles of bodies (or just step on them in a couple of places) but beyond the periphery of Union Square the sidewalks were clear. Sixth Avenue passed. Seventh. I slowed momentarily outside of Western Beef, wondering if this was where our luck ended but the dead had deserted the place. Every walking corpse in the Village must have been there at the megastore because we saw only a handful on our way back to the Hudson. Once we were past Sixth Avenue, the spell wore off—they came at us as determined as ever, but just as slowly, too.

As we ran past their rotten clutching hands I felt a certain real relief that we were back on familiar ground again. Whatever had slain the dead in Union Square had to be big and powerful and I didn't relish finding out what it wanted from me.

The thought that it might be benevolent, this unseen force that claimed the dead for its own, never even occurred to me. There was nothing truly good or clean left in this world. Anything that seemed that way had to come with strings attached.

At the river we stopped on the dock and waved our arms. The Arawelo stood out in the water about a hundred yards with no one visible on deck but we were too out of breath to think the worst. After a minute or two Mariam came up on deck, her blazer off and Osman's fishing hat perched low over her eyes. She made a frantic gesture toward the hatches and the two sailors emerged from belowdecks, looking as if they'd been caught at something naughty.

I didn't give a damn what they'd been up to. They brought the boat in to the dock and threw us lines so we could tie it up. In a minute we were on board and we cast off again.

I guess leaving the megastore in such a hurry really had been the right decision, because we all made it back. The girls looked at me with something new in their eyes. I wasn't about to go so far as to call it respect.

When I finally sat down I found I was ravenous. I called for *canjeero*, a flat Somali bread that was our staple food on the boat. Osman rubbed his head and squinted at me for a while before he decided what he was going to say.

"You in charge now, Dekalb? You're the *weyn nin*?" He glanced around at the girls. "Ifiyah didn't come back, I see."

I made no comment. Osman and I had possessed a sort of easy camaraderie on the voyage to New York. Two grown men on a ship full of children—it would have been hard not to bond. Now I was changed, though, in some subtle but very real way. I had fired a rocket-propelled grenade into a crowd of my enemies. I had ordered soldiers to shoot to kill. I had led the girls to safety—and I had also let one of the dead eat their commanding officer.

"At least tell me you got the drugs and we can go home!" He raised both hands in the air, surrendering to his disbelief. My silence left him high and dry, and slowly he lowered his arms. We both knew we couldn't return to Somalia without the medical supplies. We had failed to find them and in the process we had lost four of our number. I shook my head.

"Well, that is just fucked up, sir, yes, sir!" Osman said and flipped me a one-finger salute. I suppose there are limits to the respect that comes with leadership.

Chapter Three

Fine blue tattoos covered him from head to toe. A rope tied tight around his neck and an armband made of fur were his only clothing but he stood there unashamed and looked down at Gary with a kind of haughty pride. A particularly stuck-up teacher staring down at his best pupil from the top of the escalators.

"Come to me," he said again, and then he was gone. In his place was an image of a temple or a library or something. Lots of steps leading up to a facade of columns. Gary knew the place but its name wouldn't come to him.

Climbing the escalator took a couple of tries. Gary's brain continued to heal itself but his motor control was the slowest in coming back. Lucidity had returned like walking into air conditioning on a scorcher of a day but the simple act of putting one foot in front of the other was still mostly beyond him. The seizures that racked his body and left his brain fizzing like a well-shaken seltzer bottle didn't help either. He would progress a few yards only to find himself lying on the floor with no explanation how he'd gotten there, his hands clenched like claws and his ankles twisted beneath him.

In time he reached the ground floor of the megastore,

taking the last few steps on his hands and knees. He rose shakily and lurched for the door only to be stricken by the sight of what lay outside.

Bodies—hundreds of bodies—in an advanced state of decay, clogging up the sidewalks and slumped at random over the abandoned cars. Putrefying flesh lay in heaps under the mid-morning sun, not all of it recognizably human anymore.

Jesus, Gary thought. Had he really done all this damage himself?

These weren't like the undead he'd seen before. These were just. . . rotting meat, yellow bones pointing out of deliquescing flesh with the consistency of runny cheese.

Something stirred in the Square to the north and he dodged behind a Jeep, not wanting to get shot in the head again. He needn't have worried, though. It was one of the dead. A dead woman in a print dress stained with old blood and darker fluids. She came closer, waddling as if she couldn't bend at the knees and he saw she was badly damaged. Most of the skin was gone from her face and a clump of maggots perched in the hollow of her clavicles like a writhing scarf. Good God, how could she let that happen? Disgusting as they might be the maggots were alive. They could have given her the energy to repair her body. Instead they were feeding on her.

Others appeared behind her, mostly men. They too had seen better days. The walking dead of New York tended to have a few wounds on their bodies, sure, and maybe their skin tone was a shade paler and bluer than necessary—Gary thought furthermore of the dead veins that lined his own face—but never had they let themselves go this badly. One of these newcomers had no nose at all, just a dark inverted V in the middle of his face. Another had lost his eyelids so he seemed to be constantly staring in horrified wonder.

Gary reached out across the network of death that connected him to these shambling messes. The same connection that had let him draw their energy, that had given him the strength to dig the bullet out of his brain. The mental effort made his brain wriggle in his head and a searing white pain flashed down his back but the contact was made. He could feel the dark energy fuming out of these wretches and he understood a little of what must have happened. In his desperation he had sucked the energy out of the crowd around the megastore to save his own skin and in the process had accelerated the decay of his victims. In the new order of things the dead ate the living in a vain attempt to prop up their own sagging existence, to fuel their unlife. Gary had undone all that striving and hard work and now the rotting piles of corpses outside looked like they had been dead all along, dead and decomposing since the Epidemic began. There was no cheating death, Gary realized, only delaying it—and when it finally caught up it did so with a vengeance.

The noseless one reached out and touched Gary's face with an unfeeling hand. The fingers draped lifelessly across his cheek. Gary didn't flinch. How could he? There was no malice in the gesture. It had all the emotional resonance of a muscular twitch.

Most of the undead had lost the battle with death when Gary stole their essence. Those few strong enough to survive were left with only the barest tatters of energy remaining. Hence the broken and rigid undead he saw before him. Perhaps worse than their physical condition was their mental state. He had stolen from them the remnant of intellect that kept them hunting for food. Their hunger remained—he could feel it yawning inside of them, burning more fiercely than ever—but he had stolen from them the knowledge, no matter how vestigial, of how to slake it. He had taken what little mind they had so now they no longer remembered how to eat. They could only wander aimlessly as their bodies fell to pieces.

Gary felt no guilt. It had been necessary. He had been dying for a second and final time and only their stolen energy had been able to keep his consciousness going. Why, then, did he identify so strongly with them, why did he feel so much empathy? He was tied to them, he realized. He was one of them. He was part of the network of death. His ability to reach out and steal their energy defined him. There was no real line of division, no watershed between himself and these near-lifeless hulks that wobbled without purpose up and down Fourteenth Street. If he missed a few meals, if he didn't keep feeding himself he would become just like them.

He sank to his knees with the realization of his true nature. The ravaged dead came, drawn by some flickering instinct to gather together, and stood around him until their corrupted faces swam in his vision. They did not frighten him anymore.

He was undead. He was one of them. As their hands reached for him he knew they weren't attacking him— they no longer possessed the brainpower necessary for aggression. They were reaching for him as a gesture of solidarity. They knew what he was.

Gary was a monster, too.

The dead man with no eyelids stared at him with an

openness, an innocence that Gary was astounded he'd never seen before. There was no evil there, no horror. Just simple need. Their faces were no more than inches away from each other. Gary leaned his head forward and touched his forehead to the other's.

When he had recovered himself he commanded the faceless woman to help him to his feet, and she did. Come, he told them, just as his mysterious benefactor had summoned him. Together the small band of them, Gary and the mindless dead, headed north toward midtown. It felt so very good not to be alone anymore.

Gary had life once more, now he also had a purpose. He would find this strange tattooed man and learn what he knew. Gary had so many questions and for some reason he was convinced the benefactor would have some answers. He kept his little band heading resolutely northward, up into midtown. They would enter the park soon enough. Was that their destination? In a way it didn't matter. In some zen fashion the journey was enough.

When he saw the vision again the man's face was clogged with concern. "You're getting closer but be careful. I think you are about to be attacked."

"Huh?" Gary asked but the vision was gone. He turned to look at the noseless man on his right, wondering if the other dead had seen the apparition or if it was just some glitch in Gary's personal nervous system.

The surprised-looking ghoul stared hard at something in the middle distance. Before Gary could speak he slumped lifelessly to the ground. Gary looked down and saw the bullet wound in the back of the dead man's head long before he heard the gunshot.

The next round hit the sidewalk and sent chips of

concrete rolling across Gary's feet. He was being shot at. "Not fucking again," he whined.

Chapter Four

I shaved with an electric razor plugged into a junction box in the ship's wheelhouse. Every time I turned the shaver on or off I got a little shock but it was safer than trying to use a straight razor on a rocking boat and when I was done I felt infinitely better about myself and the mission's chances.

Which is not to say, I thought as I rinsed out the shaver with water from the Hudson, that I thought anything would be easy. Just that we might not all die.

When I'd finished I called for my maps of New York. I studied them for a long time, thinking there had to be a better way. There were hospitals all over the city. Most of them were on the East Side, which meant they were impossible to get to due to the raft of human corpses clogging the East River. All of them, I knew, would have been looted during the evacuation.

I still knew one place where we could find the drugs we needed. The UN building. My first choice. It was also impossible to access from the water.

"Osman," I shouted, standing up, "come look at this." I showed him my map and indicated our next stop: Forty-second Street in midtown. He studied the West Side, reading the names of the buildings.

"'The theater district,'" he read aloud. "Dekalb, you want to take in a show?"

I ran a finger along Forty-second, from west all the way to east. The street ran uninterrupted from the Hudson River all the way past the southern end of the UN complex to the FDR Drive. "It's a big street—wide sidewalks, less chance of getting stuck. It was one of the busiest streets in the world, before the Epidemic, so it might even be clear of stalled cars. The authorities would have tried to keep it moving when they evacuated the survivors."

The captain just stared at me. He didn't understand, or he didn't believe I was willing to do this. But until I had those drugs in my possession I couldn't go back. I couldn't see my little Sarah again, couldn't see she was okay with my own eyes. I would do anything for that.

"We can walk from here to the UN in a couple of hours. Get the drugs and walk back. It'll take less than a day."

"You are forgetting," Osman said, "that the dead are risen. In the millions. This was a busy street, once? I tell you it still will be."

I gritted my teeth. "I have an idea of what we can do about that." Now that Gary was dead. Now that we could count on the undead all being stupid. Stupid enough. I looked back at the city but not at the buildings or the haunted streets. There. I pointed at a dilapidated extrusion of weathered wood and rusted metal that stuck out into the river. "Our first stop is the Department of Sanitation pier. They'll have what we need."

Osman might have been confused by this but he bent over his controls and got the trawler moving. We pulled in alongside a half-full garbage barge, the girls in position at the rail, their rifles sticking out like oars from the side of the ship. On top of the wheelhouse Mariam called down that she saw no sign of movement anywhere on the pier.

"This is where they used to collect the city's refuse," I told Ayaan as we secured the trawler to the side of the barge. "Easy enough to get to by water but from the land side it's a fortress. They didn't want anyone getting in here and getting sick—talk about potential lawsuits—so it should still be secure."

She didn't answer. She didn't need to. We both knew it had been a long time since there had been any authorities in this city. The dead could get anywhere if they were persistent enough. They could have jumped in the water and then climbed up the side of the barge. They could have climbed over the fence from the shore side. The undead aren't great climbers from what I've seen but if there had been something alive on the pier—something they could eat—they would have found a way.

Five of the girls jumped down onto the barge and then across its stern to the pier beyond. They watched each other, one moving forward while the others covered her back. I followed behind, as always, a little creeped out but not too worried. Most of the pier was open to the air, a zone of filthy cranes and winches and massive dented steel dumpsters. Rusted metal everywhere. I told the girls to be careful—it was unlikely that they'd had the proper tetanus boosters. They acknowledged me but they were too young to worry about such things. At the shore end of the pier we found a prefabricated shed with a padlocked door. SAFETY EQUIPMENT had been stenciled next to the door in dripping silver spray paint. Just what I was looking for.

I found a piece of metal rebar about as long as my arm and fitted it through the loop of the cheap padlock. A couple of heaves and it gave, sending vibrations rattling up my arm as pieces of the lock went flying. They glittered in the sunlight at my feet.

Inside a stripe of sunlight lay draped across the floor. Dust motes twirled in the air. I spotted a desk with a small reading lamp, strewn with half-completed forms. An emergency eyewash station and a big first-aid kit. Fathia grabbed that and carried it back to the boat. We might just need it before this was over. At the far end of the shed stood a row of three freshly painted lockers. I pulled on the latch of the nearest one and the girls started screaming. Leyla lifted her rifle and fired half a dozen rounds into the human shape that came tumbling out of the locker.

"Stop!" I shouted, knowing it was too late. I picked up the bright yellow suit—the empty suit—off the ground and poked a finger through the bullet hole in its faceshield. LEVEL A/FULL ENCAPSULATION, I read from a tag attached to the hazmat suit's zipper. LIQUIDPROOF AND VAPORPROOF, it assured me. Well, not anymore.

"I'm going to open another locker. Don't shoot this time, okay?" I asked. The girls nodded in chorus. They looked terrified, as if the next locker might reveal a magical bird that would flap out and peck at their eyes. Instead it held a duplicate of the first suit, as did the third locker. I tossed one to Ayaan and she just stared at me. "Now there are only two suits. Guess who just got volunteered for this mission?" I asked her.

Cruel, I know. She hadn't exactly been the soul of warmth to me, though. She was also one of the few girls I trusted to not panic when we walked right into a crowd of the undead protected by only three layers of industrial-grade Tyvek. Tyvek, of course, being a very high-tech kind of paper.

"Normally," I explained to her, "these suits keep out contaminants. This time they'll hold in our smell. The dead won't attack something that smells like plastic and looks like a Teletubby."

"You think this, or you know it?" she asked, holding the bulky yellow suit at arm's length.

"I'm counting on it." That was the best I could offer.

We took the suits back to the boat and had Osman steam north for Forty-second Street. There was plenty to do. We had to sterilize the outsides of the suits, read instruction manuals, and then run drills on how to put on and use the SCBA air recirculator units, teach each other how to put on the suits (a two-person job) without contaminating the surface. We had to practice talking to each other through the Mylar faceshields and even how to walk so we didn't trip over the baggy legs of the suits.

I had been through a crash course in how to use a Level B suit back when I was investigating weaponized nuclear facilities in Libya. There had been an eight-hour seminar with PowerPoint presentations and a thirty-question quiz at the end. I had paid attention because a breach in that suit might have meant being exposed to carcinogens. This time the smallest tear in the suit would surely mean being surrounded and devoured by the hungry dead.

I made sure we went through all of our drills twice.

Chapter Five

Gary stepped aside and the next shot missed him completely. He glanced at his companions—at the noseless man and the faceless woman and gestured for them to spread out and find cover. They communicated their inability to do so—they lacked the brainpower to identify what was covered and what wasn't—so he wasted another second telling them mentally to duck down behind abandoned cars. The violence of the moment had sharpened him somehow, thrown everything into high contrast.

"Kev—I'm reloading—get this one!" a living human shouted. Gary swiveled to track the voice and saw a big guy with short curly black hair standing under an awning. The living man worked nervously at the action of a long-barreled hunting rifle that looked like a stick in his enormous hands. He wore a rumpled tan shirt and a name tag that read HELLO MY NAME IS Paul. There were at least two of them, Gary inferred, this Paul and another one named Kev. Gary stepped closer to the shooter and sent instructions to his companions to spread out and try to flank the assailants.

Something buzzed past Gary's eyes. A mosquito,

possibly, but when he followed its trajectory it ended in a crater in a plate-glass window no wider than his pinkie nail. Not a bullet, Gary decided, but some kind of projectile nonetheless.

He realized for the first time that he himself was completely exposed. He stepped into the shadow of a building and scanned the street for possibilities. He couldn't run—his legs felt like pieces of dead wood every time he tried. He couldn't shoot back. Even if he'd possessed a gun his hands shook too much for that. He would have to try to flank these survivors and cut them off. Reaching out along the wavelength of the dead, Gary had his companions move farther up and down the street. He had to remind them to keep their heads down. He picked up an empty soda can from the street and threw it as hard as he could in the direction of the unseen shooter.

It had the desired effect. The shooter—his name tag read HELLO MY NAME IS Kev—came dashing out from behind a mailbox as if he'd been stung by a bee. "Paul!" he shouted. "We have to get out of here!"

Paul lifted his rifle and pointed it in Gary's direction but didn't shoot. "He's over there somewhere. Do you see him?"

"Forget him! They're everywhere!" Kev rushed to the side of a derelict limousine and yanked open the door. He clambered inside the vehicle until Gary could see nothing but the long, thin barrel of a rifle sticking out. The weapon looked like a toy.

It couldn't possibly be a BB gun, could it? Gary suppressed the urge to laugh. He had a little protection there in the shadows but Paul looked ready to shoot anything that moved. The survivor wasn't about to run—

which meant Gary had worked his way into a stalemate.

He pushed his consciousness outward, tapped into the nervous systems of his fellow dead. Not just his two traveling companions. He needed reinforcements. Luckily he didn't have to expand his consciousness very far. He could feel a group of the dead just a few blocks away, clustered around the twisted remains of a burnt-out hot-dog stand. It was harder to maintain contact with these— unlike the faceless woman or the noseless man, this new group had eaten recently and were therefore stronger—but he knew how to get their attention. Food, he whispered to them, food here. Come here for food.

Paul fired his rifle and a window near Gary's head collapsed in fragments. Gary thought the big guy must be firing blind but he couldn't be sure. The reinforcements were still minutes away—too far to be of any help, probably. He would have to take a chance and strike out on his own.

Faceless stood up from where she'd been hiding. Paul pivoted with a grace none of the undead could match and put a bullet right in the middle of the faceless woman's chest. She ducked down again at Gary's order, damaged but not fatally, and Paul put a hand to his eyes, trying to see what had happened. He must be wondering if he'd got her or not.

Gary didn't plan on letting him find out. He moved as fast as he could, keeping low and dodging behind cars so that when Paul looked back in his direction again Gary was nowhere to be seen.

Kev poked his head out of the limousine but Noseless was already there. Gary sent the order and Noseless slammed the car door shut, knocking Kev backwards into the vehicle. It would take only a moment for the survivor to open the door again but in that second Gary moved even closer to Paul.

"Jesus," Paul stared as the limousine rocked on its sagging tires. "What the fuck are you doing in there, Kev? We've got dead guys out here, remember?"

The limousine's back windshield erupted in shards of tinted glass. The BB gun emerged and then the survivor started crawling out behind it. "This is fucked up!" Kev screamed. "They're organized or something!"

Gary had one more surprise left for them. He had been getting closer all the time the two of them were yelling back and forth. Now he stood up directly in front of Paul, close enough to see the survivor's dark lips moving in an unspoken curse. The hunting rifle came up and Gary grabbed the barrel. Even as Paul fired he yanked it downwards, so it exploded against his sternum. Pain—real pain—vibrated through Gary's body and his shirt caught on fire where the rifle had discharged but he didn't even wince.

Perfectly calm, Gary pulled the rifle out of Paul's hands and threw it behind him into the street. He called out for his companions and Noseless and Faceless responded, advancing on Kev. The BB gun snapped a couple of times and Noseless rocked on his feet as the tiny projectiles bounced off his forehead but soon the two undead had the smaller survivor pinned. They made no move to bite him, merely twisting his arms behind his back. Gary expressed his approval and he could feel Faceless trying to smile, the exposed musculature of her face splitting in an obscene rictus.

"So are you finished now, or what?" Gary asked

Paul. "Maybe we can do this the easy way. I used to be a doctor—"

Paul's face darkened with many, many questions. The first one to came out was "You were a doctor?"

Gary laughed. "I know, I know. I used to fight to save lives and now I take them away. It's so fucking ironic I could just rip your head off." The survivor went pale and Gary realized he must have breached some unspoken rule of tact normally observed between predators and their prey. "I promise I'll make this as painless as possible," he said. He turned to glance at Faceless and Noseless. "Was he actually trying to kill us with BBs?"

Kev answered for himself. "If I got you in the eye you wouldn't be laughing! Paul—you've gotta help me, man! Get these things off of me!"

Paul licked his lips. His eyes were very bright. "Let me get this straight. You're planning on eating both of us, right?"

"Yeah," Gary admitted, wondering where this was going.

"And nothing that I can possibly do at this point is going to change your mind."

Gary shrugged. "You did try to kill us. It seems fair, you know?"

"Sure," Paul said. "Well in that case—hey, what's that?"

Gary followed Paul's pointing finger, only to have the big survivor put one hand in his face and push him over on his ass. Gary went sprawling. By the time he recovered he could only see Paul's back tearing down the street, his feet flashing wildly as he ran.

Gary hadn't felt so humiliated since dodgeball in

middle school. But he got his revenge. A dozen or so strong, well-fed undead came around the corner just then, responding to his previous summons. Paul tried to run around them but a dead woman with enormous broken fingernails snatched at his belly as he passed her. He kept running a few more steps before stopping to look down. The front of his shirt was red with blood. He looked up at Gary as if pleading with the doctor to make it all better in the moment before his broken skin tore open and his intestines spilled out steaming onto the asphalt.

The dead converged on him. He tried to run again but a dead man picked up one loop of his small intestine and started chewing on it. Paul tripped and fell on his face. With aching slowness the dead dragged him across the street back toward them, reeling him in like a fish on a line. When he was close enough—screaming and kicking but weakened by loss of blood—the undead squatted down over his shaking body and took turns biting chunks out of his face. Eventually he fell silent.

Gary turned to face the other survivor. Noseless and Faceless stared at Gary as he came closer. He looked only at Kev. The survivor's face was glossy with sweat and his mouth didn't seem to want to close. "You—you said you would make it painless, remember?"

"As painless as possible," Gary said, "but, you know, gee"—he held up his arms and looked down at his pockets—"I forgot. I'm fresh out of anesthetic." He lunged forward and sank his teeth deep into Kev's neck, twisting his head around once he got a solid hold on the living man's jugular to tear his throat out in one bloody piece.

Chapter Six

We spotted the Intrepid from half a mile away but only I knew what it was until we were practically underneath its dull grey shadow. When Osman had gotten a good look at the decommissioned aircraft carrier he started rubbing his jaw agreeably. "Can we. . . can we just take it, do you think?" I shook my head but he wouldn't be dissuaded so easily. "I don't think your navy will miss this, Dekalb," he suggested.

I smiled at him. "It's half-buried in the riverbed. They had to dredge the Hudson just to get it in here." I looked up at the historical airplanes tethered to its deck. The military value of such a thing was not lost on me, not after all we'd been through but frankly—this was a new kind of conflict. Fighter jets and naval gunnery just no longer applied.

Just south of the carrier we nosed in to a stop at the Circle Line pier, Pier 83 at Forty-second Street. The sightseeing ferryboats were all gone, of course, and so were the tourists that used to wait for hours to sail around New York harbor. The dead had come in their place, milling through the crowd-control barriers, lining up to be the first ones to get to us.

The girls stood at port arms at the rail while Ayaan

and I helped each other into the hazmat suits. It was a two-person operation—you had to be zipped into them—but we couldn't let anyone else touch us. Any human contact with the exterior of the suits would contaminate us. It would make us smell like lunch. Osman and Yusuf watched us with an impassivity I knew was borne from their belief we were leaving them for good. I ignored them and concentrated on Ayaan. We pulled on gloves and then I poured bleach over our hands. I attached Ayaan's Self-Contained Breathing Apparatus unit to her mask and put it on her head and she returned the favor with mine. We struggled into the suits and pulled up each others' airtight zippers and then smoothed down the Velcro stormflaps. I tested my valves and seals and then switched on my internal air before the inside of my suit could get stuffy. We had twelve hours before we would have to change the tanks on the SCBAs, something that could not be done out in the field. Not a lot of time to waste. "Ready?" I asked her. She pulled her sterilized AK-47 over her suited shoulder and adjusted the strap before she nodded yes. Through the wide aperture of her faceshield I could see she looked calm and disciplined. In other words, she looked like Ayaan.

Under Fathia's command the girls lifted their rifles and fired one short volley into the crowd of *xaaraan* that awaited us. A few fell—others just spun around and looked disoriented for a moment before returning to their ravening. They fired another round and the dead grew agitated, pushing harder against the crowd barriers until some of them squeezed through and fell into the water. The shooting had the desired effect, which was to draw attention away from us as we debarked quietly.

Moving quickly but ever careful not to puncture the suits on splinters, Ayaan and I lowered a narrow gangplank to the shore and dashed down its length. Osman and Yusuf were ready and shoved the sheet of particleboard into the water as soon as we touched solid ground. We didn't stick around but instead made our way hurriedly to the promenade on the far side of the waiting area.

A dead man with gold chains tangled up in the curly hairs on his chest came at us, his arms wide, his legs flailing beneath him as he tried to run. Ayaan readied her weapon but I put one gloved hand on the barrel and shook my head. She hardly needed me to remind her of our agreement—that she should shoot only in dire necessity, for fear of alerting the dead with the noise of her gunshots—but it made me feel better. By steadying her I steadied myself and right then I needed it. I could feel my skin trying to crawl away from the animated corpse as it lumbered ever closer.

He put out one hand and grabbed at my sleeve and I thought it was over, that I had made some kind of critical error. Maybe the dead could sense the life force Gary had spoken of, maybe they could see right through the suits. I braced myself for what surely came next—the grapple, the bite, the sensation of having my flesh torn away from my bones. I closed my eyes and tried to think about Sarah, about her safety.

The dead man pushed me aside and stumbled between Ayaan and me. We had just been in the way of his true goal—the girls on the Arawelo. I listened for a minute or two to the heavy cyclic respiration of my SCBA, just glad to still be alive. Whatever special senses the dead might have they couldn't see through the suits. My plan actually had a chance of working.

"Dekalb," Ayaan said, her voice blurred by the layers of plastic between us, "we are breathing borrowed air." I nodded and together we set off.

We crossed the West Side Highway, weaving carefully in between the abandoned cars so as not to tear the suits and then the buildings of Forty-second Street closed around us like the walls of a maze. I had hoped the street would be clear of vehicles and for once I'd been right, with one exception: a military armored personnel carrier stood at an angle in the middle of the street. It had smashed into a newsstand, spilling glossy copies of Maxim and Time Out New York everywhere, their pages ruffled by a mild breeze. I wanted to check to see if the APC was drivable but Ayaan suggested, quite rightly, that if her rifle made too much noise then the sound of a big diesel engine roaring to life would be completely unacceptable.

We moved cautiously around the open back of the vehicle, probably both of us remembering the armored riot cops in Union Square. No former National Guardsmen came out at us but it didn't take us long to find them. Three of them still dressed in their Interceptor body armor and their ballistic helmets were squabbling over a trash can halfway down the block. It must have been ransacked weeks ago but still they fought over its contents. One of them grabbed an armful of trash and sat down hard on the curb, busily sniffing and licking the dry yellow newsprint and shiny Styrofoam. Another dug out an old soda can. The red paint on its side had worn off over time leaving it featureless and silver. He stuck his finger deep inside the can perhaps trying to scoop out one last droplet of sugar water but his finger got stuck. He shook his hand violently trying to get it loose but it just wouldn't come off.

It sounds almost humorous now that I describe it but at the time, well, you just don't laugh at the dead. It's not a matter of respect so much as fear. After your first few encounters with animated corpses you never stop taking them seriously. They were too dangerous and too horrible to make light of.

Unless, of course, they could talk. The thought made me wince. I'd made a bad mistake in trusting Gary. I didn't stick around to even look at the National Guardsmen. We walked on past the playhouses of Theater Row, past their colorful blandishments for entertainments that hardly made sense anymore. Beneath the marquees the dead scrabbled and hunted for food. We saw an elderly woman with blue hair and a colorful scarf around her neck lying facedown on the sidewalk. Her bony arms were stuffed down inside a sewer grating snatching up spiders out of the darkness below. Every Dumpster rattled with the dead people inside rummaging for one last morsel of food.

Most pathetic of all were the weak ones. For one reason or other they couldn't compete for the small supply of food available. Some lacked limbs or were too small or too scrawny to strive with the others. Many had been children. They were recognizable by the mottled pulpy skin on their faces, by the receding lips that had dried up and left their teeth permanently bared in broken grimaces. They did what they could to keep themselves fed but this never amounted to much. We saw a girl Ayaan's age scraping at the green lichen growing on a brick wall. Others gnawed desultorily at the bark of dead trees or chewed clumps of dry grass until green paste leaked from their grinding jaws. It was only a matter of time, I knew, before even the strongest of the dead would be reduced to these measures. There was a limited supply of food in the city, no matter how broadly you interpreted the term. For whatever unknown reason, they didn't eat each other, so this was what remained to them.

This was the future, then. The rest of history in a new paraphrase: a human face chewing on a leather boot, forever. I kept my head down and Ayaan did the same. Neither of us stopped to reflect further as we trudged eastward breathing canned air and listening to the creaking of our suits.

Chapter Seven

By the time Gary reached Central Park it had become a shambles. A sea of mud broken here and there by a pool of stagnant water slick with the rainbow sheen of chemical pollution. Shards of bone, inedible even by the loose standards of the undead had gathered in these ditchlike depressions in the earth. No grass anywhere—the dead would have devoured it by the handful. Countless broken and sagging trees raised dark supplicant limbs to an overcast sky, pulpy and white where the bark had been gnawed right off the wood. Without the root systems of living plants to hold it together the very earth under Central Park had rebelled, surging forward as mud every time it rained. The broad traverses had turned to rivers full of murky, billowing water. The fences that had divided the park into discrete zones of leisure had been overcome by the sweeping power of the water and mud and now lay twisted like long lines of barbed wire rusting in the sun. Here and there a streetlamp poked out of the dirt at a skewed angle like the gravestones in an old abandoned cemetery. The paved or graveled paths that had once woven in and out of pleasant glades had disappeared completely. A tidal wave of mud had swept out into Sixth Avenue. It had clotted in the gutters and left broad streaks of brown in elaborately ramified fan shapes down the street, carrying away cars to smash them up against buildings a block away in clumps of filthy broken metal and shivered glass.

He led Noseless and Faceless into the park's brown expanse and felt his feet sinking a full inch down into the soft soil. Within minutes of clambering across that dull plain Gary felt completely lost. He could see the tall buildings of the city around him in every direction except to the north, the rude geometry of the empty city like abstract mountain ranges pinning him in. He felt alone but not unwatched. The mysterious benefactor waited for him somewhere beyond the next hummock of earth.

Since he'd eaten he was thinking more clearly. He'd shaken off the half-trance that had lain over him like a shroud ever since he recovered his strength at the bottom of the Virgin Megastore, and now he had time to ponder just where he was headed.

Someone—some anonymous creature—had come to him in his moment of greatest peril and taught him how to open himself up to something bigger than himself, how to connect with the nervous systems of countless dead men and women. From that connection he had drawn the strength to keep himself animate even after being shot in the head. In exchange for this knowledge the unknown benefactor had summoned Gary to his presence and without a thought Gary had set off to comply. Now that he could think a little more clearly, however, he wondered what he was marching toward. It couldn't be a living person—no one living could have access to the network of death, Gary was sure of it, and anyway why would anyone living want to help a monster like Gary to survive?

Yet if the benefactor was dead, then what could he possibly want from Gary? Even if the other had somehow maintained his intellect as Gary had, he would still share the biology and psychology of all the dead. The dead only had one desire; the need for sustenance. It seemed absurd but Gary was convinced that he was walking to the place where he would be eaten. Fast-food delivery, right to your door.

If it was true, if he had been spared only to be turned into a meal for some dead man even smarter than himself, Gary still couldn't stop. He kept yanking his feet out of the mire and taking another step. Behind him, Noseless and Faceless kept pace without a word of complaint or question.

The sun had moved higher in the sky by the time they saw the first break in the monotony of the park's muddy expanse. The zoo came up on their right, its buildings still standing though they were half buried in thick silt. Grateful for any break in the visual cipher of what the park had become Gary waved his companions on and hurried into the low maze of the zoo's sunken exhibits.

There were no animals in the cages, of course—the dead would have made short work of them. Here and there a scrap of fur had caught in the mesh of a habitat or the elaborate filigree on a wrought-iron fence but that was all. Similarly the explanatory plaques and interactive displays were buried or carried away by some long-past torrent of mud. Only the barriers remained visible, a collection of untenanted cages that cut the afternoon light into long strips. Gary led his companions down long curving lanes between what had once been enclosures for baboons and red pandas and now were merely channels of mud.

Wanting to see something, he brought them to a building ornamented with the sculpted heads of elephants and giraffes. Cheerfully whimsical in another day, the reliefs had become hideous gargoyles now, stained by blowing rain and rust that ran down from the animals' eyes like tears of blood. Gary ignored the cold feeling the place gave him and touched the weathered brass handles on the doors of the building.

The doors flew open with a force that knocked him back a dozen yards on his back, his dry body gouging a great furrow in the mud. Noseless and Faceless turned to stare at him with a kind of dazed shock they might have seen mirrored in his own face. What could possibly have broken the stillness of the park so violently?

A naked dead man came stumping out of the Elephant House on calves like utility poles. He stood at least ten feet tall, a quaking mound of pallid flesh shot through with black veins. There was no muscle tone on the giant whatsoever, just great rolls of flab and doughy meat. His hands were bloated and nearly useless, human-sized nails sunk deep into the tips of his swollen fingers. His normal-sized head sat in the middle of the gelatinous mass of his body like an obscene barnacle. Gary had never seen anything like him before. He gave more than a passing second to the thought that this might be his benefactor— and his doom—but it couldn't be so. When he plucked the strings of the net that tied together all dead men and women he felt no stirring of intelligence in this beast.

What he did see in his mind's eye was horrible to look upon—dark energy, far more than seemed possible, a writhing, roiling storm cloud of it that blazed and radiated away from the giant in great gouts and yet never diminished in strength—a black star. There was hatred in there as well, raw red hatred for anyone who dared enter the precincts of the beast's domain.

The creature before Gary had not begun its life at that size. He had been a big man in life but neither a bodybuilder or an athlete. He had merely been one of the first of the walking dead to find his way to the zoo. He had fought off the weaker dead as they arrived, engaged in epic combats with the stronger ones, but always he had prevailed. His current size was due simply to eating greater quantities of more robust meat than anyone else who tried to challenge him.

There were no more elephants in the Elephant House, Gary realized, nor any giraffes, or hippopotami or rhinos or bears. He was looking at what was left of them.

The giant stamped toward Faceless and Gary sent her an urgent command to fall back. She couldn't move quickly enough and the giant slapped her to the side. Noseless tried to get around behind the thing and the giant kicked out with one leg, throwing him into a brick wall with a meaty thud. The creature wanted Gary next and would brook no delays. It would tear him apart, Gary knew—not for food, since the dead never ate the dead—but for the sheer insult of invading the giant's space.

Gary could hardly stand up to the giant physically. Instead he raised his hands before him and stroked the threads that connected the two of them in some etheric space. It hurt to touch the frenzied energy of the giant but Gary reached out and pulled hard, drawing deep until he began to siphon that mad heat away from the beast.

The giant couldn't possibly understand what was

happening but he felt it and it must have hurt like hell. He sucked a deep lungful of air, struggling against his own massive fat deposits to get the air in and then blasted it out in a wail like an air horn. Gary covered his ears—severing his connection to the giant in the process. For a moment the world was silent again. Then the giant turned to the side and started climbing up over an abandoned cage, digging his fingers deep into the metal lattice, pulling himself away from Gary as fast as he could.

Gary felt like slapping his hands together in self-congratulation as the giant hurried off across the flat plain of mud outside the zoo. He nearly did—until something gripped his aching brain like a vise. The benefactor, perhaps wondering why he had made this detour from his instructed path.

Amaideach stócach! the benefactor howled. The voice was Gary's own, the same voice he heard uttering his own thoughts but so much louder, so much more distorted that it couldn't be his own thought. Someone else—the benefactor—was shouting into his mind's ear. The words meant nothing to Gary, but they cut through him like a sword of fire and struck him down to the ground where he lay deep in a bad seizure for quite some time.

When he was able to rise to his feet again he collected Noseless and Faceless (looking a little ragged after the fight with the giant but still mobile) and returned to his uptown course. He had no intention of defying the benefactor again.

Chapter Eight

We kept to the middle of the street as we approached the Port Authority Bus Terminal. This must have been the last part of the city to be evacuated. We saw piles of luggage—sometimes just trash bags sealed with masking tape, sometimes great heaps of Prada handbags or Tumi suitcases—stashed on the sidewalk. Everywhere there were leaflets tacked up on the walls or skating along the streets like albino manta rays advising people to STAY TOGETHER and KNOW YOUR GROUP NUMBER BY HEART! At the end, the bus terminal must have been the only way out of town. I had no great desire to go inside and see what had become of all those panicked refugees. It would be depressing at best, I thought, shocking at worst.

Then we passed by the bulk of the terminal and entered Times Square and I discovered a new definition for the word "shocking."

It will sound ridiculous to some, I know, after all the devastation I'd witnessed, but Times Square was the most horrifying place I saw in this new New York. There were no piles of dead bodies, no signs of looting or panic. There was just one thing wrong with this Times Square.

It was dark.

There were no lights on anywhere, not a single bulb. I turned to Ayaan, but she didn't understand, of course, so I turned around again and stared up at the vast blank faces of the buildings around me. I wanted to explain to her—how there used to be television screens here six stories high, how the neon lights had glowed and shifted and shimmered so brightly that the night had been transformed into a luminous blue haze unlike daylight, unlike moonlight, something wholly transcendent and localized. How there had been a law requiring every building to put out a certain amount of light so that even the police station and the subway entrances and the military recruiting center had blasted out illumination like the Vegas strip. But how could she understand? She had no point of reference—she had never seen the big advertisements for Samsung and Reuters and Quiksilver and McDonald's. She would never see them now. With my mouth open I turned in place, so shocked I couldn't think. The heart of New York City— that was what all the tourist books called Times Square. The heart of New York City had stopped beating. The city, like its inhabitants, had perished and now existed only in a nightmarish half-state, an unliving undeath. Ayaan had to grab my hand and led me away.

We passed between the movie theaters and then we saw Madame Tussaud's on our right. Dozens of wax mannequins had been dragged out into the street, their paint washed off by rain and their half-melted white faces staring up at us in reproach. We could see the big ragged gouges in their throats and torsos where the hungry dead had ravaged them, obviously having mistaken them for real human beings. I was still staring at the broken forms when I heard someone speak. I looked up at Ayaan at the same moment she looked up at me. We had both heard it—which meant it had originated with neither of us.

We heard it again. "Hey, guys! Over here!" Ayaan's face set in grim planes. In this haunted city another voice could mean only Gary—but he was long dead, now, buried under an avalanche of DVD boxes, we had been there, we had done it. It didn't sound like Gary anyway. Could there be another like him? If so we were in desperate trouble.

"Living people, man! Survivors! Come on!" The voice was coming from the direction of Broadway. We rushed to the subway entrance and found it barred with steel gates. Standing just inside were three men who were very much alive and breathing. They were covered in sweat as if they'd just run a long distance and they were waving wildly at us.

"Who—" I began, but of course who they were was obvious. Survivors—New Yorkers, still alive after all this time. Had they been living in the subway since the Epidemic broke out? It seemed impossible yet here they were. They looked malnourished and scruffy but they weren't dead; they weren't dead at all.

"You must be here to rescue us, man," one of them shouted, sounding convinced this was not the case but desperately wanting it to be so. "It's been so long but we knew you would come!"

Ayaan shook her head at me but I ignored her. The drugs be damned—these were living people! I peered in through the bars. The men were armed with pistols and shotguns and hunting rifles—civilian weapons. Each of them wore a name tag stuck to his shirt: HELLO MY NAME IS Ray; HELLO MY NAME IS Angel; HELLO MY NAME

IS Shailesh. Ray held out one sweaty, desperate palm, pushing his arm through the bars up to his shoulder. He pushed the hand toward me—not to grab me, not to tear me to pieces but to greet me. I shook his hand heartily.

Shailesh asked the first question. "What are those suits for? We're not infected. We're clean!"

"They keep the dead from smelling us," I explained hurriedly. "I'm Dekalb and this is Ayaan—we've been here for a couple of days now but you're the first survivors we've seen. How many of you are there?"

Ray answered: "Near on two hundred. Everybody who was here when the Guard's last barricade broke. Listen, you didn't see any survivors at all? We've got two guys out there looking for supplies. Paul and Kev—are you sure you didn't see them? They've been gone way too long."

I looked to Ayaan as if she might have seen something I didn't but of course we all knew what must have happened to the foragers. "We have a ship on the Hudson," I told them. "We'll need to find a way to get you all over to the river but after that you'll be safe. Who's in charge? We'll need to start organizing how we do this." I planned on running this like a classic UN refugee operation—the first step was to look for the existing social hierarchy. Not only would the local boss know how to keep order among his or her people, they'd be offended if you didn't recognize their authority no matter how temporary it might be. I never thought I would be applying this kind of group psychology to Americans but the principles had to be the same.

"That'd be el Presidente," Angel sneered. He clearly had some kind of contempt for the local authority, but it softened when he realized that escape might be close at hand. "Sure, man, I'll talk to him, I'll get this moving. You want to come in, maybe have a bite? We haven't got so much, but it's yours."

I shook my head but the gesture would be hard to interpret through the faceshield, so I raised my hands in negation. "Don't open the gate. No need to endanger yourselves. We're going to head back to the ship now but we'll be back in a couple of hours. Alright?"

The three men looked at me with such open and honest trust on their faces that I had to turn away or choke up. Ayaan cleared her throat as we moved away from the subway, trying to get my attention. I knew what she was going to say but I didn't want to hear it.

"Dekalb. The Arawelo is cramped even now, with only twenty-seven of us. It is not possible to take two hundred refugees on board." She kept her voice low so the survivors wouldn't hear us arguing.

I followed suit. "So we'll make multiple trips. . . or, I don't know, maybe Osman will get his wish—maybe we'll find some way to get the Intrepid free. God damn it, Ayaan! We can't just abandon them."

"Dekalb," she said, much louder, and I turned to shush her but she had a different topic of discussion in mind. The side door of a Dumpster had slid open and a naked dead man had wriggled out. Moving on all fours he came right up to us, his nose wriggling.

"He must smell the survivors," I hissed at Ayaan. "Stay perfectly still."

The dead man crawled closer and pulled himself stiffly up to his feet. In life he had suffered from male-pattern baldness. He had tiny beady eyes. He wavered before me for a long uncomfortable minute before bending forward at the waist and craning his neck out to give me a big snuffling sniff. He seemed to find my right hand fascinating.

It was only natural to look down and see what had excited him so. That was when I noticed the sheen of dampness on my palm. Sweat, on the outside of my glove.

Two more dead men slithered out of the Dumpster. From down the street I saw movement—lots of movement.

"You shook the living one's hand! You're contaminated!" Ayaan screamed, her rifle strap getting tangled as she tried to get to the weapon. I looked from her back to the dead man as his talonlike fingers slashed down at me. They slid harmlessly off the Tyvek suit—I could feel the four hard points of contact (one for each of his fingernails) glance along my ribs—and then they caught on the seal of my glove.

I tried to pull away. Instead I got my legs tangled up in the baggy fabric of the hazmat suit and nearly fell down. The dead man gave a quick tug and my glove came off altogether, exposing my bare hand to the air.

My vaporproof integrity been compromised.

Chapter Nine

Long Mylar banners flapped wildly between the columns of the facade, their promotional messages bleached to illegibility by the sun. Snapping, snarling as the wind tore at them they were the only moving thing in sight. The Metropolitan Museum of Art stood high and alone in the mud of the park, its massive doors wide open.

"I've got better things to do," Gary said out loud. He was afraid to go in. Noseless and Faceless made no reply to his assertion. "I need to find the girl who shot me. I'm hungry, too." But he didn't turn away. Too many questions stacked up in his head.

He led Noseless and Faceless up the long flight of steps to the doors and peered in for a moment, wondering what could possibly be inside that could make him so scared. The massive lobby soared upwards to three filthy skylights that provided a trace of illumination. Enough to see that the place was empty. Gary stepped into the cool dead air of the museum and stared up at its arched and vaulted ceiling, at the grand staircase that led upward from the far end of the lobby, at the ticket and information desks standing abandoned and naked in the wan light. This was hardly his first visit to the Met, but without crowds of living tourists and patrons, without the squealing of bored children or the weary shouting of tour guides, it seemed that every step he took made the entire stone edifice of the museum reverberate like a tomb.

He had more than a sneaking suspicion of where he should look for the Benefactor, though it didn't make any sense. He turned to his right and headed through an abandoned security cordon. Noseless and Faceless followed behind, their feet shuffling on the flagstones. They passed through a long corridor lined with tomb paintings showing scenes of Egyptian daily life and then into a dark chamber lined with glass display cases.

One of the first things they came to was a case holding a mummy wrapped tight in linen bandages like an enormous cocoon. A golden mask stared up at them from the depths of the dark glass, its facial features composed in an expression of perfect serenity as it stared through Gary and into eternity. The enormous eyes seemed to be pools filled with placid understanding and a pleased acceptance of immortality. This couldn't be the Benefactor, Gary was sure of it. He placed a hand on the glass.

The mask came crashing up into the top of the case, the pale limbless body thrashing below, the pupal form of something horrible.

Gary jumped back. This was impossible. Yet here it was, the mummy convulsing in its glass cage. Gary reached out across the frequency of death and felt the barest shadow of dark heat there—rage and anguish were the only things keeping the mummy going and even those were in short supply. Soon enough this creature was going to exhaust itself and succumb to entropy. Yet it was patently impossible for it to have any kind of afterlife at all. God! It wouldn't stop thrashing! The gold mask had dented and flattened from the forceful beating against the glass, smearing and distorting the features.

Gary might be undead himself but he couldn't look at the thing in the case. It forced him every time it bent in the middle or smashed its face against the glass to imagine what its existence must be like: blind, bound, hungry—forever, not knowing how you got where you are, wondering if you were even alive or dead—it would be hell. He turned to Faceless and tried to explain to her. "No, no, this isn't right—they used to dig out the brains with a. . . with a spoon or something when they mummified people!"

What you say is truth, the Benefactor said. *As far as it goes.*

Gary looked up in a panic. The words made his teeth hurt: as intimate as his own thoughts, as loud as sirens. "What do you mean?" he demanded.

They took the brains, yes—but only in some of the dynasties. Before the Eighteenth Dynasty the practice was unknown. After the Greeks conquered Egypt, they outlawed excerebration altogether.

"How do you know that?" Gary spun around, trying to find where the Benefactor might be, but it was impossible—the voice could be coming from anywhere.

I know many things, Gary. I have seen into your heart. I know things you've forgotten and things you'll never dream of. Come to me, Gary, and I will teach you everything. Come quickly—we have much to do.

Gary edged around the display case, not wanting to get near the undead thing in its grisly chrysalis in case it finally broke the glass. Not wanting to be near it at all. He led Faceless and Noseless deeper into the Egyptian exhibit, through poorly lit rooms full of hulking sarcophagi and broken statues and scarab jewelry and stained cerements. Every time he turned around he found more mummies thumping against their enclosures—everywhere he went he saw scarabs and white eyes staring at him from the walls. In one tiny alcove a blackened mummy surrounded by the skeletal horns of long-dead antelopes smeared itself across the glass—in another a wooden coffin intricately painted and inlaid with gold shook itself until splinters fell from it like dry rain. The sense of anger and fear and horror he read off the convulsing bodies made him cringe and press his hands against his temples, unable to bear their thwarted torment.

Finally they emerged into a wide open room with one whole wall made of glass that let in grey sunlight. On a raised platform stood the Temple of Dendur—a square structure carved with hieroglyphics, a massive monumental arch standing before it. A low bench ran before the arch and on this platform someone had laid out three of the writhing mummies. Their golden masks had been torn off and lay in a heap nearby, priceless artifacts just tossed away. Crouched above them a brown form worked with a feeble hand at picking apart the cloth that bound the dead. It was the Benefactor, Gary knew it at once. He raised his head and gestured for Gary to approach.

See me as I am, Gary. I am Mael Mag Och, and I need your eyes.

He was nothing like the apparition that had come to Gary in the megastore. His skin was hard leather, tanned to a uniform deep brown, hairless and wrinkled in some places, in others stretched smooth and tight over bones that stuck out from him with sharp points. His head lolled on his shoulder as if he could not lift it and, indeed, his neck was clearly broken, fragments of the uppermost vertebra of his spine exposed at his nape. He had only one arm and his legs were horribly mismatched. One looked strong and muscular, the other withered and skeletal. He wore no clothing except a rope tied tight around his neck, and a band of matted fur around his arm.

"You're not. . . like them," Gary said, staring down at the twitching mummies.

Not half so old, nor as wise. Come, come here. No, I was never in Egypt, lad. I hail from an island off what you would know as Scotland. Please, look here. This is one reason I called you, to help me see this.

Gary had no idea what that meant—and then he saw. Mael Mag Och had no eyes in his head, just gaping sockets.

I can see what you see, through the eididh that makes us one. I had no idea how ugly I had become. Here.

Gary looked where Mael Mag Och pointed. "The eididh?" he asked.

What you call the network, though it is so much more than that. A thick wad of stained wrappings came away from the mummy and an arm was revealed, a thin arm terminating in five bony fingers. The hand snatched at Mael Mag Och's face but lacked the vitality to do any damage. The eyeless corpse reached for another strip of linen and started peeling it back, his fingers fumbling with the rotten cloth. *We must get them free. They were promised immortality, Gary. These wretches believed they would wake in paradise, in a field of reeds. I cannot bear their shock. Help me.*

The gentleness, the compassion of the act moved Gary in a way he had no longer thought possible. He knelt down to help remove the bandages and called Faceless and Noseless to do the same. With so many hands they soon had the mummy free of her constraints. She rose slowly from the bench, a skeletal form shrouded in tatters of her linen. A glinting golden brooch sat just above her heart in the shape of a scarab beetle while other amulets and charms dangled from her side or hung from cords around her neck.

Her face remained hidden by the wrappings except for a ragged hole where her mouth had once been. *Their final ritual made that—the wpt-r, the "Opening of the Mouth." It was done with a chisel and a hammer.* The cloth around the wound was stained brown and yellow by long-dried fluids. *Fucking barbarians*, Mael Mag Och muttered. She moved on unsteady feet away from them, hobbling to the arch where she slouched against the weathered sandstone as if reading the hieroglyphs with her body. Gary would have crushed her, smashed her head to pieces if he had found her in a glass case still wrapped so tightly as she had been. Mael Mag Och had seen the animate creature, the humanity, below the bandages.

"What are you?" Gary asked.

A humble Draoidh. The way Mael Mag Och pronounced it sounded like "Druid."

"Well, okay, then who are you?" Gary asked.

Well, now, that's an easy one. I'm the fellow who turns off the lights when the world ends.

Chapter Ten

The undead man stared at my bared hand as if uncertain what it could possibly be. I backed away cautiously but he came right after me, his nose wrinkling in his bluish face. His mouth opened wide and I could see his broken teeth slick with drool and then he pounced, his arms swinging shut like a pincers to grab me around the waist. I tried shaking him off but the hazmat suit limited my mobility. I tried bringing my knee up and caught him directly under the chin but if I connected with enough force to hurt him, he showed no sign. His teeth snapped shut on a fold of my suit and he shook his head violently, trying to rip it away. I was in danger of falling backwards, which would almost surely mean my death—with the heavy SCBA unit on my back it would take me far too long to get back on my feet. The other two dead men from the Dumpster were approaching. If I lost my footing now I would have three of the things pinning me down.

Where the hell was Ayaan? I swiveled at the waist and saw her fumbling with her rifle. She couldn't seem to bring it to bear, the bulky suit's shoulders were too thick to let her bring it up to her eye. She could probably shoot from the hip but if she did she'd be as likely to hit me as my attacker. I was on my own until she could figure it out.

My breath made plumes of condensation on the inside of my faceshield, limiting my visibility as I twisted and tore at the undead man clutching my midriff. He held me in a grip of iron as I pried at his arms with my gloved hands. Every time I thought I had a good grip on him a layer of his dead skin would slough off and my hands would slide free. His teeth had failed to puncture the Tyvek of my suit—it was pretty tough stuff—but I knew eventually he would go for my bare hand with his teeth and then it would be over. Even if I got away after being bitten I would be prey for any number of secondary infections. I could still remember the panic in Ifiyah's glassy eyes as her leg swelled up and her heart began to race.

Desperation forced my fingers deep into the dead man's armpit. Finally I had some leverage. The bones in my hands felt like they would snap as I clawed him away from me, finally breaking his grip. I lifted one clumsy leg and kicked him off me, his fingers flickering in the air like scuttling claws. He landed on his back and immediately rolled to all fours again, clearly intent on coming for me once more. Then the top of his head exploded in a powdery puff of vaporized grey matter.

I turned, my lungs heaving, and saw Ayaan. She had managed to unzip her suit down to the waist, freeing her arms so she could use her AK-47 freely. As I stood there staring she lifted the weapon again and fired two quick shots, eliminating the pair of dead men that had been coming up right behind me.

Hurriedly we shed ourselves of the now-useless suits. There were more of the dead coming, a loose crowd of them from the west moving as fast as the undead could. The one in front was missing both arms but his jaw worked hungrily as he advanced on us. There were too many of them to fight off—we had to run.

I grabbed Ayaan's arm and we ran north onto Broadway but they were there as well, the weakened kind, the kind we had seen licking mold off stucco walls. Their clothes dangled from their emaciated frames, their withered necks and sparse hair horrible to see. They looked far less pathetic now that we were unprotected. From the south came a dead woman with long black hair in a full bridal gown with a train, her hands covered in bloodstained gloves, her veil back to show us the long sharp teeth exposed by her withered lips. We would have to take our chances, I decided. We would have to gun down the bride and hope there were no more of the dead behind her. I didn't relish meeting the rest of the wedding party.

Ayaan had her rifle up and was merely waiting for my order to shoot when a blur of orange light shot past our feet and straight into the biggest pack of undead with a yowling noise. It was a cat—a tabby, a mangy, half-starved rabid-looking cat. A living cat.

On reflection I couldn't remember the last time I'd seen a live animal. Not so much as a stray dog or even a squirrel loose in the streets of New York. This couldn't be a coincidence but to me it was a startling mystery.

The cat's effect on the undead was electric. Ignoring us completely, they turned as one to reach for the running feline, their hands stretching down to grab at its patchwork fur. It dodged left, feinted right and the dead fell over each other—literally—trying to get a handful of the orange streak.

Whether they were successful or not I didn't find out till later. As I stood there mesmerized by the sight Shailesh, one of the survivors from the subway station, came up behind me and grabbed my arm. I shrieked like a child. "Come on already," he said, "we don't have a lot of bait to spare, you know?"

"Bait?" I asked. Sure. The cat. The survivors must have let it loose specifically to distract the undead long enough for Ayaan and myself to get inside. Following hard on the heels of our guide we bolted past the steel gate at the entrance to the station—I heard it clang shut behind us—and down a flight of murky stairs. In the gloom I saw litter boxes everywhere and a few angry-looking cats and dogs sleeping in ungainly heaps. A single incandescent bulb lit up the turnstiles. We clambered over them since Shailesh assured us they had frozen in place when the trains stopped running.

Beyond the turnstiles we were met by an earnest-looking survivor wearing a pair of faded but immaculately clean jeans and wire-framed glasses. He held a black combat shotgun in his hands, the barrel pointed away from us. The weapon moved in his hands as we approached him, his hands subconsciously keeping it at a safe elevation. It all happened in such a reflexive way I knew he had to have Armed Forces training. No one else would be that disciplined with a firearm. There was a sticker on his white button-down shirt, one of the increasingly familiar HELLO MY NAME IS labels but the white space below had been left blank.

He turned to Shailesh. "Are we secure?" he asked.

Shailesh laughed. "Dude, it's the first rule of staying alive. They go for the fastest moving object they can see.

The faster it goes the more excited they get! You should have seen them, Jack. It was like a Jim Carrey movie out there."

Jack didn't raise his voice but what he said next made Shailesh break eye contact. "I asked if we were secure or not," he repeated.

Our guide nodded obediently. "Yeah. Listen," Shailesh said to me, "Jack will take you inside. I have to, you know, watch the gate. Welcome to the Republic, okay?"

"Sure," I said, not fully understanding. "Thanks."

Jack looked at me for a moment and I knew he was sizing me up. He gave Ayaan the same inspection but said nothing to either of us except, "This way."

Chapter Eleven

One of the mummies—a Ptolemy and a cousin of Cleopatra, according to Mael—ran his partially unwrapped hands over the glass of a display case and then started beating on it with his palms. Mael hobbled toward him but couldn't stop him from shattering the glass. It cascaded down his bandaged legs in a torrent of tiny green cubes. Long shards of it stuck into his arms and his hands but he ignored them as he bent to retrieve a clay jar from the exhibit. Hieroglyphs covered its surface and the stopper was carved wood in the shape of a falcon's head. Mael tried to pull the mummy away from the jagged glass but the undead Egyptian refused to be led. He was far too intent on cradling the jar against his chest.

It was the first time Gary had seen a dead man motivated by anything but hunger. "What's in that jar that's so important?" he asked.

A spectral smile twitched across Mael's leathery lips. *His intestines.*

Gary could only grimace in revulsion.

They don't understand this place, Gary. So much has changed and so quickly. They think they're in hell so they cling to the things they know and understand.

"I imagine the same could be said of you." It was a taunt but a halfhearted one.

Perhaps. I am a little better off than them. I have access to the eididh. It's how I learned your language and everything else I know about Manhattan. That flickering smile again.

"I've only been able to see the energy, the life force. You can get information out of the network?"

Oh, yes. Our memories go there when we drop, lad. Our personalities. What our elderly friends here would call the ba. It is the storehouse of our hopes and our fears. Indra's net. The akashic record. The collected notions of the human race. You and I can read anything there, if we open ourselves to the possibility.

"You and me. Because we can still think. You need to make a conscious effort to reach into the network and the others—they, the dead out there—they can't make that leap, not with what they've got for brains."

Aye.

"But there's a difference between you and me, as well. I can feel it. You—your energy, it's more compact. Like a living person almost but dark like mine. I can't explain it so well."

You're doing fine. The mummies and me, now, we don't share your hunger. Our bodies are incorruptible, in the old palaver. We don't rot. That twitchy smile again. Then there's the fact that you chose this. You did it to yourself.

"I can't be the only one, though. You found me from a distance, you must know if there are others like us."

Mael nodded. *A few. Mostly of my sort but you were not the only one to abuse yourself like this. There's a boy in a place called Russia. Very promising. Struck down by a speeding vehicle. He suffered for years with machines pumping his heart for him, but his parents wouldn't let the doctors pull the plug. They could not know, of course, what they were creating. Another one is here in your country. In California, she calls it. A yoga teacher hiding out in an oxygen bar. I have no idea what that means. She had the same brilliant idea you did, but it didn't work as well for her. Woke up with a bad headache and found she'd lost her multiplication tables and plenty more besides. Such as her name.*

Gary nodded. Russia. California. Without a car, without planes, he would have to walk to them. They were so far away. "They might as well be on the moon. It's funny. A couple of days ago I thought I was the only one and that was okay. Then you contacted me. It's like I only got so lonely when I knew I wasn't alone." He reached into the broken display case and picked up a jewel in the shape of a jackal-headed god. It was beautiful—worked by loving hands. A made thing. All that was over now. Nobody left to create beautiful things. Nobody left to appreciate them, either. There were survivors but all they cared about was not getting killed. He supposed he couldn't blame them. He put the jewel back in its case. "What happened to us, Mael? What caused the Epidemic?"

The Druid scratched his chin. Thinking hard, the gesture said. Mael was a master of body language, even with just one arm. *I know what you think it was. A disease same as the grippe or the pox. It's not, though. The old ones, the fathers, what you would call gods, they brought this on us as retribution. It's a judgment.*

"For what?"

Take your pick, lad. For what you've done to the earth,

I might say, but then I'm just an old tree-hugger from way back. For what you did to each other, maybe. I know that sort of thing won't sit easy with you. In your world things just happen, eh? Accidental like. Random. In my time we thought otherwise. For us everything happened for a reason.

Walk with me, Gary. I have but a little time to converse with you. There's dark work that needs doing. Fighting. Slaughtering, before this is through.

"Huh?" Gary demanded. It was all he could think to say.

We'll get to that in proper time. Let me show you something first.

Mael led him back through the Egyptian wing of the Met. The liberated mummies had taken it over and Gary saw for the first time how morbid the place was. An inside-out graveyard where the dead were put on display for schoolchildren. Gary saw a mummy trying on jewelry in one room, the turquoise and gold necklaces glinting against the stained linen at her throat. In another room a truly ancient mummy who was little more than rags and bones was trying to pry open a massive sarcophagus with his splayed fingers. It looked like he was trying to return to the tomb.

Mael stopped at a room partitioned off by a folding screen. The exhibit beyond was only half finished: clearly the curators had been working on it when they abandoned the museum during the Epidemic. The walls had been painted a sky blue and in white italic script above a row of empty display cases was written MUMMIES AROUND THE WORLD. The bodies in this room were truly dead. SIBERIAN ICE MUMMIES were little more than incomplete skeletons with clumps of hair attached to their broken skulls; MOUNTAIN MUMMIES OF PERU showed hollow darkness through their sunken orbits, their brains having long since rotted away. At the back of the room sat a long, low case that had been shattered from the inside. Gary crunched glass underfoot as he approached it. A CELTIC BOG MUMMY FROM SCOTLAND, he read. This must have been Mael's sepulcher.

"The mummy in this case," Gary read from a plaque on the wall, "lived in the time of the Romans. Most likely he was sacrificed by his own people. From the artifacts found with him, archaeologists believe he must have been a priest or a king."

A little of both, actually. Also a musician and an astronomer and a healer, when the need arose. Yes, Gary, I too was a physician in my day. You would probably consider my methods crude but on the whole I did more good than ill.

Gary squatted down to study the display. There was a re-creation of how Mael would have looked in life—pretty much exactly like the apparitions that had appeared to him downtown. They'd gotten the tattoos wrong—they made them look more tribal, more modern. Next to this was a picture of Stonehenge, which the museum assured Gary was not built by Druids but which they had used to predict solar eclipses. "How did you die?" he asked.

Now there's a tale to tell. Mael sat down on a display case full of partially preserved skulls and ruminated for a while before-continuing. *We took turns, is how. The burnt bannock cake came to me in my twenty-third year. That's how we chose the anointed ones, drawing bits of cake out of a bag. The-summer had been too cool for the corn and my people were in danger of starvation. So they took me to the oaks above Móin Boglach and hanged me until I gurgled for breath. When they cut me down and I plunged into the black water below the peat, I had a prayer to Teuagh on my lips. The father of tribes, we called him. O Lord, please make the grains to grow. Something of the sort. Down under the water he was waiting for me. He told me how disappointed he was. He told me what I had to do. Then I woke up here.*

Gary noticed for the first time that the rope around Mael's neck wasn't for decoration. It was a noose. "Jesus," Gary breathed. "That's horrible."

Mael came alive with anger as he responded, his head shaking so violently that Gary worried it might fall off. *It was glorious! I was the soul of my island in that moment, Gary, I was the hopes of my tribe made agonized flesh. I was born for that dying. It was magical.*

Gary reached out and put a hand on Mael's arm. "I'm truly sorry—but you wasted your death. Teuagh, whoever that was. He couldn't make the crops grow."

Mael stood up hurriedly and hobbled out of the room. *Maybe so, maybe so. Luckily for me then that's not how the tale ended.*

My world was a few score houses and a scrap of planted field. Beyond that lay only the forest—the place where the nasties roamed in the night. We had none of your technological advances but we knew things you've forgotten. Aye, true things—valuable things. We knew our place in the landscape. We knew what it meant to be part of something larger than ourselves.

When I woke here I was blind. Parts of me were missing. I didn't understand the language of my captors nor why they would shut me up in a tiny glass coffin. I knew only that my sacrifice had failed—they don't work, you know, if you survive. The father of tribes had other plans for me but I did not comprehend them at first. It took me far too long before I opened myself to the eididh and finally understood. I had served one purpose in life. I would serve another in death.

I had become the nasty in the night.

Which brings us up to date, my boy, and to the time when I turn things around and ask you a question. I've work to do and only one hand of my own. I could use you, son. You'd be a great help.

"Work? What kind?"

Ah, well. I'm going to butcher all the survivors. The Druid's voice had taken on a melancholy weariness Gary could barely stand to have echoing in his head. This was not a task that he wanted, definitely not anything he'd asked for. It was a duty. Gary got all that from the Druid's tone of voice. I spoke to you about judgment, well. I am the instrument of that judgment. I'm here to make it happen.

"Jesus. You're talking about genocide."

He shrugged. *I'm talking about what we are. I'm talking about why we were brought back with brains in our head—to finish what's begun. Now, lad.*

Are you in or out?

Chapter Twelve

Jack led us down a long hallway lit only sporadically by light streaming down from gratings set into the ceiling. On the other side of those grates were thousands of undead and the light in the tunnel changed constantly as they wandered the sidewalks above us, their shadows occluding the sun. For someone who lived here, like Jack, the walk might not have been so unnerving. After a minute of it there was icy sweat pooling in the small of my back. I felt a little better about it whenever Ayaan would spot a dead man walking overhead and lift her rifle in a spasmodic reflex. Once one of the dead dropped to the ground and stared in at us through the grating, his fingernails scratching at the metal. I could feel the wiry tension in Ayaan's body even though I was standing three feet away. It was all she could do not to fire off a shot, even though it would most likely ricochet off the grate and hit one of us.

We were rats in a cage. The dead had us trapped.

Finally, just when I thought I couldn't take any more, the hallway ended in a wide aperture. Beyond was open space and some light. As we came around the corner I could hardly believe my eyes. The concourse of the subway station looked almost the same as I remembered it—almost. The white pillars made of girders were there, still holding up the low ceiling. The walls were still lined with advertising posters behind thin plastic scratched with endless graffiti.

There were still too many people in the low space but they weren't moving. Normally this station would have been crowded with great surging tides of humanity moving from one platform to another. Now the people sat on the floor in groups of five or six, on a blanket or lounged against the walls, refusing to meet our gaze. Their clothes were brilliantly colored or expertly cut or lined with thousands of dollars' worth of fur but their faces were sunken and pale. Their eyes showed nothing but the exhausted boredom that comes from living in fear. I'd seen that look everywhere in Africa.

I looked up at the ceiling and saw something surprising. "You have electricity," I said. A few scattered fluorescent tubes sputtered up there. Most were dark or the fixtures were bare but enough light was generated to see our surroundings. "I thought the power was out."

"There's a hydrogen-fuel-cell system. It got put in after the blackout in 2003, when people got stuck down here in the dark. It was meant only for emergency use, but we've nursed it along."

"How long have you been down here?" I asked. It had not occurred to me before. "Since the evacuation?"

Jack squinted at me. "There was no evacuation."

I shook my head. "We saw piles of luggage outside of Port Authority. Signs telling people to keep together."

He nodded. "Sure. Because people went there and tried to get out, and maybe some of them did. But there was no large-scale evacuation. Think about it. Where would people go to? There's no place safer than this. Except maybe where you came from. The Guard closed the city down block by block, protecting what they could but it was a losing battle. Times Square was the last place there was any kind of real authority. It lasted until maybe a month ago. Those of us smart enough to know that civilization was over came down here. The rest of them got eaten."

We were interrupted before I could ask any more questions. A woman came up to us, a living woman (I still felt the need to qualify her as such) wearing a full-length Louis Vuitton logo-pattern coat over a baby T that read DON'T LOOK NOW. Even in the gloom of the station she wore peach-tinted sunglasses. She had to be at least six months pregnant, judging by the way her belly swelled out from under the shirt. Her name tag read HELLO MY NAME IS *fuck you*.

"These are our rescuers?" she asked Jack. He shrugged. "They didn't get very far." Apparently word of our exploits had already reached the survivors. "Still, it'll give us something to talk about. Stories of abysmal failure always make for great gossip."

Jack's mouth had been a tight line before. His lips disappeared entirely now. He was bristling with disgust or hatred or rage or something but he wouldn't let himself show it. "They had a good plan, Marisol. It showed real ingenuity."

"So did plastic belts, darling, but they're gone now." She reached out and touched Ayaan's head scarf. "Britney Spears meets Mullah Omar. How fetching. I suppose I should welcome you to the Grand Republic but it wouldn't be sincere. There is food for you if you need it. We can probably scare up a blanket without too many fleas in it if you want to take a nap." She sighed and brushed stray hairs out of her face. "I'll be right back."

Jack led us into one of the concourse's less-crowded corners and squatted down on his haunches. I sat down on the floor, glad for the chance to rest. Ayaan stayed on her feet, occasionally fingering her rifle. I don't know what she made of any of it. Jack clearly did not intend to talk to us so I broke the ice myself. "That's a nice shotgun," I said, indicating his weapon. He pulled it toward himself as if he thought I was going to try to take it away. Probably just a reflex left over from his training. "It's a SPAS-12, right? I didn't recognize it with that coating."

He looked down at the dull black enamel paint on the weapon. "I put a police coating on it because the standard finish glinted too much."

I nodded agreeably. Just two gun nuts talking here. The SPAS-12, or Sporting Purposes Automatic Shotgun 12-Gauge (the name was meant to fool Congress into thinking it was a hunting weapon—a complete lie, the thing was a military shotgun, a "streetsweeper" in the most violent sense) had been pretty high on my list of weapons systems I'd have liked to outlaw before the Epidemic but I could see its utility in protecting the station against undead attack. "You fire standard shells or do you cut them down to tactical strength?"

"Tactical." Jack looked away from me for a while. Clearly a man given to poignant pauses in conversation. Finally he gestured at Ayaan with his shoulder (his hands being busy with the shotgun). "She's a skinny, right? A Somali?"

"A 'skinny'?" I demanded.

"Just Army slang. No offense meant. I was a Ranger with the 75th."

He didn't seem to feel the need to elucidate on what that might signify. Judging by the way Ayaan tensed up and even let out a little gasp I was able to tentatively fill in some blanks. The 75th Ranger Regiment, as I later confirmed, was the outfit that tried to capture Mohammed Aidid at the Olympic Hotel in Mogadishu back in 1993. The outcome of that mission saw the first time in history that a dead American soldier was dragged through the streets of a foreign capital.

"She's proven herself to be a valuable ally," I protested, but he quieted me with a look. This, it seemed, was something he wanted to talk about.

"I wasn't on that detail at the hotel, I was back at the base playing cards all day. I saw plenty of other shit, though. The skinnies were smart. With all of our training and discipline they still got the better of us. Committed, too. I saw skinnies get shot and drop their weapons and other guys—kids and women even—would run out into fire to pick up the weapon and shoot at us some more." He shook his head and looked right through me. "We were occupying their land, and they wanted us gone. We should never have been there and when Bill Clinton broke contact I was so glad to come home."

He stared at Ayaan as if reading her, as if her very presence were a report from another place that he could study and analyze. "What I'm getting here is it's the skinnies who made it through this plague okay, that they didn't get overrun like we did." I nodded in confirmation. "I'm not surprised at all. Just do me a favor and keep it to yourself. If these people knew our only hope was signing up with Somalia. . . I don't think a lot of them would want to go there."

I guess that was all he wanted to say. I kept prodding, using my dated knowledge of Army acronyms and slang to try to draw him out but he would only answer in monosyllables after that. Finally he got up without a word and wandered away. Eventually Marisol came back with a couple of blankets for us and a can of creamed corn that Ayaan and I gratefully devoured. It was clearly the best the survivors had to offer. They must have been living out of cans the whole time.

"I see how impressed you are with our accommodations," Marisol said, watching us eat. "You simply must stay for the show." Something seemed to change in her, a mask falling away and she sat down next to me. "I hope Jack didn't hurt your feelings. He can be a bastard, but we need him."

I had actually wondered about her, not him. What could her bad attitude and lousy jokes actually accomplish down here? I asked a different question. "He's in charge of your defenses?"

"Sweetie"—she batted her eyelashes in a halfhearted attempt to regain her studied insouciance—"he's in charge of everything. He fixes the generator when it goes down. He organizes the search parties that bring in our food. Do you know how much food two hundred people go through in a day? Without him we would die. Horribly." She took the empty can from my hand when I'd finished eating. "Of course, I shouldn't underemphasize the importance of my little hubby. The old man does a pretty bang-up job himself. I hope you'll stay for his big address."

Night was falling and we no longer had any way to protect ourselves against the undead. It looked as if we didn't have any choice.

Chapter Thirteen

"You...you can't be serious," Gary said. Mael kept moving deeper into the dark museum, through a sculpture garden lit only indirectly by windows on the outside. "You honestly expect me to believe that you're going to walk out there into the city and start killing survivors?" As the Druid hobbled along the mummies began to emerge from the Egyptian wing, clutching canopic jars and heart scarabs to themselves. A supremely frustrated Gary called for Noseless and Faceless to come as well—he didn't necessarily want to get outnumbered just then. "Anyway, this isn't where you would do it. There are maybe a handful of people left in this city—"

There were over a thousand of them, when last I took a peek.

Mael pushed open a door and they stepped through into a spray of colored light. Stained-glass windows high overhead showered the radiance down upon them, while massive Gothic arches invited them to press on. Mael stopped and turned to face Gary. *The lot of them are in poor shape, lad. Starving—holed up so tight they can't get out again, or just too terrified to go out scavenging for food.*

"So just let them starve to death!"

That'd be cruel. I'm all about mercy, lad. The human race is done for, nobody can question that. It's taking its time on the way out, though. Imagine how much suffering I'll save. Here!

Mael had found a glass display case exactly like the hundreds of others Gary had seen. With the help of two mummies he opened it and lifted out a sword. It had been beautifully wrought, once, though over the centuries it had corroded to a dull green patina and the blade had fused with its scabbard. The hilt was worked in the shape of a howling Celtic warrior. Mael twisted it through the air in a wide cutting motion.

She's not the Answerer, but she'll do.

"You're going to kill people with that?"

Mael's head sagged forward. Try not to be so literal. I just want to be kitted out properly. You won't help me, then. It's not 'your thing.' Very well. Will you play at being my enemy, then? Will I need to go through you to complete the Great Work? Or will you stand aside and leave me to it?

Gary entertained the notion for a moment but it was pointless. He was no fighter—and he had seen how strong Mael was despite appearances. Mael's dark energy was enormous and powerful, too. It felt like a sunless planet, vast and round and self-contained, something so big and deadly it had its own gravitational field. "I. . . I don't suppose I could stop you. I can try to talk you out of it."

There's no debate, Gary. This is what we are. Uamhas. Monsters. There's good in this world and there's evil, and we're the evil. Now either come with me or leave me be, lad. There's work to do.

Using the sword as a cane Mael lurched forward through the Medieval exhibit and passed into the museum's great hall. Not knowing what else to do Gary followed, his mind reeling.

Saying no had been his immediate reaction and he knew he should stick with it, but Mael's conviction was a powerful argument on its own. After all, Gary had come to the Druid with his questions. Did he have a right to pick and choose among the answers, discarding the ones he didn't like?

It wasn't as if Gary felt any particular allegiance to the living. They'd treated him shabbily enough. He remembered the moment of recognition he'd had when he first saw Noseless on Fourteenth Street, when they had seemed like reflections of one another. Gary had called himself a monster, then, and meant it.

He'd spent so much time trying just to survive. He'd made himself a dead freak because it seemed like the only way forward. He'd tried to befriend Dekalb to get himself out of a bad situation. Yet what was he existing for? Simply going on had seemed like a good enough motivation before but now—if he did nothing with this second chance he'd been given, had he deserved it in the first place?

He didn't believe any of this crap about judgment and retribution. But maybe there were other reasons for signing on. Revenge, for one. Destroying all humans included killing Ayaan, and Dekalb too. The fuckers hadn't listened to him—they'd just shot him like a dog, not even giving him a chance.

Then there was the hunger in Gary's belly, a wild animal in there kicking at the walls in thwarted need.

Working for Mael he'd get plenty of fresh meat.

"How are you going to start?" Gary asked timidly.

Mael stood framed by the open doors of the Met, the sunlight streaming around his leathery flesh. *I've begun already*, he said, and stepped out into the day. Gary followed and found uncountable eyes staring right at him.

The entirety of Fifth Avenue was clogged with the dead. Their bodies filled the space like a forest of human limbs. In clothes dulled of color by dirt and time, with hair torn or matted or falling out they became a single entity, a featureless mass. White, black, Latino, male, female, decrepit skeletons and freshly slaughtered corpses. Thousands of them. Slaver dripped from their sagging jaws. Their yellow eyes turned in terrifying concert to look upon the Druid. They awaited his command. Mael had assembled an army—he must have been calling them the whole time Gary was asking his questions and miring himself in moral dilemmas.

Gary had never imagined so many of them together in one place—it seemed impossible, as if the world couldn't support so much weight. Their silence made them sphinxes, unknowable, implacable. No force could stand against them.

For the first time Gary wondered if Mael could actually pull it off. There were so many more dead people than living ones. The few survivors had stayed alive by out thinking their opponents, but if the undead were organized—if one person could lead them, then what chance did the living have? It was time to choose sides.

Mael raised the sword and pointed and the dead surged as a mob up and down the street, splitting as they streamed around the sides of the museum and into Central Park. The sound of their feet pounding the flagstones was like a war drum beating out a savage tattoo. Mael and the mummies fell in behind the throng and Gary caught up with them as they passed a statuary group of three bears modeled in bronze. Gary had seen the sculpture before but had always thought it had something to do with a children's story. It looked like a totem now, an emblem of a conquering force.

For good or for evil, Gary, I do what I am meant for. It doesn't matter what we choose. It simply matters what we are.

Though Mael stood only a few feet away Gary was surprised by the sudden entrance of the thoughts into his mind. In the thundering footfall rhythm of the marching dead he expected all words to be swallowed up.

Instead they seemed to echo. For good or for evil: two sides of the same duty. I used to fight to save lives, Gary had told the survivor Paul. Now I take them away.

Do you feel you have some other cause to serve? What else is more important to you? What could be more important than the end of the world?

The mud of the park boiled under the tramping feet of the dead, jumping up in great clods that Gary had to stumble through. They came to a great open space devoid of trees—it must have been the Great Lawn, once—and the dead spread out, forming a wide circular clearing in their midst, an open patch where Mael stood with the mummies. The Druid turned around a few times and finally scratched a mark in the soil with his sword. He gestured at the dead all around him and they went into action. From a distance Gary heard a great rumbling crash and a column of dust rose above the branches of the denuded trees to the south. A bomb must have gone off or a gas main exploded or—Gary had no idea what it was.

"What's happening?" Gary asked.

The construction has begun. I must have a broch from whence to issue my orders. A fortress, with a throne room.

Which wasn't exactly helpful, but Gary soon understood. The crowd rippled at its edges and then the movement drew closer. The dead were passing bricks forward, hand to hand. Clumps of mortar stuck to the bricks, some of which were ornamented with fragments of graffiti. The dead must have pulled down a building— that was the crash—and now they intended to use the liberated building materials for Mael's headquarters. One by one the bricks were laid down, the dead pushing them deep into the mud with clumsy hands. They swarmed around the spot where Mael stood like a hive of ants, totally focused on their task. This was far beyond what the dead were capable of in Gary's experience, not without an intelligence organizing them from afar. Could Mael actually be controlling them all at the same time? The Druid's power must be enormous.

Give me a chance, Gary. Work with me for one day. Maybe you'll like it. Maybe you'll feel at home being who you really are.

He had felt so much guilt over eating Ifiyah, because he had tried to live up to the standards of living men—in spite of what he had become. The euphoria that had followed his devouring of Kev had been the most natural thing he'd ever experienced.

Gary started to refuse but he couldn't. In the face of so

much concerted effort, not to mention Mael's certainty, it seemed impossible to deny what was happening. "One day," he said, the most defiant thing he could force out of his mouth. "I'll give it one day and see how I feel."

Mael nodded, careful not to put too much strain on his broken neck.

Chapter Fourteen

Shailesh led us to a good spot where we could lean against one of the station's pillars. It was the best place to watch the speech, he said. I still had very little idea of what was going on. The lights dipped and the buzz of conversations around us dropped to a low murmur. We were seated looking at an empty patch of station floor. Above our heads we had a good view of the famous Roy Lichtenstein mural. In primary colors and thick comic-book lines it showed a New York of the Future: finned subway trains blasting on rockets past a city of spires and air bridges. At the far right a serious-looking man in a radio helmet supervised the trains with glowing pride.

From underneath the mural a man appeared, smiling and waving at people in the crowd. Applause broke out and somewhere a violin started playing "Hail to the Chief."

The man was probably sixty years old. He had a scruffy gray beard and a few wisps of hair on his head. He wore a charcoal grey suit with a tear on one sleeve and a name tag that read HELLO MY NAME IS Mr. President. A discrete American flag pin gleamed on his lapel.

Marisol stood up from one side of the room and bellowed out an announcement. "Ladies and Gentlemen,

I give you the man of the hour, my beloved husband and your President of the United States of America: Montclair Wilson!"

The crowd went wild. Wilson clasped his hands above his head and beamed like a searchlight. "Thank you, thank you," he shouted over the roar of the crowd. When they finally calmed down he cleared his throat and crossed his arms behind his back. "My fellow Americans," he said, "it has been a hard month. Yet we must remember that spring has come and with it the promise of a new morning in America."

I grabbed Shailesh's arm. He had to forcibly break himself away from looking at Wilson. "Is this serious?" I asked.

He shook his head to try to shut me up but then he sighed and said, "Without strong leadership we'd be doomed."

"But who is this guy?"

"He was a professor of political economics at Columbia before the, the you-know. Now can I please listen? This is important!"

I let him go and turned back to hear the speech, some of which we'd missed.

"—kept or exceeded all my campaign promises. I am proud to say that we now have enough hot water for everyone to have a shower each week. You asked me for more working fluorescent tubes in the sleeping concourse and with Jack's help I brought a thousand points of light to our benighted country. We have also added five more volumes to the library, including a Tom Clancy novel I personally recommend."

I looked at Ayaan, a sarcastic grin on my face, but

she was as rapt as the rest of them. She'd been raised by demagogues and political-indoctrination counselors so I suppose it was no real surprise she was susceptible to this kind of rhetoric. I leaned back against the pillar and studied the zip-a-toned mural, sinking into a reverie for a future that would never be, now. I sat up again, though, when the President got to his roundup of current events.

"We have all heard the rumors. It would appear to be true—there is a boat in the harbor, I have learned it is a diesel-powered fishing trawler repurposed as a troop carrier. Now, we don't want to start using the word 'rescue.' I know we're all tired and bored and we want to get out of here but our rescue is not something I'm going to talk about tonight. I will never promise you that you will be rescued until I can guarantee it. I will be leading a fact-finding committee myself to see what our chances of rescue really are. My results will be made public as soon as they are available. I can promise you one thing, though. When we are rescued, we will all go into that new and promised land. We will leave no child behind.

"Good night, America—and God bless!"

The crowd exploded in a roar of excitement as Wilson left the "stage," his fists pumping in the air as the violin broke into a raucous rendition of "It's a Grand Old Flag." Marisol ran to take her husband's place, her hands clapping in time. When the song ended she called up the violinist and had him play requests. He was a slender teenage boy no older than Ayaan with a bad case of acne and a T-shirt that read WEAPONIZED 2004 WORLD AUTOPSY TOUR. A blurrily menacing nü metal band looked out with scorn from the faded cotton. The requests he got were mostly for songs by Sinatra and Madonna, which he played with feeling.

It was the first music I'd heard since leaving Somalia and I have to admit it stirred me, even bitter, cynical, crusted old Dekalb. I sang along with a couple of the tunes, remembering my youth in the States. I had run away from my home country, I had requested fieldwork the second I got hired by the UN. But America hadn't been so bad, had it? In my memories it was just fine. There had been a lot of cars that constantly broke down, as I remember, and a lot of hanging out in front of McDonald's hoping cute girls would walk by, even though they never did, but it seemed like paradise compared to what was going on over our heads. When the kid broke into an arrangement of Avril Lavigne's hit "Complicated" for solo violin, however, I rose from my numbed haunches and headed to the back of the concourse, where a set of card tables held refreshments. I helped myself to some punch (watered-down Kool-Aid mixed with bathtub vodka) and a cookie full of clumps of baking soda.

The survivors wouldn't talk to me. I tried various conversational gambits—complimenting the snacks, asking about the weather, even just introducing myself cold; but I guess they didn't want to hear what their chances of getting out with us were. If they just stared at me they could maintain the illusion that I was a free ticket to safety.

Well, maybe I was. The Arawelo was still out there somewhere in the night. If we could reach it there was a chance. And I thought I might have an idea how to reach it.

I went looking for Jack and found myself in a deserted corridor. Up ahead it ended in a short flight of stairs. I could hear people down there so I went to investigate and found Jack. Marisol, too. He had one hand inside the drawstring of her pants and his mouth was nuzzling her neck.

She saw me and for a second the look in her eyes was one of simple defiance. Why not? she seemed to ask, and in truth I could hardly fault her. Death was always near us. More to the point it was none of my business. She seemed to recall herself after a second, and she pushed Jack away angrily. "You fucking asshole, get off of me!" she screamed. "You know I'm married!"

She dashed past us. I watched Jack carefully, wondering if he would be angry at me for discovering them. Instead he merely turned around, very slowly, and opened his eyes. "What can I do for you, Dekalb?" he asked. Before I could answer we heard a squeal, maybe a scream—the white tiles of the station played hell with acoustics—and we raced back to the concourse.

The cat had returned. The mangy tabby that Shailesh had released as bait so that Ayaan and I could come inside. It must have found its way through the dead on its own and then returned via some hidden entrance too small to need to be guarded. It looked confused and very bedraggled as it walked across the open floor of the concourse, its tail flicking back and forth cautiously.

A girl with braces and thick glasses bent down and patted her knees. "Come here, baby," she cooed, and the cat turned to face her. In an instant it was on her, its vicious teeth sinking deep in her arms as she tried to protect herself. We could all see now the hole in the cat's side, a ragged wound through which its ribs were clearly visible.

Jack rushed for the girl as the rest of the crowd fell back in terror, nearly trampling each other as they tried to get away. Jack flicked a combat knife out of his boot and impaled the cat through the head. Then he turned to the girl. He grabbed one of her arms roughly and yanked it upward. It was covered in small bites, pinpricks of blood and cat saliva. "Come on," Jack said. His voice was neither cruel nor kind—just empty. He had nothing left in the way of emotions to give her. He led her away through one of the concourse's many passages.

After that the air in the concourse felt like something solid and foul-tasting. Like the place had been poured full of rubber cement. Any of the feeling of festivity was gone—which was apparently Marisol's cue to take the stage once more.

"Famous movie scenes!" she shouted. The words had a brittle quality but they got the attention of the crowd. "Famous movie scenes! Who's got one?"

Perhaps numbed by horror the survivors just looked at one another, trying to think of something. Anything. Finally Ayaan stood up. She looked as if she might die of embarrassment and her command of English declined sharply with her stage fright, but she managed to pipe out: "May we have the famous scene of Ms. Sandra Bullock and Mr. Keanu Reeves in the Speed?"

Marisol nodded eagerly and called Ayaan up to act it out with her. "There's a bomb on the bus!" Ayaan shouted, smiling a little. "I need to know, ma'am, if you can drive this bus!"

So that's what they needed Marisol for. I left them to it and turned to follow Jack out of the concourse.

Chapter Fifteen

Gary knelt down in the denuded mud of Riverside Park and looked across the river at the Seventy-ninth Street Boat Basin. A few sailboats still rode at anchor there, their masts splintered and their hulls sagging lifelessly in the water. A speedboat smoldered away in their midst, acrid smoke leaking from its engine compartment to drift across the night air to Gary's twitching nose. One vessel, a big racing sailboat with its boom tied down, looked as if it was still seaworthy. A pair of huge wheels stood at its stern, lashed to the deck. A single electric light blared from its bow every few seconds. Someone had raised an upside-down American flag to the top of its mast.

Mael had been certain there were survivors in the boat basin. They wouldn't be hard to find.

Gary kicked off his shoes and leapt into the Hudson, Noseless and Faceless following close behind. They sank to the bottom like rocks while Gary bobbed up and down like a cork in the water. He realized he was holding his breath. He let it go—he didn't need it—and drifted down to the bottom. The water was cold, very cold if he could feel it through his thick skin, but it didn't bother him. It was dark, too, murky and dismal so that he could barely see a few feet in front of his face. It would be easy to get lost down there. What little moonlight penetrated the surface shifted and shimmered so much it was more-or-less useless. He could make out currents of silt flowing past him and he could see the soft outlines of centuries worth of dumped junk—old cars, fifty-gallon drums that had rusted open, piles on piles of black plastic trash bags sealed off with metal crimps. A mat of slimy algae covered everything, fronds of it drifting in the river's flow. Every step that Gary took required real effort but he didn't tire. His feet sank into the mud of the riverbed but he pressed on, looking for the sailboat's anchor.

Noseless appeared through the gloom just to Gary's right. The dead man looked more at home under the water than he had on land, a white pulpy thing with floating hair and billowed-out clothes. Silvery bubbles leaked from his shirt. Gary watched with approval as his companion grabbed a fish out of the dark water and sank his teeth deep into its side. Clouds of blood blossomed around him, temporarily hiding Noseless from view.

The dead man was coming along nicely. After the day's bounty, the walking corpse who had once been unable to feed himself was now acting of his own volition again. Faceless was making slower progress but at least she had managed to clean herself of the insect fauna that had been nesting in her collarbones.

They had all fed well under Mael's scheme. Gary had found he had a real talent for killing. He exulted in it.

Their first mission had been an elderly woman cowering in a brownstone up in Harlem. She had sequestered herself on the second floor, filling up the stairs with broken furniture and bundles of old magazines tied up in twine. The hard part had been climbing over all that refuse. When they reached the top they found her in her bathroom, crouching behind a wicker hamper. Gary had expected moral qualms to rear themselves as she pleaded for her life but in fact she had trembled so badly that she couldn't speak. There had been no difficulty at all as Gary moved in for the kill, no hesitation on his part, just cold mechanics until the hunger had taken over and he could not have resisted if he tried.

They had moved on when it was done, stopping at the 125th Street train station. The terminal and its elevated platforms had been deserted but next door sat a building that had been boarded up and abandoned since as long as Gary could remember, the burnt-out shell of a red-brick office building ornamented with elaborate coats of arms. A banner offering used laptop computers for sale hung limply from its side. From the platforms he could see sunlight leaking through the building's gaping windows and trees growing from the spars of the broken roof. He could also see a twisting curl of white smoke coming from the top of the building—smoke that disappeared almost as soon as he spotted it. Someone up there had a fire going and must have extinguished it quickly.

The building's street-level entrances had been barricaded for decades but the three of them made short work of the plywood covering a low window, their shoulders smashing into the obstruction in concerted force. Inside triangular patches of light showed through from the sky three stories above. The interior of the building had imploded leaving a three-dimensional maze of collapsed lathing and dangling floor beams. They climbed upward, ever upward, moving from plank to plank with their hands, falling back as the boards gave way, making progress when they didn't. With the patience of the dead they kept trying and they kept making progress. Whoever had taken refuge on the roof could have thrown down debris or shot them from above at any time but as they reached the top floor they met with no resistance whatsoever.

Someone had thoughtfully left a stepladder under the hole in the roof. They climbed up through torn tarpaper and emerged into the bright light of day. Gary saw a makeshift lean-to mounted on the last stable corner of the roof. The embers of a campfire burned nearby, complete with a spitted rat waiting to be roasted. He heard something crumble and the patter of stone chips hitting the street below and turned to see a living man perched on the edge of the rood, one step away from oblivion. He looked like one of the homeless, his face smudged with dirt, his clothes colorless and torn.

Gary took a step in the man's direction and he leapt. Better that, he must have thought, than what Gary intended for him. From his perspective that was probably accurate thinking. Noseless and Faceless scampered back down to the street to get to him before he could rise again. Gary took his time. It wasn't meat he wanted anymore, it was the life force, the golden energy of the living that could make him strong.

Four hours later he stood on the bottom of the Hudson with his hands on the anchor chain of the sailboat. He wouldn't let these survivors get away, he promised himself. He began to climb, hand over hand, his minions following. When his head burst through the surface once more he reached up and dragged himself onto the wooden deck of the boat, water streaming from him in gouts. He rose to his feet and felt himself swaying as the current rocked the vessel. A cabin sat in the middle of the deck, its hatch recessed into the wood. That was their destination. Before Gary could cross half the distance to the door, however, it opened and a living human leaned out. He held what looked like a toy pistol in his hand, bright orange with a barrel wide enough to shoot golf balls.

The gun made a loud fizzling noise and smoke leapt across the deck. Faceless looked down at her stomach where a dull metal cylinder hissed and spat. With a burst of red light like a firework it exploded, knocking her backward into the water.

"A flare gun?" Gary asked aloud. "No shit, a flare gun? What's next? A starter's pistol?"

"Jesus," the living man said. He wore a blue fleece with the collar up around his neck. "You can. . . you can talk." He put the flare gun down on the deck and raised his hands in supplication. "I am so sorry! I thought you were one of those dead things!"

I am, Gary thought, and prepared to pounce on the idiot. But before he could get into position the sailor ran up onto the deck and leaned on the railing, staring down at the turbulent water. "Jesus Christ, what have I done! I'm so sorry—I have a life preserver here somewhere. Can she swim?"

Gary looked down into the water. He could see Faceless under the surface, illuminated by the sparkling flare, twirling as she drifted toward the bottom, struggling to pull the incendiary out of her midriff. "She'll be fine," Gary said, as much menace as he could get dripping from his voice. "You, on the other hand. . ."

"Oh. You are dead." The sailor's face went blank.

"But you can talk. Listen. Come belowdecks. We'll, we'll discuss this like rational people. Please."

Gary felt like laughing but he just nodded. He went down into the belly of the ship, leaving Noseless to help Faceless get back aboard when she could. Gary ducked his head to get through a low galley and followed his guide into a cramped cabin at the fore of the boat. "You want some coffee?" the sailor asked, pouring himself a mug from a tiny electric coffeemaker. "No, I guess you wouldn't. I'm Phil, by the way, Phil Chambers from. . . from Albany originally. Things were bad there. We came down the river hoping to find a safe place. . . Saugerties was on fire and now, New York City, this is it, I mean, there's no place else to go but out into the Atlantic. This is the end of the line."

"Yes," Gary said. It would only take a moment to kill this man. One quick bite on the throat. A deep laceration on the carotid artery.

Chambers pulled some charts out of a pigeonhole and spread them across a table. He stared hard into his mug as if he had discovered an insect inside. He didn't seem able to drink. "Please don't do this," he said. "My kids are in the stern. They've got nobody else. Oh, Jesus, no. No, you won't take my kids too. Please."

Gary stepped closer until he could feel the man's body heat. Chambers was shaking and he stank of bad sweat. Gary grabbed him by the hair on the back of his head.

"I'm begging you, guy, I'm begging. I'm begging."

Real tears rolled down the man's cheek. Gary could taste them on his neck when he bit into the yielding flesh.

He'd thought it would be difficult when they pleaded

for their lives. He had dreaded the moment when the old woman started blubbering.

It turned out to make no difference at all.

Chapter Sixteen

Jack looked at me over his shoulder as I approached. He had the girl—the one who had called the cat and been bitten by an undead feline for her trouble—behind a locked steel gate at the bottom of a stairwell. She looked more sullen then afraid. "Hold on, Dekalb," Jack said. "I've got to see to her first."

I nodded and sat down on a crate. We were at the last safe barrier on the Number 7 train platform, according to a sign written in Sharpie pen and taped to the wall. The tunnels themselves couldn't be closed off so the survivors had simply sealed off all the platforms, sticking to the concourses and their connecting passageways where they could be assured of their safety. Shailesh had told me that they had never actually seen one of the undead down on the tracks but that Jack refused to take the chance.

The girl—her name tag read HELLO MY NAME IS Carly—had been put out on the platform to see if she died or not. If she didn't, she could come back in. If she did, Jack would put a bullet in her head. Either way he would be spending the night sitting next to her. He did what he could, passing a first-aid kit through the bars. She dabbed Mercurochrome on her arms until they turned bright orange.

"Did you forget what I taught you?" Jack asked in a flat voice. As if he was simply asking for basic data. "You never touch anything that's been outside. Not until it's cleared."

"It looked so scared and I just wanted. . . " Carly shrugged. "It's not like it matters. We're all going to die anyway."

"You can't give in to that attitude now. Especially not now, when we've actually got a chance to get out of here. You haven't heard about his boat?"

The girl stared at me. There was nothing but naked antipathy in her eyes, a complete refusal to connect with me. "Yeah? Well, thanks for making my death extra ironic, Grandpa."

"You don't talk like that to your elders," Jack said. He didn't raise his voice but his tone made my skin crawl. "Are you listening to me?"

"Yes, sir. I just don't give a fuck, sir." She turned around and started walking away from the gate. "Enough of this," she shouted back. "I'm going to Brooklyn!" Only a single fluorescent tube still burned out there and she was quickly swallowed up by shadows.

Jack didn't call after her. Instead he slumped down on the tiled floor, his back to a wall so he could keep an eye on the gate. He picked up his SPAS-12 again and laid it across his knees. Reaching into his pocket he took out a shell—a two-and-a-half-inch tungsten slug, unless I missed my guess.

"What are her chances?" I asked.

"About ninety-ten, based on what I've seen. Talk to me, Dekalb. Tell me why you keep chasing after me while

I'm just trying to do my job." The words were too open and vulnerable to belong to this man. He was clearly under immense stress. I thought about leaving him alone and coming back the next day but I had a feeling all of his days were like this.

"You sent out two people a couple of days ago. Paul and Kev, I think." Ray had mentioned their names to me back at the gate.

He nodded and pressed the magazine cutoff of his weapon and opened the slide. He snapped the slug into the barrel and closed it back up again. "Yes," he confirmed.

"So you're not trapped in here. You can send people out when you need to—to get supplies, say, or whatever. I'm not saying it isn't dangerous but it can be done. You must know some tricks to staying alive here that we don't."

Without moving his gaze away from the barred gate in front of him he raised the corners of his mouth. I wouldn't call it a smile. "Sure. We know one great trick. It's called desperation. When we get hungry enough somebody always volunteers to go out and get more food. Sometimes people just get bored and go up on their own. Some of them even come back. We're running short of everything, Dekalb. I don't know if you noticed, but one resource we're real low on is single men, eighteen to thirty-five. They're the ones who volunteer first."

"Wow," I said. I had thought there must be some secret.

"There's nothing to do down here but wait. Some people can't take that."

I understood, kind of. "I have an idea but it's dangerous. Very dangerous. We need to get your people to the river. There's an APC just west of the Port Authority."

Jack nodded. "I've seen it. I've even thought of that myself. It would still run, assuming the fuel hasn't evaporated and the battery still has a charge and none of the belts in the engine have rotted away. Sure, we could back it up to one of the gates and load people on board hassle-free. We'd have to make a bunch of trips but yeah, it would get us to your boat just fine."

Warming to the idea I pointed out the flaw. "Somebody would have to go out there, get it started, and drive it back here, though. If the engine didn't work on the first try they'd have to try to repair it. The dead would be on them the entire time. I have some soldiers I can bring in—Somalis—but they don't know how to maintain an American armored personnel carrier. I'm thinking that maybe you do."

"Correct."

Okay. We were getting somewhere. "There's just one hitch. None of this can happen until I complete my original mission." He looked over sharply and I held up my hands for patience. "Look, there are political issues. Somalia's in the hands of a warlord. I need a good reason to convince her to accept a bunch of white refugees who aren't soldiers, who are going to be a drain on her resources. We need to be realistic."

If I wanted to manipulate him that was the word to use. This was a man who had stripped himself of all pretense, all sentiment. Realism was his only philosophy. He nodded once. I tried talking to him about what I needed to do and how he could help but he was done with that conversation. He just shut down—conserving energy, maybe. It was an unnerving trick but it served him well—the ability to just ignore another human being, even if they stood right in front of him and tried to get his attention. He was the hardest man I ever met. It gave me hope, though. If anybody could get me to the UN building, it was Jack.

We sat in silence for quite a while. I thought about heading back up to the concourse, to Ayaan and the other survivors, but I just couldn't. I couldn't handle the way they looked at me—as if I was a tasteless joke, their fondest hope dangled before them after weeks and weeks of being told that nothing good could ever happen again. I couldn't face their weird games based on a popular culture that had ceased to exist.

The silence was just starting to really get to me—I was ready to start talking to myself, just to hear something— when it was broken by Carly. We couldn't see her. She stayed to the shadows, but we heard her footsteps echoing on the deserted platform. Jack raised his shotgun to track the sound. That felt callous to me but then we both knew that she might be coming back changed.

"I threw up," she said from the darkness. "That's bad, right?"

"Probably. It might just be nerves." Jack rose slowly to his feet, the weapon still in his hands but not necessarily pointing at her anymore. "Come here. You're probably cold and hungry. I can help with that."

Ifiyah had been cold and hungry after she got bitten. I wondered how many times Jack had sat this horrible vigil. Carly came up to the bars and we saw at once she was going to die. Her face was covered in a sheen of sweat and her eyes were completely bloodshot. Her arms, where the cat had scratched her, were puffy and dark with congested blood. Jack offered her a blanket and a can of chipped beef. She took them both without comment. I watched her face as she ate. The braces shredded the sensitive inner skin of her lips as she wolfed the food down. She noticed me staring and stopped for a second. "Get a good look, perv," she said. "I'm not going to get any prettier."

I looked away, flushing with embarrassment. I'd been thinking about Sarah, wondering if she was going to need an orthodontist soon. I couldn't very well explain that to Carly, though. She wouldn't have understood.

We sat with her all through the night. I dozed off now and again but I would always wake to find Jack sitting perfectly still. The shotgun never strayed from its position athwart his knees. Each time I looked Carly had taken another turn for the worse. She started panting, her lungs struggling to keep up with her body's demand for oxygen. Her fingers turned into painful-looking sausages, so thick the skin split around her nails and they bled dark blood. She started raving about four in the morning—begging for water and her mother and, more and more frequently, for meat.

Twice Jack offered to end her suffering but both times she refused without a moment's hesitation. "I think I'm feeling a little better," she said, the second time. Her breathing had, in fact, calmed down. Her eyes fluttered closed and I thought maybe she would actually make it— maybe her immune system would win this fight.

"Lie down if it's more comfortable," I told her. "Keep visualizing how much better you'll feel tomorrow. If you can sleep, you probably should."

She didn't respond to me. We waited a few minutes and then Jack kicked the steel gate, hard, with his boot. It clanged loud enough to hurt my ears but she didn't so much as wince. "Okay," he said. "I'm going to do it.

Stand back."

I shook my head. "No. No, she's just tired—"

Slowly she stood up from where she'd been sitting on the tiles. Her legs were unsteady beneath her and her eyes were still closed.

"Look," I said, "she's okay." I knew I was wrong but I said it anyway. She came for us hard and with all the strength she had, smashing her bloated hands and her sweat-damp face against the bars, smashing her shoulders and her hips against the steel. The cartilage in her nose snapped as she collided face-first with the barrier, her cheekbone broke and her features smeared across her face. I did step back, then. Jack raised his SPAS-12 and fired, the slug entering her left eye and coming out the back of her head with part of her skull. She stopped moving, then. The shotgun clicked as the gas-powered mechanism automatically loaded another round. He didn't need it.

I was breathing hard and my body was buzzing with the chemistry of panic. Jack brought the weapon up to his chest and looked over at me. "Sometimes," he said, slowly, quietly, "I think they'd be better off if they all died in their sleep one night. Then they wouldn't be afraid anymore. Some nights I stay awake and think about how to do it."

He shook off the thought and when he spoke again it was with his usual confident tone. "We'll commence with your mission tomorrow, after we've both had some sleep." Then he turned and headed up the stairs.

Chapter Seventeen

Gary marched into the compound at Central Park like a returning hero. He felt he should be wearing a cape. Behind him Noseless and Faceless kept easy pace with his stride.

The work on Mael's broch was coming along well. Two triangular support vanes rose a dozen yards in the air while one curtain wall was already higher than Gary's head. The undead workers on the scaffolding looked unsteady at best but they lifted and carried their building materials as if they were precious relics and placed the bricks so closely together that Gary would have had a hard time getting a piece of paper between them. Groups of dead men sat in pits around the construction site preparing bricks, scraping the old mortar free of the bricks with their fingernails. Some used their teeth.

Other work parties erected the scaffolding, lattices of metal pipes torn off the facades of New York's buildings. There had never been a shortage of the stuff. The ladders and platforms thrown up by the dead were rickety and precarious, and accidents were common—in the short time Gary had spent on the building site he had more than once heard the sudden crump of an undead body falling thirty feet to the mud. Their bones shattered and their limbs useless these victims would be put to work wherever it was possible—if they could still walk, they could drag sledges full of bricks, while if they could still use their arms they would be put in the cleaning pits to scrape mortar.

Those few sorry wretches who were effectively paralyzed in accidents were still useful to Mael as taibhsear, or seers—in the most literal sense. Hoisted up and tied to the rising walls of the broch their eyes scanned the park for their master. Eyeless himself he depended on these assistants, without whom he would be blind. Dead men climbed up on ladders to feed bits of meat to these lookouts, keeping them fresh.

The Druid sat on a mound of piled rocks at the very center of the compound. His honor guard of mummies stood arrayed behind him, slumped against one another, clutching at their amulets and heart scarabs like a court of mentally deficient wizards. In front of Mael spread out on the ground lay a folding gas-station map of the city with tokens marking the location of all known survivors. One of the mummies knelt over the map as Gary approached, removing tokens for the three locations he'd raided during the night.

Leaning forward on his sword the color of verdigris Mael shooed the mummy away and raised his head to greet his champion.

My gowlach curaidh returns! You're looking hale, lad. The Great Work must agree with you.

"I have a right to exist," Gary demurred. "Which means I have to feed."

Aye, and you've done well. The Druid's head slumped

against his chest. *Maybe too well. Did you have to be so vicious with the wee bairns?*

Gary could only shrug. "You said yourself that we're evil, and that we need to act like it. I was just following my orders." Gary squatted down and studied the map. There were plenty of survivors left—hundreds. He could keep this up for months and not run out of food. Any compassion or sympathy he might have once had for the living was draining out of him, perhaps as a result of being shot at every time he met them. Or maybe he really was becoming the creature of absolutes Mael had asked him to be. "This is what I am, right? A monster. Don't criticize me for being good at it."

Mael studied him for a long moment before agreeing. *Aye. Forgive an old wizard for his sentimental maundering. I've another task for you, lad, one I imagine you'll take to. It's a big job and it'll take a thoughtful man to pull it off.*

Gary nodded. He was ready, whatever it might be. Mael had promised him that he would feel at peace once he had accepted the role fate had cast him for and as usual the Druid was right. He felt strong, so much stronger than when he had crawled out of the basement of the Virgin Megastore with a hole in his head. Even stronger than when he'd first awoken in a bathtub full of ice.

A dead woman in a stained pair of jeans and a low-cut halter top that showed off her withered blue breasts stumbled forward, nearly stepping on the map. She would have been pretty, once, a Latina with a massive mane of curling hair. Now her face showed blossoming sores and clouded eyes. She looked at Gary and then at Mael and finally let her gaze drift out of focus. Not particularly strange behavior for a walking corpse, but to Gary she seemed more dazed than she should be. As if she'd been drugged or put into a trance.

You'll need more than your usual retinue for this job. You need to learn to read the eididh, and how to lead troops into battle. This one has knowledge I want to impart in her head, if you can get to it.

Gary licked his lips, more than a little excited. Mael had powers beyond his own, far beyond, but so far the Druid had been stingy with teaching his attack dog any new tricks. "How do I. . . " he asked, but he knew what the answer would be.

Open yourself, as I've told you before.

Gary nodded and reached out to grab the dead woman by the back of the neck. He tried to do what he'd done before—stroking the network of death, just as he had when he took control of his companions, just as when he had summoned the crowd that devoured the survivor Paul. He pushed until his brain was throbbing and white daggers of light leaked in around the corners of his vision but only succeeded in gaining her attention. She stared at him wide-eyed, as if fascinated by the dead veins in his cheeks.

You can do better than that, man, Mael mocked. *It's not something you see or hear or taste—forget those things and try again!*

A little annoyed, Gary tried again—and only managed to develop a buzzing in his ears. He could feel the dead blood quivering in his head and he thought for sure he would give himself an aneurysm. But then—finally— something snapped and roiling shadows blossomed in his mind, streaks of darkness, of dark death energy that resolved into rays, into threads. Strands of a web that linked him to everyone around him—the dead woman, Mael, the seers hanging from the walls. He could sense Faceless and Noseless behind him.

Then he saw the back of his own head.

He was looking through the eyes of his minions, seeing what they saw—even as he continued to be able to use his own eyes. He turned to look at the Latina and felt the connection that bound them together, the unity of death. He could feel thoughts and memories bubbling around her—information she herself could not access any more because her brain had suffocated when she died.

His hadn't. He saw at once what Mael had wanted him to find. Something she'd seen while scavenging for food, something important. A street—a square—a doorway, a steel gate. Human hands, living hands clutching the bars. White noise hissed and crackled around him, he tasted metal in his mouth, copper, dried blood, but he fought it back. More living humans, more on top of more of them— hundreds. He saw their eyes peering out of darkness, their frightened eyes. Hundreds?

Hundreds. Their bright energy seared him. He wanted to take it from them.

When he returned to himself he was down on all fours and a long string of shiny drool ran from his lower lip to the mud below. "Now?" he asked.

Aye.

Gary pointed and dead workmen came down from their ladders to gather before him. He reached out with his mind and summoned others—an army of them—from as far away as the reservoir. It was easy when he had the knack down. He didn't need to give them detailed instructions, as he had with Faceless and Noseless. He didn't need to micromanage. He simply told them what he wanted and they did it without question. It felt good. It felt amazing. He called on more of them, as many as he could reach.

Leave me a few to put a roof over my head, eh, lad?

Gary nodded but he was too busy assembling his army to pay much attention to the Druid. "So many of them," he said, unsure whether he was referring to the living or the dead.

Chapter Eighteen

Jack handed me a cell phone that looked like something from the early nineties. A real brick—two inches thick with rubberized grips on the sides. The antenna was almost bigger than the phone itself, eight inches long and as thick as my index finger. "Motorola 9505," I said, trying to impress him. "Sweet." Most cell phones would be useless in New York—the towers that dotted the city's rooftops were unpowered now—but this beast could tap into the Iridium satellite network. It would work anywhere on earth as long as it had a charge and a good line-of-sight to the sky. Which meant you needed to be near a window— or one of the gratings that ventilated the subways from above. The UN used Iridiums, but only sparingly, handing them out to field operatives as if they were Fabergé eggs. In America they were standard issue for military units, and in fact Jack had retrieved them from an abandoned National Guard checkpoint a few blocks away.

Two more phones sat in a multiunit charger which had been built to hold six. The rest had gone out with scavenging parties and had never returned.

One of the great features of this particular model was that it could work as a walkie-talkie, so I could contact the

Arawelo's radio set. I made a quick call to Osman, letting him know we were still alive.

"That is too bad, Dekalb," he said, the signal degraded and clipped through the thick ceiling of the station but still audible. "If you were dead I could go home."

I rang off to save the phone's charge.

"Next stop is the armory," Jack said. He unlocked the door of the station's twenty-four-hour token booth. Behind the bulletproof glass sat rack after rack of long-barreled rifles, some of them still in their boxes. Too bad they were just toys. Paintball rifles, BB guns, pellet shooters guaranteed not to penetrate human skin. "There are more toy stores in New York than gun shops," Jack explained. It didn't sound like an apology. "We took what we could get. They're useful as distraction weapons. You hit a corpse with one of these and he'll feel it. He'll come looking for you, which gives your partner enough time to take him down."

Your partner, theoretically, would be holding a single-action hunting rifle, of which there were exactly three in the booth, or a pistol—there were dozens of those, though only a couple of cardboard boxes of ammunition for them. There were plenty of knives, though, and sledgehammers, and riot-control batons. "I'm guessing you're not much with a firearm anyway," Jack said, looking over his arsenal. He settled on a machete with an eighteen-inch blade—originally a gardening implement. It felt well balanced in my hand and the grip was rubberized for comfort but I didn't relish using it.

"You're kidding," I hoped.

"Sharpened it myself. Let me do the fighting, alright? You can be the radioman." He locked the booth up again and we went off to find Ayaan. She was with Marisol, who was painting her fingernails. The girl soldier snapped to attention when she saw Jack, but she couldn't stop from bubbling when she addressed me.

"She used to be a movie star," Ayaan told me, and I had to fight the urge to laugh. "She was in The Runaway Bride, with Julia Roberts but her scenes were cut out in postproduction. I think she is the most beautiful woman in the world, now."

Ayaan was sixteen years old. When I was her age, I dressed like Kurt Cobain and memorized all the lyrics to "Lithium." I guess we take our heroes where we find them. "We're going for the drugs," I told her. That broke the spell. She immediately set about cleaning and checking her weapon and gathering up her pack. She didn't even wait for her nails to dry.

I tried to be discrete as Jack and Marisol said good-bye but I was itching to get started. Jack had a plan, and while he hadn't let me in on it yet I knew it would be good.

"If you don't come back," Marisol said, pushing Jack's glasses back up his nose. She couldn't seem to finish her sentence.

"Then you're all screwed." Jack put his arm around her hips.

"Dekalb," she said to my turned back, "do you begin to see why I had to marry a politician? At least Montclair knows how to lie. Get out of here. I'll be listening on this end. Not that I can do anything if you get into trouble, but at least I'll be able to hear your dying screams."

Jack actually laughed at that, something that had seemed impossible the night before. He gave Marisol a final probing kiss and then led us deep into the bowels of the subway station and right to the S train platform. The gaping twin mouths of the tunnels like the business end of a double-barreled shotgun lay just beyond a steel gate.

He expected our shock, of course, and he tried to explain as he fished a mammoth set of keys out of his pocket. "The tunnel runs all the way to Grand Central, nonstop. The power's off so we don't need to worry about the third rail. Yes, it will be dark in there but it's also unpopulated, as far as we can tell. We've never seen a stray corpse come out of that tunnel."

"It's a deserted subway tunnel and the dead have come back to life," I said, as if he might have missed the obvious.

"It'll take us halfway across the city," Jack insisted, unlocking the gate. "Almost right to the UN and it's a closed environment the whole way."

"Have you never seen any horror movie?" Ayaan demanded, but she filed through the gate just as I did.

Jack locked the gate behind him and started off down the platform at a steady clip. I rushed to keep up. Electric lights shone from the ceiling and the white tiles of the walls were no more dirty than the ones in the concourse but the platform felt tangibly different—colder, less inviting. There was no protection here from the city at large.

When we entered the right-hand tunnel the feeling grew into a creeping dread. Jack stopped to peel open a chemical light for each of us. He bent them in the middle and shook them until they started to glow, then snapped them to our shirts so we could keep track of each other in the blackness of the tunnel. He had a halogen flashlight duct-taped to his SPAS-12 and he switched it on, revealing railroad tracks that marched off in a perfectly straight line—a depiction of infinity straight out of seventh-grade geometry class, if your junior high happened to convene in Hell.

Time pretty much lost all meaning as we moved down the tunnel. We walked on the tracks, our feet settling into a rhythm of stepping on every other railroad tie. I tried counting my steps for a while but got bored with that quickly. I looked over my shoulder from time to time, watching the glaring light of the station behind me shrink, wishing I could go back, but soon it had become no brighter than a bright star. We made no more noise than we could help, trying not to even breathe too hard.

The tunnel revealed by Jack's flashlight was uniformly black, or even more than that. A dull dusty color that absorbed the light and gave back little to focus on. Now and again we would come across an electrical junction box on the wall or a signal light but these seemed to float in space, unmoored from reality. Reality was the tracks and the third rail that ran alongside us and countless alcoves and recesses and emergency doorways built into walls pierced with Roman arches to cross-ventilate the twin tunnels. Holes where anything at all could be hiding.

Jack stopped abruptly ahead of us, his yellow green chemical light nearly smacking my nose. I moved around him to see what had brought him up short.

A dead woman was down on all fours on the tracks, scooping cockroaches into her mouth. When she looked up her cloudy eyes were like perfect mirrors, dazzling us with reflected light. Most of her upper lip was missing, giving her a permanent sneer. She climbed to her feet and started stumping toward us, the bull's-eye pattern of Jack's light making strange watery shadows in her faded dress.

She was nearly on us before I realized that neither Jack nor Ayaan was going to shoot her. I stared at them and saw he was holding the barrel of her AK-47, pointing it at the ceiling. He looked back at me with an expression of indifferent curiosity.

One of the dead woman's arms was bent up painfully under her breasts but the other stretched out to snatch at us. Her mouth was open wide as if she wanted to swallow us whole.

"Just like a baseball bat, Dekalb," Jack said, reminding me of the machete in my hand.

She was so close her stink was on me, permeating my clothes. "Jesus," I shrieked, and lunged forward, swinging with both hands, putting my weight into it. I felt her bony frame collide with my chest as the blade went right through her head, all resistance taking the form of a bad shock in my shoulder as if I'd been hit by a car. But then she was lifeless, a rattling inanimate heap that slid down my pant leg. I gasped, wheezing for breath, bending forward to see by the light of Jack's flashlight that I had taken off the top of the dead woman's head in a big diagonal slice that included one eye. She wasn't getting back up.

"Why?" I asked.

Jack bent down beside me and put an arm around my shoulders. "I had to know if I was going to be carrying you. Now I know you can hold your mud."

"And that's a good thing?" I spat out everything in my mouth—my fear, her stink, the look on Ayaan's face that showed real approval for the first time. Approval I fucking didn't need, if that's what it took to get it. I had just been hazed, of all things.

Jack squeezed my bicep and headed down the tunnel. I watched his chemical light recede for a moment, then jogged to catch up.

Chapter Nineteen

We followed Jack's flashlight up a never-ending series of stairs and stalled escalators. It got easier to see as we went along. I thought my eyes were adjusting to the darkness but in fact we had merely arrived at Grand Central and light—real sunlight—was streaming through the terminal's high windows. When we emerged into the marble-lined corridors leading to the main concourse I could suddenly see everything again and I blinked rapidly, my eyes watering.

Ayaan dropped into a crouch and scanned the empty terminal from behind her rifle. Jack kept close to the walls but I was just so glad to be out of the tunnels that I couldn't maintain that level of healthy paranoia. I led them past empty newsstands, empty shops selling men's shirts or CDs or flowers, past a deserted shoeshine stand until we entered the big main concourse and I could look up at the green-blue ceiling and the gold diagrams of the zodiac, at the enormous windows through which streamed visible rays of yellow light. There was no sign of any life or movement anywhere.

The emptiness of Times Square had shocked me and this should have, too. Grand Central had never been anything but crowded in my experience. Yet something about the place—its cathedral scale or its gleaming marble, perhaps—lent itself to a kind of somber peace. I didn't have time to sightsee, really, but it was hard to tear myself away from the massive quietude of the terminal. This was a place built for sleeping giants and I longed to rest a while in its megalithic grace.

I led them down the Graybar Building passage to a row of glass doors. They were locked at the top and bottom but Jack had a police pick gun. It looked like a pistol grip with a thick needle sticking out where the barrel should have been. It could open almost any lock in the city. It used to be that only civil authorities could have such things, but the Internet had made them publicly available—Jack had got his from the same outfit that sold him the SPAS-12. "Check the street," he said, as he crouched down to get at the bottom lock on the door. It was a tricky operation— you had to fire the gun to retract the cylinder pins at the same time you used a tension wrench to turn the plug.

I peered out through the glass at Lexington Avenue and saw abandoned cars and dead buildings but nothing animate anywhere except a flock of pigeons wheeling between the glass walls of a pair of deserted office towers. It looked as if our luck was going to hold. From here it was just a few short blocks to the UN buildings. If we were quiet and didn't draw any attention to ourselves we just might make it. It was almost as if something had cleared out this whole section of the city. Perhaps the National Guard had put up barricades to keep the dead out. Maybe they were even still there. Maybe there were living soldiers protecting this last bastion of New York, just waiting for us to come and find them.

"Anything?" Jack asked. The lock released with a loud clang that startled the pigeons outside. They leapt into the air, their wings snapping out as they rode up into the sky, one after the other. Jack stood up and started working on the top lock.

"Negative," Ayaan said. She watched the birds, entranced as I was, perhaps observing how they relied totally on each other, each one mirroring the movements of its neighbor so that each time the flock changed its position a wave of motion seemed to go through them, as if they were a single entity with many bodies.

The second lock shot open and Jack put his tools away. He pushed on the door's latch bar and it swung open, letting in a cool puff of air from outside.

Air that stank of decay and rot.

"Get down!" Jack shouted as the flock of pigeons swung through the air, pivoting to dive headlong through the open door. The ex-Ranger slammed the door shut as dozens more of the birds smacked up against the glass, their filmy eyes showing nothing but naked desire. Hunger. One of them lay twitching just inches from my face, separated from me by only a thin piece of safety glass, and I saw the marks on its spine where it had been pecked to death, disarranging its iridescent feathers. Its beak snapped at me against the glass door, desperate for a bite of my flesh.

I heard wings flapping behind me and Jack rolled up into a sitting posture, his shotgun in his hands. He fired and the noise echoed wildly off the marble walls. Birds fell out of the air right and left as those pigeons that had made it inside doubled back for another go at us. He fired again, and again, and Ayaan opened up with a volley of fully automatic fire that blew the undead birds into clouds of blue feathers and wet gore. My ears ached with the noise and I worried they might start bleeding.

I felt pressure on my back and looked to see pigeons colliding with the door behind me, trying to bludgeon it open with their bodies. I put my shoulder against the door while Jack finished off the last of the intruders, stepping on the heads of the ones his shots had only crippled. Ayaan put her rifle over her shoulder and helped me as the birds outside redoubled their efforts.

"This is crazy!" she said. "Fucked up!"

Jack hurriedly relocked the door with shaking hands. The attack had surprised even him. "Undead animals. . . you don't see a lot of them. Most of the city's wildlife got eaten in the first couple of weeks. I can't remember the last time I saw a squirrel."

"What do we do?" I asked, stepping away from the door as another pigeon smashed itself against the barrier. The glass was cloudy with the grease of their bodies. "This is ridiculous. What do we do?"

Jack shook his head. "So close. If we abort now—"

"No one is aborting this mission." Ayaan scowled at us. "I have lost my commander to get here. I have lost my friends. Now is not the time to stop. There will be a way, if we look."

In defiance of her words a shadow passed across the sidewalk outside. I looked up and saw a new flock of birds approaching. It was almost as if they were organized, as if they could plan their attacks. It was just instinct, though, something in the bones that they didn't even need their tiny brains for. Pigeons were social animals, taking their cues from one another just as they always had. I could imagine how they had come to own this part of the city. One of them must have been bitten by a dead human looking for a quick meal. It had escaped, but had died of its injuries. Returning to its flock, it would have attacked its fellows—who would attack the ones next to them, who would turn to do the same. The flock that flies together dies together, I suppose. The Epidemic must have spread through the avian population of New York even faster than it had through the humans.

I wondered for a moment what they were all doing here, so close to the East River. Then I understood and my blood went cold. Hungry things went where the food was. The dead humans had eaten pretty much everything on the land. The last big source of food was clogging the river as far south as the Brooklyn Bridge. I'd seen it from the deck of the Arawelo.

There had been hundreds of thousands of pigeons in the city before the Epidemic—now they had joined forces, an instinct stronger than death. "If we go out there," I said, "we'll be pecked to death in seconds." It sounded hilarious but nobody laughed. "There are tunnels around here, though. There's one that leads to the Chrysler Building, I know that. If we came out of the ground somewhere else, somewhere they weren't expecting."

Jack nodded. "Sure. And if the wind is just right they won't smell us. And if we take off our shoes we can walk silently. Sure. We'd make it one or two blocks before something changed and they realized where we were."

I stared out through the doors, looked between the buildings. I couldn't see the Secretariat Building of the UN from here, not quite. But I could almost feel it, no more than ten minutes away by foot. We were so close.

Fate made up our minds for us. The Iridium cell phone in my back pocket rang, a strident pulsing chime that annoyed me so much I grabbed at it and answered the call. "Dekalb here," I said.

I expected to hear Marisol's voice but it was a man who answered me. "No shit? Dekalb? I just found this phone and hit star sixty-nine. I must have just missed you. This is awesome! Is Ayaan there with you?"

"She is—who is this?" I asked. Osman? Shailesh? It didn't sound like either of them but I knew I recognized the voice, even with all the electronic distortion on the line. Then I had it and my back rippled with icy fear.

"Who am I? I'm the guy who just ate the President of Times Square."

"Hello, Gary," I said.

I hit END hurriedly, as if he could come through the satellites and get at me. "Jack," I said, trying to sort it out, "there's a problem at the station. The dead—"

He didn't wait for me to finish the sentence. He turned on his heel and bolted back toward the subway entrance as fast as he could go. I called after him and Ayaan ran a few steps but then she turned and looked at me. Her face was a question I didn't want to answer.

Chapter Twenty

Gary climbed up the side of the Armed Forces Recruiting Center in Times Square and steadied himself on the roof. A wandering breeze snatched at his hair and his clothes. He looked up and saw the darkened signs, just as I had done, but for him the dead neon wasn't so much a shocking portent as a monument to what the world—and, by extension, he—had become. Dead but still standing. A reflection in a distorted mirror.

He let his gaze fall to the street level. To his troops. He had brought hundreds of the undead with him and though they wore no uniform nor carried any weapons they were an army. They awaited his command, still and passionless. He looked across the ranks of their slack faces and their hanging limbs and thought about how to begin.

From behind the steel gate of the subway station living faces peered out at the army. A rifle barrel poked through the bars and a shot snapped out. One of Gary's soldiers collapsed backwards onto an abandoned car, rocking it on its tires. Gary just laughed. He cupped his hands around his mouth and shouted. "You in there—why don't you come out and play?"

The faces at the gate drew back into the shadows.

"You'll never get through," one of the living warned. If they were surprised to hear a dead man talking they made no sign. The rifle cracked again and another walking corpse slumped to the pavement.

Gary reached out with his mind and the ground began to shake. The giant from the Central Park Zoo—tamed now, and under Gary's control—came shambling around a corner and grabbed at the bars of the gate with his massive hands. The rifle barrel disappeared. With a shriek of metal fatigue the gate warped in its hinges, then released with a reverberating clang that sent the giant stumbling backwards.

Hordes of the undead surged forward and into the station. Gary could see through their eyes as they tumbled down the stairs, pushing each other out of the way in their hurry to get to the living meat inside. There were animals down there, living animals. A big dog sank its fangs into the thigh of one of Gary's soldiers but three more just tore the animal away and devoured it.

The mob poured into the main concourse of the station, flowing over and under the turnstiles. The humans had fled, though they'd left behind some strange tokens of their occupation. Half a dozen translucent garbage bags hung from the ceiling like industrialized egg sacs. Visible through the thin plastic were thousands of nails and bits of gravel and random pieces of hardware—screws, nuts, bolts, washers. Mixed in with the scrap metal was a coarse black powder. Gary couldn't figure out what it meant.

Old blankets and empty cans had been strewn around the floor by the living. Among the refuse was a single brown paper bag, just another crumpled piece of trash unless you noticed the wires emerging from its open end.

One of the dead stepped on the bag without so much as glancing at it.

A dust storm erupted in the concourse, Gary's vision turning to blue murk that howled and rattled as the hardware in the plastic bags shot out in every possible direction, nails and screws gouging the white tile walls, washers and nuts tearing through the dried-out brains of the dead. When the smoke had turned to billowing dust and Gary could see again, his army lay twitching and broken on the floor.

Clearly the living had planned for this invasion. They had studied the dead for weeks, learning their weaknesses—hence the improvised fragmentation grenades hung from the ceiling, at head height, where they could do the most damage. Land mines would have been far less effective. This wasn't going to be as easy as Gary had thought.

No matter. He called up another wave of troops and sent them deeper into the labyrinth, climbing over the bodies of the twice-dead on their decomposing hands and knees. Gary closed his eyes and listened through their ears, smelled through their noses—there. Under the reek of homemade gunpowder and the shit stink of torn-open intestines he smelled something fainter but far more appetizing. Sweat, fear sweat—the perspiration of the living. He sent out a command along the network, the eididh, and his dead warriors shambled forward into a long hall ending in a ramp.

The secondary concourse which served the A, C and E trains had once been a shopping arcade. The boutiques and gift shops had been pillaged long hence and transformed into simple dormitories. They lay empty and pathetic now under the fluorescent lights, rows of cots stripped of their sheets, piles of expensive luggage abandoned in the haste of the living. Gary sent his troops deeper, streaming toward the stairwells that led to the platforms.

He completely missed the second trap.

Near the entrance to the concourse stood a simple, unmarked doorway, formerly closing off a janitorial-supplies closet. The dead had passed right by it and had their backs to it when it opened on oiled hinges. Three men bearing power tools on extension cords leapt out and opened fire.

Undead fell like wheat before a scythe, dropped from behind by projectiles that made a chugging pneumatic hiss every time they fired. Gary had his troops wheel around to face the assailants and saw they were using nail guns—heavy-duty roofing models that fired like automatic rifles. The nails they spat out were hardly as damaging as bullets but they didn't need to be. Even one puncture wound in an undead skull was too much. The average ghoul couldn't take a head shot the way Gary had. He needed to eliminate those shooters. He sent his troops stumbling forward into their own destruction, intent on taking out this threat as quickly as possible.

Suddenly more of the living emerged from the stairwells, rifles and pistols in their hands. The dead who had turned to attack the nail gunners were easy marks for the more heavily armed survivors behind them. The dead couldn't move quickly enough to overrun their attackers so they were sitting ducks for the crossfire.

It looked bad—the living had created a perfect kill zone—but Gary simply called up reinforcements and sent them hurrying as fast as they could shamble toward the fight. In the end, it was a matter of simple mathematics. Each of the living might destroy ten of their enemies, but there were ten more right behind. The last of the defenders to die was an elderly man in a torn suit and a bow tie. He had a name tag on his lapel—Gary remembered the adhesive tags that Paul and Kev had worn—that read HELLO MY NAME IS Mr. President.

"I will not negotiate with the undead!" the survivor screamed, brandishing his nail gun.

No matter. Gary had his soldiers tear the leader of the living apart and move on. The dead marched steadily onward down the stairway to the platform, where their noses told him the living had fled. No survivors presented themselves—they must have moved into the actual tunnels. Gary directed his troops to leap down onto the tracks and got a nasty surprise that made his scalp itch. The living had powered up the third rail.

It seemed like a worthless sort of trap—only a couple of his soldiers had actually touched the current-bearing rail. Their flesh sizzled and their bodies shook wildly but only a fraction of the dead were affected. In short order smoke from their burning flesh rose to the ceiling and the sprinkler system kicked in, dropping hundreds of gallons of liquid on the heads of Gary's army until it dribbled down their faces and soaked their filthy clothes. Of course the living had taken the time to replace the water in the sprinkler system with gasoline. Fumes that rose from the dead like steam reached the third rail. In an instant the undead soldiers lit up like so many Roman candles. Gary blinked wildly as he watched them burn through their own melting eyes.

"Shit!" he said, with a sudden realization. The trail led

down off the platform and into the downtown tunnel. Of course. Whoever had designed the traps had been one step ahead of Gary all along.

They must have known how many soldiers he could call on, and how willing he was to sacrifice as many as it took. It was a losing battle no matter how they looked at it—so they had chosen not to fight him directly. The station's defenses had been designed not to stop the dead but simply to slow them down while the survivors escaped through the tunnels. Directly to the south, one subway stop away, lay Penn Station—a perfect fallback position should Times Square be compromised.

Gary led his final wave of soldiers from the rear, pushing them onward through the ruined station, urging them forward into the stygian tunnel. The dead could see no better in the dark than the living and they stumbled and fell as they tripped on rails and railroad ties but enough of them kept moving forward. Soon enough Gary could see dancing light ahead—a greenish radiance that came from hundreds of glowsticks.

"Keep moving!" he heard a woman shout. "We can outrun them!"

Oh, they could have indeed—if Gary had let them. Instead he sent a command forward to Thirty-fourth Street. There were plenty of the undead there. It was easy to mobilize them and send them down into the subway tunnels. Soon Gary had the survivors trapped between two hordes of hungry dead. The survivors closed ranks and tried to fight—after all they had nothing to lose—but their pistols quickly ran out of ammunition. Knives and hammers and other hand-to-hand weapons came out but they were lost and they knew it.

Gary climbed down from his command post and hurried as fast as he could through the devastated station to catch up with his army. He moved through the undead crowd and came before the survivors to look over his victory with his own eyes. There were hundreds of them, as promised. Mostly women and children and old men, wearing backpacks or shoulder bags. They huddled together in their terror, some of them sobbing, some of them actually wailing. One of them stood apart from the crowd. A woman dressed in expensive-looking clothes. Her name tag read HELLO MY NAME IS fuck you. She was very, very pregnant and rested her hands on her belly.

"You win, motherfucker," she said. "Now come on. Eat me. Do me a favor!"

Gary came closer. He looked down and placed a hand lined with dead veins on her belly. The life force thrummed in her, bright energy radiating outward from the center of her being like a warm fire. He could see it glowing through his fingers, tingeing them red as if he held his hand up to the sun.

"Actually," he said, "I've got a better idea."

Part
Three

Chapter One

Smoke and acrid fumes swirled across the surface of the scorched platform. The tiles from the walls had cracked and fallen during the inferno and lay in piles of shards that clinked against my shoes. Jack's light stabbed out in a wan cone that couldn't penetrate the dust and soot suspended in the air. Bodies—grey piles of sacking, mostly, but with a telltale hand here or a charred tuft of hair there—had been shoved onto the tracks in long untidy heaps.

"Good girl," Jack said.

He ran up a stairwell two steps at a time. We tried to keep up but in the thick air we could hardly breathe and we fell behind until we were abandoned in the near-perfect dark, only our glowsticks illuminating our way. Ayaan tossed hers to me so she could have both hands free for her Kalashnikov. I brandished the two sticks above my head like torches. We came to a place where the bodies were piled up like unliving barricades and I picked my way carefully through, terrified that one of the twice-dead would rise up behind me and grab me around the neck. Ayaan let the barrel of her weapon swing from left to right, up and down, sighting on each punctured head in turn. In time we emerged into the main concourse where we'd seen Montclair Wilson give his State of the Union address. It was unrecognizable as a place where hundreds of people had once lived. The walls had been scraped bare, leaving chipped concrete behind. The ceiling had collapsed in places, dropping tons of plaster across the twenty-four hour token booth which sat twisted and abandoned. The dead there had been pushed rudely to the sides, making a wide aisle toward the stairwells that led up to the street. The light from above beckoned and we didn't stick around.

At the street level we found Times Square deserted, emptied of its shambling corpses. Every undead thing in midtown must have been in on the invasion of the subway station but they were long gone now. Only Jack was there, turning in circles looking for signs or clues or something. I could see no sign of the struggle at all but Jack bent and picked up a random piece of paper trash off the street. He handed it to me without a word. It had been a flyer for a Broadway show once but someone had scribbled notes in the margin with a ballpoint pen:

ALIVE = CAPTURED

DEAD = ORGANIZED!

LEADER = "GARY"

MOVING UPTOWN

"Jack," I said, holding on to the note because I didn't want to just throw it away, not when it might be Jack's last connection to the people he had helped lead. "There was nothing you could do. You couldn't save them."

He stared at me while his mouth worried at a grimace. "They're still alive," he said, finally, and waved away my protests. "If the dead just wanted to kill them, they would have done it here instead of dragging them halfway across the city for it. They've been taken for a reason. Who is this 'Gary'?" he asked. "Is he a survivor?"

"He's—he's undead, but different from the others. He could talk, and think. He was a doctor and he knew how to avoid brain damage when he died, he. . . we met him a while back, I would have mentioned him, but—"

Jack stared deep into my eyes. "There was a threat I didn't know about and you forgot to tell me." He took the note out of my hands. "I'm too busy to kick your ass right now, but I'll get to it."

It was so unlike him to say such a thing I was rendered speechless. Luckily Ayaan could still talk.

"He is dead! Gary is dead! I put a bullet in his head. I did it myself. We watched him die. He is back now, though, and very dangerous."

"Yeah, I got that." Jack surveyed the empty square. He turned to the west, toward the river, and started walking at a good clip. I ran after him. He had questions. "It would have taken an army to get through the defenses we built. It should have taken power tools and a lot of electricity. How he got through the gate—do you know how he could do that?"

I shook my head. "He couldn't hold things. . .he was a doctor, before he—well, before. He tried to help one of our wounded but he couldn't even wrap a bandage himself, his hands were too clumsy. I don't think he could have used power tools."

"These dead people were organized. Is he capable of that?"

"He never—I mean, we didn't see him organize anybody," I said. "Nothing like that. He seemed harmless when we met him."

"They didn't organize themselves. It sounds to me like this guy has some tricks he didn't show you. Mind-controlling the dead. Surviving a head shot. Tearing a carbon-steel gate off its hinges with no tools. Now he has my people but apparently he's not going to just eat them or he would have done that here. He's creating facts on the ground and we've got no intel at all."

In no time we had reached the old National Guard barricade near the Port Authority. Jack reached under the hood of the abandoned Armored Personnel Carrier there and popped a latch. He peered down into the big truck's engine and grunted. "They've got at least a half-hour lead on us and it's getting longer while I talk to you. We're going to fix this, Dekalb. We're going to go after them and find them and I'm going to get Marisol back. You can help me with that or you can leave. Your choice." He reached deep into the engine and twisted something. His arm went stiff with effort for a second and then he let go in a hurry as the engine turned over and coughed. It sputtered to silence again.

"Jack—you're talking about suicide," I tried, knowing that if anyone knew better than to play cowboy against these kinds of odds it had to be the ex-Ranger.

"I'm not stupid, Dekalb. I'm talking about recon. We don't aggress on them until we know what the facts are—that's SOP. For now I'm just going up there to take a look." He popped open a repair kit mounted on the APC's nose and took out a long white fan belt. He had to climb up on top of the engine to install it, his arms deep in the mechanism. He tried the starter again and the vehicle roared and whined and finally settled down into a bone-rattling chug of life. He jumped down to the street again and then clambered up into the driver's position. I started to climb after him but he shook his head. "No. Just me. This thing'll get me close but it's hard to keep inconspicuous. Eventually I'll have to abandon it and then I'll be tracking them on foot. You'll be no help to me then."

That was fair enough. When it came to moving stealthily in an urban environment he'd had the best training in the world and I'd had none at all. He gunned the engine, flooding the street with black smoke, and put the APC in gear. He had to shout over the noise.

"Take Ayaan and get back to your boat. Go to Governors Island. If I'm not there in twenty-four hours you're on your own."

I nodded but he didn't wait for my reply. He engaged the vehicle's treads and headed north—toward the survivors, assuming they were still alive.

Chapter Two

Two mummies awaited Gary when he returned to the broch. They gestured for him to follow them—alone.

There would be trouble, of course. Mael would already know what had happened. As they entered the compound the workers on the walls of the big tower had turned to see the procession, their hands dropping to their sides, the bricks they carried put aside to watch as hundreds of living humans marched fearfully into the very midst of undead central. The dead on their own had no curiosity—for all the eyes turned on Gary and his raiding party there was only one intelligence looking through them.

Gary could understand Mael's surprise. The dead army was under strict orders not to let a single living thing enter Central Park, much less a crowd of them. Gary was breaking a serious taboo.

He commanded his army to guard the prisoners and then stepped inside the shadowed spaces of the construction site. The walls were rising steadily: The dead never rested, and Mael had a multitude of them to draw on. At the center of the building the Druid waited for him on his cairnlike throne. He did not look pleased.

Now, lad, I know you're a smart one, so you'll have

no trouble explaining this: why my best servant would disobey my instructions so completely. You didn't forget what we're at, did you? The killing and all?

"I didn't forget." Gary came closer until he was face to face with the bog mummy, staring directly into the dark hollows of his eye sockets. The Druid didn't lift his head but the taibhsearan hanging from the walls craned their necks around to follow Gary as he moved.

Then maybe you've gone soft again. Is that it? Did you go all pale when you were in the catbird seat? I don't blame you feeling a little compassion, son, to be honest. If you want then I'll send my own creatures to do the dirty deed.

Mael rose from his seat and hobbled toward the exit from the room. As he drew close to Gary he seemed to sense something. He stopped and raised his hand to pass it slowly over Gary's face.

It wasn't compassion, then, oh, no. Gary knew what the Druid felt—the energy that ran through Gary like waves on the ocean, massive and deep and strong. It buzzed and shook within him and he felt as if he might split open at any moment. *You ate what, twenty of them? Thirty?*

"I needed the strength. Otherwise I would have spared even them." The men he'd slain had been old or unfit one way or another. They couldn't help him achieve his desired end. "Mael. I've been thinking."

Have you now? And what grand notion has you in its grasp?

"I need to know. . .I need to know what your plan is for me. For me and all the undead like me, the hungry ones. When the work is done and all the survivors are dead, what will become of us?"

The Druid stroked his chin and paced back to his chair as the taibhsearan followed Gary's every fidget. *You'll be rewarded, of course. I'll be giving you peace, peace and the satisfaction a man feels on completing a job of work.*

"Peace? The only peace I know anymore is a full stomach," Gary tried.

Oh, lad, don't be dense. I know what you're driving at and it's unnatural. No creature should have to live forever. It's a curse. Take the peace I'm offering. I wish it could be otherwise, but there's only two sides in this thing: You're either with me or against me.

Gary circled slowly around the throne, the seers on the walls craning their necks after him as he considered his next move. "You're talking about the peace of the grave. When there aren't any people left there'll be no food for us to eat. You'll let us starve until we wither away to dust. Or no—no, you would see that as heartless. When the work is done, when the last living man is dead, you'll just cut us off. You'll suck out our dark energy and let us just drop where we stand like so much meat."

Do you see another option, then?

"Yes!" Gary crowed. "It starts with those people, those living people out there. We stop killing them, at least, we stop killing all of them. Some of them we cull out for food but the rest we keep alive and safe from the dead. It's a renewable resource, Mael—they'll keep making babies. It doesn't matter how awful things get. Even in the middle of Arma-fucking-geddon they'll still make babies. I can keep this going for—for as long as I care to."

And if you do that, boy, my sacrifice will be wasted. My life and my death will have been for naught. No! I won't let you make me meaningless! Now do as you've been told!

"I'm done, Mael. I won't work for you anymore," Gary said, looking down at his feet.

The two mummies came at Gary with their hands up, clearly under orders to attack. Gary ducked under the arms of one of the mummies and saw an amulet tucked into her wrappings in the middle of her chest—her heart scarab. He tore it free and threw it away from him as hard as he could.

In his head he could hear the mummy wailing for her magic charm. She ran after the amulet, leaving her partner to take care of him. It was easy enough to block the bandaged arms he tried to use like flails. Gary head-butted him hard enough to crack the Egyptian's ancient skull and the mummy went down in a heap.

Then Mael waded into the battle himself. The green sword crashed down against the back of Gary's head but he was ready for it and rolled with the impact. He dodged sideways and looked for an opening. He knew he had only a few seconds before Mael thought to call for reinforcements—thousands of them. Despite the energy blazing away inside Gary's dead veins he couldn't hold his own against an army of the undead. He also knew how strong Mael was and that given a chance the Druid could snap his neck with one hand. He needed an advantage and he needed it fast.

Mael swung and the sword came down hard against the floor, shattering bricks to powder, missing Gary by inches as he rolled away. *Take what's coming to you, boy!* Gary covered his face with his arms, but he knew that if Mael connected with the sword the blow would shatter his bones.

Another swing—Gary dashed out of the way and felt

his back collide with a stone wall. There was nowhere left to retreat. Mael came after him, looking down at him through the eyes of the taibhsearan.

The weapon rose again and then stopped in mid-swing. *In Balor's name,* the Druid shrieked, *it's gone dark as night! What have you done, lad?*

Gary held his hands tight across his face as he manipulated the eididh. His voice was softer than he meant to be when he spoke. "I've just told every ghoul in the park to close their eyes," he said.

The sword fell from Mael's hand. The Druid reached up to touch his empty orbits. He started to moan, a low, mournful sound that rattled Gary's teeth so much he nearly lost his grasp on the dead. He could feel Mael trying to undo his command, mental shrieks probing at the *taibhsearan* up on the walls, desperate cries going out for the workers outside to come in and serve their master with their eyes. But Gary had become too strong. He had eaten too many of the living.

Gary rose slowly to his feet, careful not to make too much noise, and stepped up directly behind his erstwhile benefactor. It wasn't easy with his own eyes closed but he had made a point of memorizing where the Druid stood.

"I have a right to exist, Mael," he whispered.

Oh, lad, and it's a wondrous clever thing you've become. Gary could feel emotion radiating from the Druid's form like warmth. There was fear in there and some hatred and quite a bit of pride in his apostate pupil. Mostly though it was sorrow, genuine sorrow that his work was over.

With shaking hands Gary reached out and grabbed Mael's head below the ears. It hung from his broken neck by little more than a flap of leathery skin. With one swift movement Gary tore it free. Mael's emaciated body slumped to the floor, as dead as when it had drifted in the cold water under a Scottish peat bog. The head buzzed in Gary's hand like something that might explode. It felt hot and cold and wet and dry all at the same time and he had a real urge to just cast it away but that would be real folly—Mael wasn't dead quite yet. Unsure if what he planned next would actually work, he raised the head to his lips as if it were a pumpkin and bit down hard. The ancient skull fragmented in his teeth and then a black flood of screaming, sparking fluid tore through the world and carried Gary's consciousness away in its unrelenting current.

Chapter Three

We had no trouble getting back to the river. It looked as if every dead person in midtown Manhattan had been drafted into Gary's army. The girls were thrilled to see Ayaan again. They laughed and wiped tears from their eyes and pressed their cheeks against hers. There were plenty of questions for her, of which I understood only "*See tahay?*" and "*Ma nabad baa?*" the standard greetings. Her answers met with rapt attention and genuine delight.

As for me, Osman took one look at my slept-in clothes and my haggard face and shook his head. "At least nobody died this time," he said. He grabbed an old plastic milk jug full of green hydraulic fluid and then went back down into the engines of the ship to get us ready to sail.

It wasn't a long voyage to Governors Island, but we took our time. The teardrop-shaped island lies just south of the Battery at the tip of Manhattan, close to Ellis and Liberty islands. It was a Coast Guard base for most of my life, but in 1997 the government decommissioned it. What Jack wanted with the place I had no idea.

I didn't mind going there, though. New York. It was so good to be back on the water, back where I wasn't constantly in danger. You stop noticing how edgy you get in a sustained combat situation. You start thinking it's normal to get muscle cramps for no reason or to feel like something is creeping up behind you, even when your back is to a wall. It's only after you return to safety that you realize just how crazy you were becoming.

Which maybe explains why I asked Osman to take the long way 'round. He put the Arawelo through her paces, sailing at half steam in a full circuit of the tiny island while I watched its tree-lined shore go by. Docks and wharves lined most of the coast, while in other areas walkways had been built up overlooking the harbor. The gunports of round-walled Castle Williams were empty and I could look through them into an abandoned courtyard that shimmered in the heat of the day. The girls were fascinated by the biggest structure of the island, a perforated steel tower that sat in the water just off the shore like the skeleton of a high-rise. It provided ventilation for the Brooklyn Battery Tunnel. I ignored it and kept scanning the shoreline. Ayaan eventually came up to the rail beside me and asked what I was looking for.

"The dead," I told her.

"And have you seen them?"

I shook my head. I hadn't. It seemed impossible that a place in this world could be so tranquilly unaffected by the Epidemic, but Governors Island appeared to be not only deserted but thriving. The greenery that dipped down to brush the water shook with the warmth of the day, and the cheerful breezes off the harbor didn't smell like death at all. The sun bounced off of unbroken windows and gave everything a wholly unnatural sheen of health.

Jack had sent us to a safe place, it seemed. Somewhere quiet where we could make plans. I signaled for Osman to bring us in to the ferry slip. The docks there were the only ones on the island big enough to accept the Arawelo. We pulled in between a pair of retaining seawalls lined with old tires and felt the ship lurch with a creaking wail as she bumped in to a complete stop. Fathia and I cast lines up onto the dock, and two of the other girls made them fast against big concrete planters full of dusty miller and coleus. We had the gangplank ready to deploy when the noise of a gunshot made us all wince.

A man in a navy blue windbreaker and a baseball cap stepped onto the ferry loading ramp and looked down at us. I shouldn't have been shocked to see a survivor at this point, not after my experiences in Times Square but this guy had my attention. For one thing he had a shiny metal badge on the front of his coat and the letters DHS painted in yellow on his back; for another he had an M4A1 carbine with a night-vision sight like an oversized telephoto lens and an M203 grenade launcher slung under the barrel. He wasn't a tall man and it looked like that much weaponry might topple him over, but I didn't laugh. The weapon was trained on my forehead. I could look right up into its flash hider.

"We're alive," I said. "There's no need for that."

The rifle swung to my left and I ducked down by reflex. "Why don't you just stay right there, towelhead," the survivor announced. He was covering Ayaan, who had started to reach for her Kalashnikov. Great, I thought, just what we needed. Geopolitics played small at the worst possible moment.

"You're with the Department of Homeland Security, right?" I called.

The survivor didn't turn but he scratched at his unruly

stubble with his left hand. "I'm Special Agent Kreutzer of the DHS, yeah, and I'm going to commandeer your vehicle under the emergency provisions of the Patriot Act. You can go ahead and start throwing your weapons over the side, now. You're not going to need them anymore."

I breathed deeply. "Listen, my name's Dekalb. I'm with the United Nations Mobile Inspection and Disarmament Unit. I think we all need to just stand down."

"I don't take orders from any mushy-headed one-worlder fucks, thank you very much. Now start obeying my fucking instructions! I've got an objective to meet!"

"What's your objective?" I tried to keep the dialogue open. This guy was going to shoot somebody if I didn't calm him down.

The agent raised his arms to the heavens as if beseeching a beguiling fate. "To get my hairy white ass out of here! Now disarm, motherfuckers!"

It was the opening Mariam needed. Unbeknownst to me (and, thankfully, to Kreutzer too) the girl sniper had climbed on top of the wheelhouse and lined up the perfect shot. When Kreutzer's arms lifted and he was no longer aiming directly at anyone on the ship she held her breath and squeezed the trigger on her Dragunov. His top-heavy M4 carbine dropped to clatter on the concrete as Kreutzer grabbed at his right index finger. "Jesus!" he screamed. "She blew my finger off!" He stared down at his bloodied hand with wide eyes and then looked at me again. "Jesus!"

In a second I was over the rail. I scooped up the weapon he'd dropped, intending to cover him with it while the girls secured the perimeter. Ayaan had a similar idea but a simpler one. It mostly involved clubbing the survivor across the face with the buttstock of her AK-47. He fell to the ground and rolled into a fetal ball.

"Goddamn it, Ayaan, that was unnecessary," I shouted. "And dangerous, too. What if he had a partner—or a whole platoon of them hiding behind those trees?"

Ayaan nodded thoughtfully. Then she jabbed Kreutzer in the gut with the barrel of her rifle. "This towelhead wants information, *futo delo*. Is there a platoon of fools like you hiding there?"

"Oh, glory, no, oh Lord, I'm the only one here, Jesus protect me in my hour of misery, I swear it, I swear it!"

She looked up at me with a smile and a shrug.

I called for the girls to come and bandage the poor asshole's finger (Mariam hadn't blown it off at all, merely cut it enough to make him drop his weapon) and start looking for a secure place to set up operations. It looked as if Governors Island was ours for the taking. I examined the weapon Kreutzer dropped and put it on safety, then handed it to Ayaan.

"You ever think about upgrading?" I asked her.

She gave the weapon about a second's worth of examination, sighting down the overloaded receiver and hefting its considerable weight. She pulled out its composite buttstock to full length and then slammed it home again. Then she glanced from the black plastic and electronic doodads of the M4A1 to the varnished cherrywood and solid steel of her rifle. Kreutzer's weapon looked like a futuristic toy. Hers looked like a weapon out of the Dark Ages.

"Everyone knows about this M4 weapon. Urban warfare version of the M16, yes?" she asked. "It is known to jam at a bad time. The barrel overheats when you fire one full clip." She tossed it back at me and I staggered as it collided with my arms. "No sale, Dekalb."

Chapter Four

One of the mummies brought the pregnant woman to Gary. They had tied her into a wheelchair after she attempted to beat in the skull of one of her captors with a brick. A valiant attempt, surely, but Gary wondered how far she expected to get through a city full of the dead when she couldn't run or do more than waddle quickly. Her swollen belly lay in her lap as if she'd stuffed a bowling ball up her shirt.

The mummy pushed the wheelchair over to where Gary sat on a pile of bricks and waited patiently for his next command. He took his time issuing it. He'd been in a peaceful mood all morning, just contemplating the sky and the unfinished broch behind him and the new structures he had ordered built on the Great Lawn, not really thinking about anything. After the previous night he supposed he deserved a chance to rest.

His body had been rigid with seizures for hours after he snacked on Mael, the dark energy he had liberated from the Druid sloshing back and forth in his belly and his head and his fingers until black lightning shot from his eyes and mouth. At least a hundred dead men outside the broch's walls had been consumed as he thrashed about trying to hold on to his spark—Mael's energy threatened to sunder him, to physically tear him to pieces and he reached out for their fleeting life force to sustain his scorched and bruised frame. Somehow he managed not to explode. After a few hours of shivering in a corner, his arms wrapped around his knees as his brain iterated through endless hallucinations and his eyes blind with the phosphor glare of the dark light he'd seen, he was finally able to stand upright and walk around a little bit again.

"You've gained weight," the pregnant woman said. Marisol, her name was Marisol. "I guess that's what happens when you binge and forget to purge."

"Hmm?" Gary looked up. He rubbed his temples and tried to snap out of it. These frozen times when he became locked in contemplation of his own navel were too much like death, like real death for comfort. "I beg your pardon. I was miles away," he told her. He needed to do something, something physically real or he was likely to sink into reverie again. "Let's take a stroll, shall we?"

The mummy pushed her wheelchair along as Gary ambled alongside the fifteen-foot wall that surrounded his new village. "Did you enjoy your breakfast?" Gary asked. He'd made sure the prisoners were given plenty to eat. Canned foods were commonplace in the emptied city but they were useless to the undead, who lacked the manual dexterity to use a can opener.

"Oh, yeah," the woman said, stroking her belly as if it pained her. "I just love cold clam chowder first thing in the morning. We need access to cooking equipment if you want us to eat. You ever heard of botulism?"

Gary smiled. "Not only that, I've seen it. I used to be a doctor. You can't have a fire because I can't risk you hurting yourselves."

"You can't watch us all the time. If we want to kill ourselves badly enough we'll do it. We'll just stop eating or. . . or we'll climb on top of this wall and jump off." The woman wouldn't meet his gaze.

"You're right. I can't stop you." Gary led her out into a furrowed patch of earth. The mud of Central Park would grow just about anything—after decades of fertilization and aeration and intense loving care by professional gardeners, the soil was rich and dark. Now that Gary was present to keep the dead from consuming every living thing they saw, rows of dusty weeds had already sprouted in the denuded earth. "This area will be your garden. Eventually we hope you'll be able to produce all your own food. Fresh vegetables, Marisol. You can have fresh vegetables again. Imagine that."

"Are you deaf? I said we would kill ourselves rather than help you!" The woman thrashed against the cords holding her into the chair. The mummy reached forward to restrain her but Gary shook his head. By rocking back and forth and throwing herself against her straps, eventually Marisol managed to overturn her chair, spilling herself sidewise across the moist dirt that smudged her face and flattened her hair.

Gary helped her up himself with his hands under her armpits. "I heard you. And I believe that maybe you would take your own life. Others will make their own choices."

He led her down a narrow lane between two rows of makeshift brick houses that were still under construction. He showed her the double thickness of the walls and the fiberglass installation stuffed between the two layers. They would be cozy in the winter and cool in the summer, he explained to her. Mostly they would be safe—the perimeter wall would keep the dead out. "How could you not be happy here?" he asked.

"For one thing there's the smell," she spat back.

Gary smiled and squatted down on his haunches so he could look her in the face. She still wouldn't meet his gaze but it didn't matter. "When I was working at the hospital, I watched a lot of people die. Old people whose time was up, young people who barely knew where they were, struck down in accidents. Kids, I saw kids die because they didn't know any better than to eat Drano or jump out of windows. Just before they went, they would always call me over to ask one last favor."

"Yeah?" she sneered.

"Yes. It was always the same thing. 'Please, doctor, give me one more hour before I go. Give me one more minute.' People are easily frightened by death, Marisol, because it is so very long and our lives are so very short. I'm offering your people a chance to have long, full lives. I can't bring back the world we've lost. I can't give them gourmet dinners or luxury vacations or American Idol. But I can give them a chance to not be afraid all the time. A chance to start over fresh. A chance to have families— big families. That's a lot more than you offered them in your spider hole."

"And in exchange for all this? What do you get? My baby? You already ate my fucking husband!" Her hair had fallen across her face and she blew it away, puffing out red cheeks hot with anger.

"Everything has a price. I only need about one meal a month, maybe even less if I'm careful. That's not a lot to ask." He thought of Mael and his tribe in Orkney. They had taken turns being human sacrifices. It was something people could accept if you made it a necessity.

"Marisol, I'm going to give you an option right now. It was your pregnancy that inspired all of this generosity I'm feeling so I want to give you something really special. I can make you the mayor of the last secure human village on Earth." He bent close and let her smell his fetid breath. "Or I can eat your face off right now. Don't answer yet, though, there's more! I'll make it painless. You won't feel a thing. I'll even make sure you don't come back. You'll just be dead." He grabbed the handholds of her wheelchair and spun her around and around. He was enjoying this. "Dead, dead, dead forever and ever and ever and ever and your body will rot away on the ground until the flies come and lay their maggot eggs in your cute little cheeks."

When he stopped she was breathing hard. Her body shook visibly as if she were very cold and he could smell something stale and sharp rising from her pores. Nothing special, really. Just fear.

"So what'll it be, hmm?" he asked. "Do I get an early lunch today—or should I start referring to you as Ms. Mayor?"

Her eyes were thin lines of hatred. "You bastard. I want the biggest, silkiest sash that says MAYOR on it in rhinestones. I want people to know who sold them out."

Gary smiled real big so she could see his teeth.

Chapter Five

Kreutzer led us through a lush park where trees rolled in the breeze, their branches sheltering brightly painted clapboard houses and cobblestone avenues—the old officers' quarters back when Governors Island was a military base. The Coast Guard logo was everywhere, on monuments and plaques and chain-link fences, even on the street signs.

The DHS agent swore the houses were empty and that he'd checked them out himself. "Honest, there's not even a stick of furniture in there and no goddamned food at all."

Unconvinced, I sent squads of girls into every building we passed. "There must have been other people here," I said. "Nobody posts a field agent to a place like this if there's nothing for him to do."

"There were more," Kreutzer said, clutching at his bandaged hand. "There was a whole fucking garrison. When the Epidemic broke out we needed a hardened location for emergency-management ops. We reactivated the base here and staffed it with Operations Directorate irregulars. The kind of people who are used to flying in and out of airfields with little or no notice. Some useless fucking moron in the Pentagon thought you could fight dead fucks with helicopters and law-enforcement aircraft."

I looked around at the trees rattling in the wind, at the yellow houses. "That would take some pretty serious infrastructure."

Kreutzer tilted his head toward the far part of the island. "Over that way. This is all touristy crap. When the city took over in 2003 they spruced up here and started letting visitors in. They kept the real stuff out of sight."

I nodded and signaled for the girls to regroup. We headed across a lush green lawn past the star-shaped stone edifice of Fort Jay.

"So like I was saying—me and Morrison, my partner, we got detailed here to run sigint and systems while the Guard pilots ran their flyovers. We were Systems Directorate before we got rolled up into Homeland Security. At first I was pissed to get stuck in this latrine while guys I outranked were doing a real man's job in the city. Then the choppers started turning up missing—whole crews never came back—and I figured maybe I had it okay after all. Finally we got a call from Washington— they needed all our units for a tactical event along the Potomac. Morrison and me stayed behind to keep the site maintained for when they came back."

Kreutzer had brought us to the side of Liggett Hall, an enormous brick dormitory building that cut the island in half. A line of trees behind the structure hid a chain-link fence topped with barbed wire. A gate stood open, revealing a dirt pathway to the other side. "I'm guessing they never did," I said.

"Well two points for you, shithead. They got slaughtered,

from what we could hear on the blower. They were useless up in the air, and when they put down they got fucked, royally fucked." Kreutzer stopped before entering the gate. "I don't know about this. This is a restricted area."

I pushed past him and entered the real base. A broad central lawn ran most of the way to the far shore, dotted here and there with baseball diamonds. A concrete airstrip had been laid down across this lawn, which was flanked with dilapidated prefab buildings of the kind I associated with American military bases. Time and rust had been unkind to most of the structures but I could see a few hangars that still looked operational as well as an air-traffic control tower.

"We held on the best we could. Occasionally one of those dead assholes would climb out of the ventilation tower but we took 'em down by the numbers. We managed to close off the louvers eventually, so that's not a problem anymore."

I nodded absently, too busy cataloging the island's assets. There were a few Coast Guard cutters bobbing in the water but they were useless to us. Gary wasn't about to just come down to the water and let us blow his head off with a .50 caliber machine gun. I spotted a few things that might come in handy, including a fully equipped armory replete with M4s and small arms and made a mental checklist to go over with Jack when he arrived. If he arrived.

We made camp on the lawn. At first I was tempted to sleep in one of the yellow officers' houses or even in one of the barracks buildings; but when night fell they became infinitely creepy. There's something about being inside a windowless room with no electricity that truly bugs my modern soul. The girls didn't mind camping rough at all—it was what they were used to back home. They kept Kreutzer under guard all night but mostly left him alone. We made a big campfire and ate bread and thin porridge—our staple foods.

"There's not a bean or a fucking carrot left on this dunghill," Kreutzer informed us as he tore into the flat loaves of canjeero the girls offered him grudgingly. "That's what happened to Morrison."

"I was wondering when we'd get to that," I said.

Kreutzer nodded. "Morrison got hungry faster than I did. He was a big guy, liked to lift weights when he was off duty and he needed more calories, I guess. He took a rigid-hull inflatable boat and headed over to Staten Island to resupply. That was two weeks ago. I don't expect to see him again."

"And what about you? You were just going to starve here?"

Kreutzer scooped a fingerful of porridge out of a pot and stuffed it in his mouth. "I'd rather not eat than get eaten. I could have left anytime I wanted, but where would I go? Until I saw you over at the ferry slip I thought I was going to fucking die here." He handed the pot back to Fathia. "Thanks," he said.

I woke to the sound of water slapping the side of a cutter and a fresh breeze that lifted my eyelashes and played with them. I was grinning, stupidly grinning because I felt so good. Then I sat up and remembered everything. Pulling my pants on, I started looking around for a latrine when I heard a buzzing sound coming from the water.

It was Jack.

I don't know where he got a Jet Ski in New York but

he was wave-running hard for the coast. I ran down to the water and waved my arms and whistled and finally he saw me and cut in to meet me. I held a hand down and helped him climb up onto the boardwalk. He took off his life vest and unzipped the tote bag he'd used to keep his weapons and gear dry and then finally he said hello. "He took them to Central Park. I couldn't get very close—the wind was blowing toward them and they would have smelled me, but I saw them enter the park. There's something going on there, something huge, and I have no idea what it is. I can't just go in there guns blazing and hope to rescue anybody. That's what I'm going to do, though."

I nodded sagely. I badly needed to urinate but I also wanted to show him something, something that just might solve his problem. I led him around the back of a hangar and let him see the thirty-foot trailer crowned with radar dishes and the four coffins—slang for the storage crates of the UAVs.

"Good," he said, and started prying open the coffins.

"Jack," I asked, because the question had been bothering me, "why did you send us here? How did you know Governors Island was deserted?"

He stared at me. "I didn't. For all I knew this place was crawling with the dead. I just knew you could handle yourself regardless."

"We could have been headed into a trap!" I cried.

Jack looked to one side and then the other. "Looks like you did fine. Now help me with this crate."

Chapter Six

The controls for the Predator RQ-1A Unmanned Aerial Vehicle were simple enough. They'd been designed for the average twenty-first-century soldier and were a near replica of the game pad for the Sony PlayStation. You used one thumbstick for the throttle and the other to steer while vehicle systems were mapped to the face and shoulder buttons—raising the landing gear, moving the nose-mounted cameras and so on. Child's play, I figured. I had studied the weapon system back in the old days, back when I had a life and a career. I felt confident and alert as my little plane leapt into the air off Governors Island and streaked toward Manhattan.

"Watch out for sudden updrafts," Kreutzer said. "They can be a real bitch." He had the second seat in the cramped, overheated trailer. As systems specialist, he had to keep the aircraft's avionics and telemetry streams coming in clear and legible. He faced three big monitors where he could display and manipulate his "product."

The Standard Oil Building came up on my right and I slewed over a little to avoid its spire. Then something went wrong. The Predator kept trying to flip itself over, its right wingtip popping up again every time I tried to bring it down. I poured on a little more throttle to try to break free of what I thought was mild turbulence and suddenly a wall of wind slapped the vehicle across the nose, sucking it down into a superfast spiraling descent that could more rightly be called "falling out of the sky."

The UAV smacked Broadway at an angle and skipped like a stone across the roofs of several parked cars, finally skittering to a halt in the middle of Bowling Green on its back. The camera showed us a shaky view of the Charging Bull statue and a partially cloudy sky.

Kreutzer's face curled into a look of infinite smugness as he showed me what I'd done wrong. On his product screen he showed me the last few seconds of the Predator's flight as a PowerPoint slideshow. I saw the spire on the Standard Oil Building and the column of air beyond where Morris Street butted up against Broadway. Then he maximized the infrared view of the same scene and showed me a false color vortex spinning madly at the corner of the two streets—wind shear generated by the difference in temperature between the sunny and shaded sides of the buildings.

"Okay. Lesson learned," I said. My heart was still racing a little from the excitement of piloting the Predator. When Jack came in to find out what was going on I let Kreutzer explain. Suddenly I shrieked. They both turned and stared at me.

A dead man with no skin on the top of his head had come to investigate the Predator where it lay in Bowling Green. His inverted nose wrinkled as he sniffed the downed plane's optics. I had become so immersed in flying the UAV that I'd forgotten it was half a mile away and the walking corpse couldn't get me through the screen.

I switched off the view and rubbed my hands together. "Let's get another one assembled," I said. "I'm ready to go again."

An hour later Ayaan's crew had Vehicle Two ready to go. It had a wingspan of fifty feet and its nose instrument package looked like the head of one of the aliens Sigourney Weaver used to fight in the movies. I ran through my preflight and initialized the optics. I hit the throttle hard—we were using a shorter-than-regulation airstrip—and let the Predator race down the lawn, the view on my screen bouncing as it picked up speed. At just the right time I yanked back on the yoke and the nose jerked up into the air. The UAV surged up into the sky and easily cleared the top of Liggett Hall. I remembered to retract the landing gear and we were on our way.

I brought the UAV up to cruising speed and let it fly itself, mostly, only banking a bit to bring it in over Castle Clinton in Battery Park. I kept my altitude low, balancing the possibility of one or two undead spies hearing the propeller against flying high and letting millions of them see it. That meant flying between buildings—something the Predator was built to do, although it was also supposed to have a highly trained pilot at the controls. When faced with the brick walls of lower Manhattan I aimed for a narrow funnel at the top of the Battery where Bowling Green opened up to the wide canyon of Broadway.

"Easy this time—don't try to force her." Kreutzer leaned toward me and I could smell his breath as I neared the vortex that had brought me down before. This time I just let go of the throttle at the crucial moment and the Predator shot through like a floating cork going over a wave, yanked along by the edge of the wind shear instead of trying to punch through it. I was leveling out over the abandoned cars of Broadway when the Iridium cell phone started chirping.

"What do I do?" I asked. "What do I do?" Jack rushed into the trailer and booted up a secondary pilot's terminal. He knew only one person had my phone number. He took control of the vehicle and I rushed outside into the sunlight and the green grass and answered the call.

"You're spying on me now?" Gary asked.

I was stunned. "What are you talking about?"

The dead man laughed in my ear. "I see all, Dekalb. Every walking corpse in Manhattan can be my eyes or my ears. I assume it was you who just dropped an airplane on my perfectly good island. You're getting some bright ideas, aren't you? You're planning to come up here and rescue the prisoners. It won't work."

I tried to bluff. "We were just looking for the drugs. Scoping out hospitals, looking for a way in to complete the original mission."

"Nice try. My brain is dead, not damaged. You want to kill me. I know I would do the same thing in your place. I'm a threat—a serious threat—and you want to neutralize me. Obviously I don't want that. I'm willing to make a deal."

I sat down hard on the lawn. "Talk to me. The survivors—"

"Are mine now," he interrupted. "There's no room for negotiation there. What I will give you is safe passage. I know you had some trouble with pigeons the other day. They're gone now. I'm going to let you enter Manhattan just long enough to get to the UN building, get your pills, and leave. Nobody will come close to you—I can keep them back. I can protect you. You do this and then you get on your boat and you leave here forever. Sound doable?"

"And if we try to take back the prisoners anyway?"

"Then you get to find out why a million dead men can't all be wrong. This is what I'm offering, Dekalb, and nothing else. Get the drugs and leave. Oh, and one other thing. Ayaan."

I looked over at the girl in question. She was posing for pictures—Fathia had found a Polaroid camera in one of the barracks and all the girls wanted a souvenir of their visit to New York City. She turned to look at me and smiled.

Gary purred in my ear. "Ayaan stays here. I want to cut the skin off her in little pieces and eat them one by one. I want to have some quality time with her viscera. She shot me in the head. Nobody gets a free ride after that."

I put a hand over my mouth to hold in what I wanted to say to that. Not going to fucking happen, asshole. Instead I waited a moment and said "I'll have to get back to you." I hit END and put away the phone.

"Dekalb," Kreutzer said from the door of the trailer. "We've got image." I followed him back into the stuffy enclosed space to see what Jack had found.

Chapter Seven

Gary flew with the undead pigeons on First Avenue. Through their eyes, he watched as they fell, whole flocks at a time, tumbling through the air, their wingtips spinning lifelessly. Gary was a man of his word—if Dekalb wanted to take him up on his generous offer, the way to the UN building would be clear. Gary wasn't so much afraid of Dekalb as concerned. While his team of Somali killers could hardly make a dent in Gary's defenses, they could conceivably do something so random it would endanger Gary's breeding stock. If they were to fire missiles at the broch, for instance, Gary would almost certainly survive but Marisol's people could be hurt in the ensuing chaos and debris. A thousand such scenarios had gone through Gary's mind and he didn't relish any of them. Getting Dekalb out of New York as quickly as possible was just good common sense.

Gary sucked the life out of the birds until only one remained, banking unconcernedly over the great piles of its former wingmates, the greasy iridescent blue feathered masses of them clogging the streets. Gary spilled air across a pair of fluttering wings and wheeled toward the river and Long Island. He dug deep with the bird's pinions and soared until he could see Jamaica Bay burnished by the sun, until he thought he could see the earth curving away beneath him but. . . enough. He gave the bird a hard squeeze and its vision dimmed. A barely noticeable spark of dark energy flowed into Gary's being.

In a soft and shadowed place he shifted in his king-sized bathtub and fluid seeped into the hollow of his collarbone. He reared up, the briny liquid falling away from him in torrents, and grabbed his bathrobe. There was work to be done.

Marisol vomited noisily across the brick floor. "Morning sickness?" Gary asked, lifting the living woman to her feet by one elbow.

She shook him away. "I'm suffocating in here. What is that stuff, pickle juice?"

"Formalin," Gary responded, looking down at the pool of straw-colored liquid he'd just clambered out of. "I'm preserving myself for future generations. You should be grateful. The more I protect myself from bacterial decay, the fewer of your people I have to eat. Let's go get some air if it bothers you so much."

As he led her up the spiraling staircase hidden in the tower's double wall he summoned one of the mummies to clean up the sick. It gave him a real—if petty—pleasure to make Mael's former honor guard do janitorial work, but honestly, somebody had to clean the broch and only the mummies retained the necessary manual dexterity. Gary's own hands acted as if they were encased in fur-lined mittens—he couldn't even button his own shirt. At least the Ptolemies from the museum could use simple tools.

"How are your people settling in?" Gary asked. The

dead were still hard at work constructing the wall around the prison village but the living had already been moved into their simple houses. Gary had provided as much help as he could with books from the New York Public Library down on Forty-second Street and archaic tools taken from the Museum of the City of New York (known for its period rooms), but it couldn't be easy for twenty-first–century people to suddenly be forced into an eighteenth-century existence. Gary had no way to provide electricity or running water, much less television and online shopping. Rude survival was all that he offered. Still, it beat the alternative.

"They're scared, of course. They don't trust you."

Gary frowned. "I'm a ghoul of my word. Anyway, it's in my best interest to keep them safe."

Marisol gave him something approaching a defiant smile. "They didn't trust Dekalb, and he had a boat in the harbor. Jesus, do you even know what you look like these days? It's not a logic thing, okay? They see a dead guy who smells like pickles and who still has scraps of skin in his teeth, they want to run the other way. Give them a break. In time, I guess. . . I guess you can get used to anything but for now they've been herded into a corral in the middle of an army of bloodthirsty monsters and now they're being lorded over by a cannibal in a bathrobe. They're scared. Most of them. A couple still think they're going to be rescued."

Gary scratched himself. "Rescued? What, by Dekalb? If he wants to do the smart thing he'll leave me the fuck alone."

It was a hard walk to the top of the broch, probably too much for a pregnant woman with a bad stomach (she did seem to be panting a lot when they reached the top) but Gary took the steep stairs easily, nearly running up two steps at a time. "Of course, he won't do the smart thing," he told Marisol. Noseless and Faceless were waiting for them on the unfinished tower's ramparts. Noseless brought forward a silver tray with a dozen sticks of beef jerky fanned out for Gary's pleasure. He took one and chewed vigorously. Grudgingly Marisol took another, staring at it in her hand for a long while before biting into it, perhaps wondering if it was dried human meat. It wasn't—Gary was no savage. "Dekalb is an idealist. He'll come here even if he has to come alone, even if it means his death."

"Maybe he'll have some help," Marisol suggested. "You haven't met my Jack yet."

Gary gestured for her to look over the park. Below them, arrayed in their thousands, stood the dead—their shoulders slumped, their bodies wasted, but there were so many of them. They covered the ground like locusts, their constant movement like the waves of a sea.

He reached into the eididh, seized the throats and diaphragms of thousands of the dead in his spectral fist. The air sighed with their spasms as, for the first time in weeks or months, their esophagi opened and air flowed into them. Gary let it out like air spilling from the neck of a balloon.

"Hell. . . o. . ." the dead moaned. The noise was like tectonic plates shifting, like an ocean draining away through a crack in the world. A real dead-end sound, a symphony for solo apocalypse. Gary's lips split open he was smiling so hard. "Hello. . . Marisol. . ."

"I don't need any more males," Gary told her. "If your Jack comes here he'll die."

Chapter Eight

The thirty-foot trailer barely had room for a crew of three. With the girls all struggling to get in and have a look at the monitors the air inside quickly became too muggy and close to be breathable. I mopped sweat away from my forehead and nodded when Kreutzer asked if I was ready. Jack still had the Predator in the air, making wide circles around Manhattan at about twenty thousand feet but even he couldn't help his curiosity. We all wanted to know what the spy plane had seen.

I blinked rapidly as the display shot images rapid-fire at me of buildings passing far too close and fast on either side. I nearly lurched forward in my chair as the view opened up dramatically, the Predator gliding over the head of the Columbus statue at Fifty-ninth Street. Beyond the barrier of Central Park South the view changed again, and dramatically, into a landscape of mud laced with junk. The park had become unrecognizable, even the green grass torn away by the changes of the Epidemic. I hadn't even considered at that point that the dead might eat the vegetation there, and I felt my head shaking from side to side in doubt and distaste to see what had come of one my favorite places in the world.

In silence we watched as the plane sped uptown. Jack had kept it low so we could get a better view—maybe five hundred feet off the ground. At that height, when we saw the first of the dead people in the park they looked like pieces of popcorn scattered on a dark tabletop. Kreutzer froze the frame and ran an image-enhancement algorithm to zoom in on one. Its hair had fallen away in patches and its skin had turned a kind of soft and creamy white. Its clothes hung in tatters from its twisted limbs. We couldn't tell if it was a man or a woman.

Kreutzer, who had seen only a handful of the dead, had to turn away for a moment. The rest of us just ignored the corpse and studied the background—looking for places to entrench, fortifiable positions from which to stage an assault.

Then the Predator's nose camera swung forward to show us the skyline and our eyes went wide.

The dead filled half the park. They were close enough to one another to have trouble swinging their arms as they pressed closer and closer to something round and grey in the middle of the Park. They filled what had been the Great Lawn, and the Ramble, and the Pinetum. They covered the ground like a writhing sea of whitecaps. No. That was far too pleasant an image. They looked more like a maggot mass. Disgusting as it might be that was the only analogy I could think of—their colorless, pulpy flesh and their constant mindless motion could only call up images of fly larvae seething across the stretched dry skin of a dead animal.

There was no way to estimate how many of them there were. Thousands, definitely. Hundreds of thousands was an easy bet. I went to a peace rally in midtown just before the first Gulf War. According to the media, my war-hating colleagues and I had numbered at least two hundred thousand and we filled up only a few dozen blocks of First and Second avenues. To completely cover half of Central Park like that, well.

Gary had mentioned a million dead men. It looked like he wasn't far off.

"What's this feature?" Jack asked, scraping his chair across the floor of the trailer as he moved in for a closer look. He tapped his finger against the monitor with a soft, dull sound that shook me out of myself again. He was indicating the round grey shape at the very center of the crowd.

Kreutzer's fingers flickered over his keyboard as he called up a three-dimensional rendering of the object, extrapolating details from hundreds of frames of two-dimensional video footage. The trailer's hard drives chunked and rumbled for a minute, and then he put his product up for display. What we saw was a sort of squat tower, a circular structure rising with tapering walls to a ragged top. It must have been unfinished. It rose a good thirty yards in the air and was wider than the Met that sat next to it. What Gary could possibly want with such a structure was a mystery.

Its outbuildings made a little more sense. The dead had erected a wall about four meters high that surrounded a space the size of the Great Lawn. The wall attached directly to the main structure, forming a kind of corral. Inside this enclosed area was what looked like a tiny village of stone buildings with red terra-cotta roofs. It looked like something from Europe in the Middle Ages. The only way in or out of the village was through the main structure.

"Why did Gary want to rebuild Colonial Williamsburg here?" I asked, very confused. Ayaan stared at me curiously. "Those houses"—I pointed them out for her— "I guess that's where he keeps the prisoners, but they hardly look like jail cells."

"No, they don't," Jack said. "They look like barns."

Barns—where you keep your cattle. I got what he was saying. Gary needed to keep the prisoners alive and healthy—perhaps even happy—over the extreme long term. How long he could survive on the meat locked up in that corral was anybody's guess but clearly he meant to drag it out as long as possible.

I got up from my chair and headed outside for some fresh air. On the way out I squeezed Ayaan's shoulder. She followed me out onto the grass and out of earshot.

"There's something," I tried, not knowing quite what to say. "Something you should know. I intend to go after him. I can't go back to Africa until he's dead. Dead for real. That means going inside of that tower. In the process I'm going to try to free the prisoners, but my main goal is to separate his brain from his body."

She inhaled noisily. "That is impossible."

I nodded. "I saw how many of the dead he has under his control. I'm still going to try. Will you help me?"

"Yes, of course." She gave me a strange smile. "There really is no choice, is there? He will not let us approach the United Nations building, not while he still has control. If we are to finish our mission then he must be removed."

Did I tell her? It could only disturb her—and frankly, she didn't need the pressure of knowing she actually had an option. In the end, though, I decided I knew Ayaan well enough that I knew she would want to know.

"He called me," I told her. "He said he would make the way clear for us. Give us free passage. There's a price, though. He wants to eat you personally. It's a revenge thing for the time you shot him."

Her eyes went very wide but only for a moment. Then she nodded. "Okay. When do I go?"

I stepped forward and put my hands on her shoulders. "I don't think you understand. He wants to torture you. To death. I won't let that happen, Ayaan."

She pushed me away. I'm pretty sure that my touching her like that had violated Sharia law but mostly she just didn't like my attitude. "Why do you deny me this? It is my right! So many others have died! Ifiyah died just so that we could learn a lesson. That girl—the one with the cat—she died for being stupid! You will not let me die for my country? You will not let me die the most honorable death possible? Even if it means our mission is a success? Even if it means you can see your daughter again?"

I opened my mouth, but come on. There are no words after something like that. None at all.

Chapter Nine

"Sure." Kreutzer scratched vigorously at his unkempt hair. "It makes sense. She's a Shiite, right? They actually want to become martyrs. It's a good deal for them—one quick death and then you're in fucking paradise with your seventy-two virgins." He considered that for a second. "Or maybe she gets to be one of somebody else's virgins. Face it, blowing themselves up is what they do best."

I glared at him. "That's the most asinine thing I've ever heard. For one thing the Somali brand of Islam is based on the teachings of the Sufi sect, not the Shia. And anyway, it's only a tiny fraction of Shia who subscribe to that kind of nonsense." I waved my hands in the air. "She's a teenager, that's all. She doesn't understand what dying really means but she knows for a fact that life sucks. She's got all these hormones and energy and weird bad culturally created bullshit, fucked-up sexuality projected into glamorous ideas of death as transcendence—"

"She's a soldier." Jack peeled apart a blade of unmowed grass and put it to his lips. He blew hard and it made a reedy sound, like a mournful bassoon starting a dirge.

"She's a child." I said. But of course, she was much more than that. Jack understood her better than I did right then. She was a soldier. Which meant that she could submerge her own self into a larger idea, a context of community that had to be served—her national identity as a Somali, her place as a kumayo warrior fighting for Mama Halima. The good of all humanity.

It was a distinctly un-American sentiment but I had felt it myself. When we returned from the ill-fated raid on the hospital, dragging what was left of Ifiyah behind us, I had felt it. My own needs and wants and shortcomings no longer applied. When we got back to the boat and Osman started making wisecracks I had felt so disconnected from him and his selfish cowardice.

It takes us years to learn to surrender to what is larger than ourselves. Jack had spent much of his life having it drilled into him. Parents were supposed to get it instinctually as soon as the babies showed up, but some never really learned to put their families ahead of themselves.

Ayaan had figured it out in grade school. It was insulting, not to mention pointless, to deny her the belief she held closest to her very soul.

The girl herself must have heard us—I hardly kept my voice down after Kreutzer started spouting off— but she was busy and didn't feel the need to break into the conversation. She was preparing herself, you see. Preparing herself to be eaten alive.

Of all the fucked-up things I have seen since the dead came back to life and the world ended in grasping, hungering horror, the very worst was a sixteen-year-old girl touching her forehead to green grass on a sunny day and communing with her god. I could understand her motivation for throwing away her life—I could even go along with it, if I had to, by gritting my teeth—but I knew it would haunt me forever.

This was it, though. All I could ever hope to achieve. I would get my drugs and I would go back to Africa and I would see Sarah. I would hold her in my arms and pray she never had to make decisions like this, never had to watch people annihilate themselves for the sake of corrupt politicians half the world away again. We would build some kind of life and I would make myself forget what had happened. For Sarah's sake.

My mission was about to be over. The price: one sixteen-year-old girl. But it was over. "I didn't think it would be so easy," I muttered, smacking myself in the thigh with one tense fist.

"Dekalb," Jack said. "You're forgetting something."

Oh, no, I wasn't. I knew perfectly well that Marisol and the others were still being held as a food supply in that castle in Central Park. I knew that I had a personal responsibility to kill Gary.

I also knew that Ayaan had just gotten me off the hook. She had made those things unimportant. Ignorable. I could finish my mission and barely have to lift a finger. The price went up: two hundred human lives. Two hundred and one, if you counted Ayaan. Still, I doubted the two hundred were as excited by the prospect.

Jack wasn't done. "I've got some ideas, but I need every man I can get in on this one. I need you, Dekalb." He stared at me even as I steadfastly refused to meet his gaze.

Eventually I followed him into the trailer without a word and sank down into one of the comfortable chairs. Kreutzer lingered in the background, all but rubbing his hands together in nervousness while Jack studied high-res images of Central Park and the things Gary had built there.

"We have to start with a couple of assumptions," he said finally, that last word sounding like something with too many legs that had just flown into his mouth. This was a man who thought that hard data was a necessity in buying an electric toothbrush. Staging a suicidal rescue attempt would require notarized affidavits from signal-intelligence operatives and a signed letter from the Joint Chiefs of Staff describing in perfect detail exactly what his mission was. He didn't have that luxury now, of course. "We start by assuming that this is possible. Then we assume that we have the gear and the personnel to pull it off."

I nodded but still refused to look at his screen.

"We have to assume that he's still human enough to share some of our limitations. That he can concentrate on only one thing at a time."

I rubbed the bridge of my nose. "You want to use Ayaan's sacrifice as a diversion." It made sense, of course. Gary wanted one thing very badly, and that was revenge. If he was handed it on a silver platter why would he notice us sneaking up behind him with a chain saw to cut his head off?

I could think of a bunch of reasons why he would notice that. He wasn't stupid. We had underestimated him before and it had cost us so much. Jack was thinking in the realm of possibilities, though, not in terms of what might happen but what could happen. Even I knew that was dangerous territory.

"We have to assume one other thing. That he didn't

know this was here when he built his fortifications."

That made me look up. Something Gary had overlooked? Something that would solve all of our problems? Jack was tapping the screen, indicating a featureless rectangular shape just inside the boundaries of the park. It sat immediately downtown from the Seventy-ninth Street transverse, formerly a well-paved road and now a ribbon of muddy water. I had no idea what it was.

When Jack told me, I had to seriously think about what we were going to do. About how we were going to sneak inside Gary's fortress and somehow make it back out alive with a couple of hundred living people in tow. It couldn't be done.

We were going to do it. "How do we start?" I asked.

Chapter Ten

They were walking in the garden between the dormitory buildings, the mummies keeping a discreet distance from the living when something white and fast blurred across Gary's vision and collided with his temple, making his eyes shiver in their sockets. His brain squirmed in his head as he sent out a dozen commands at once, drawing in clumps of soldiers to cover his blind spot, sending Noseless clambering up the stairs of the broch to get a clear view, rushing Faceless out to where the wall of the enclosure wasn't quite finished.

His own eyes, however, solved the mystery. Looking down, still shaken by the blow, he saw the missile that had struck him so violently. It was a softball, soiled and dented from long use. Looking up again he saw a little girl standing stock-still a few dozen yards away, her eyes very wide. She wore a catcher's glove and her nose was running unheeded. Her bright energy thrummed inside her with the adrenaline coursing through her veins.

Gary knelt down before the terrified eight year-old and tried to smile. Considering the state of his teeth, maybe that wasn't the best idea. The girl trembled visibly, waves of fear rippling through her gooseflesh.

"Come here, baby. I'm not going to bite." Not this one, anyway. She had plenty more years ahead of her as a breeder before she would be culled. If she was a threat, he might have to eat her father or someone as an object lesson.

At his side he could feel Marisol, barely able to control herself. She wanted to hurt him, he knew. Violence had been done to his person and she felt as if she should take it as a sign to begin a violent rebellion against her captivity. He also knew she wasn't that stupid. The others who stood around him in a wide circle looked ready to run away at the slightest provocation. There would be no mutiny today.

"Did you throw this?" he asked, holding up the softball. It took both of his hands to keep a grip on it. "Did you throw it at me on purpose? Don't worry, I'm not angry. Did you throw it on purpose?"

Perhaps too quickly, the girl's head swiveled right and left in negation. Gary smiled again.

"Playing ball is fun but we have to be careful," he said. "Maybe you remember how there used to be doctors and hospitals, but they're gone now. If one of us gets hurt or sick there's nobody to look after them. Do you—"

He stopped in mid-thought. His death-numbed senses had picked up something, something distant and faint, a kind of rumbling that he felt more than heard. Like a distant earthquake. Gary queried the taibhsearan hanging from the broch's walls and his own scouts out in the park. There was a generalized sense of agitation from the crowd of dead outside but no real information to be had.

A living man came out of the crowd and hurried the little girl away. Her education would have to wait until

Gary knew what was going on.

"What was that?" Marisol demanded. The living around them shook their heads in confusion. Gary wasn't just losing it, there had definitely been a sound. He touched Noseless's mind and had him study the dead trees of Central Park, the tombstone tenements beyond. There—a puff of brown and grey smoke rolling over some trees on the western edge of the park. Over by the American Museum of Natural History, almost directly across the park from the Met where Mael had reanimated. Gary reached across the eididh and sent a wave of his dead soldiers moving in that direction. Those closest to the museum were engulfed in a cloud of dust that dissipated quickly. They staggered onto the museum grounds and tripped over fallen pieces of stone and brick. That wasn't altogether surprising—the dead had demolished a good half of the Museum of Natural History in their quest for bricks with which to build Mael's tower. Maybe the rest of the building was just collapsing.

A honking, shrilling blare rolled across the park. The dead nearest the museum covered their ears in defense against the noise. The sound rose and fell and flared out into a high-pitched shriek that made Gary's skull hurt. When it finally stopped he ordered his dead to get closer, to surround the museum. That had been a man-made sound. Feedback on a speaker system, perhaps.

Or from a bullhorn. "Hello! Mr. Asshole *Xaaraan*!"

That word wasn't English but it sounded familiar. Oh, yes, of course. One of the Somali girls had used it to describe him. She'd had a bayonet impaling his chest at the time.

"Hello, dead man, are you out there!"

There was still dust in the air near the Museum of Natural History. It vibrated every time the girl spoke. Gary possessed the throats of his army.

"Yesssss," he made them hiss with rotten vocal cords. "I'mmmmm heeerrrreee."

A figure appeared on the roof of the Museum of Natural History, on top of the glass-walled Hayden Planetarium. Noseless could just make her out with his cloudy eyes—plaid skirt, blazer, head scarf. The girl soldier raised the bullhorn to her mouth again and her words blasted across Central Park, bouncing off the hardened mud, ricocheting off the twisted iron streetlamps. "You said you would take me as your payment for the drugs. I have come."

Ayaan—it was Ayaan, the bitch who shot him. Gary felt his dessicated salivary glands swell with excitement. He hadn't really expected Dekalb to accept his offer. He urged his dead scouts forward, into the broken province of the museum. Inside in the shadowy space hot dust roiled in great clouds that reduced visibility. Piles of broken rubble clogged the corridors and broad exhibit spaces. Ayaan must have demolished all the stairwells—there was no way up to the roof anymore, as far as Gary could tell. The only part of the museum that hadn't been damaged was the planetarium itself, a metal-clad sphere suspended inside a self-contained structure of tempered glass. There was no way inside the glass cube without going through the main body of the museum, and the glass was shatterproof.

Gary pulled his troops out of the ruined building and had them swarm around the sides. They reached up across the glass but could find no handholds, nothing at all to help them climb up. Ayaan had picked an incredibly defensible location to make her last stand. There was no way up—but she was also cut off from escape.

"Here I am!" she called, her words chased by rubbery echoes. "Come and get me!"

Clearly she didn't intend to go down easy. Alright, Gary thought. Alright. This might be fun. He urged his army forward, the great surging mass of them. They moved silently like a wind passing through tall grass, but their footfalls made the ground shake. Gary thrilled with the power he commanded, only to have his ego shaken a moment later.

From behind ventilation hoods and elevator-shaft heads the rest of Ayaan's company emerged, a dozen, two dozen girls with heavy packs on their backs and assault rifles in their hands. Some of them held large cardboard boxes. These girls ran to the edge of the planetarium roof and upturned their loads over the heads of the encroaching ghoul army.

The boxes were full of live hand grenades. They fell like fruit from an orchard in a thunderstorm, tumbling through fifty feet of air to bounce around the feet of Gary's soldiers. They went off in rhythmic fountains of pale smoke that hid the army from Noseless's view and made Gary wince as he felt the distant pain of each dead man as they were blown apart.

"Goddamn it," Gary howled. He headed back to the broch, calling the mummies to follow him. It looked as if Dekalb still had some surprises for him after all.

Chapter Eleven

Six hours earlier:

Osman handed me a limp kif cigarette and a pack of matches before he jumped back onto the Arawelo and started barking orders at Yusuf. "It will calm your nerves," he told me. I guess I looked like a ghost—people had been telling me all morning how pale I was. I didn't think Osman's weak hashish was going to help so I shoved the joint in my pocket after waving him my gratitude.

The boat pulled away from the Coast Guard dock with a rattling of pistons and a blast of hot exhaust from its diesels. Osman brought it around slowly, backing and filling with a series of slow-motion turns. The girls on the deck held to the rails or to lashed-down boxes of armaments and looked wistfully over the green grass of Governors Island. I had hoped not to see Ayaan before she left but there she was on top of the wheelhouse like a homecoming queen on a particularly rusty parade float. She looked down at me and I looked up at her. Our eyes met for perhaps the last time and we seemed to communicate on some nonverbal level, some wavelength of respect I couldn't really define. Finally she shot me a smile that made me queasy and then she turned to face the harbor.

I headed back toward the aircraft hangars at a jog—timing was a big part of Jack's plan and I wouldn't be the one to screw it up. The big tubular Chinook helicopter—a CH-47SD, the newest and fanciest cargo helicopter the armed forces had—sat on the lawn waiting for me. I dashed up the rear loading ramp and hit the switch to close it behind me, then jogged forward through the cabin, cavernous now that we'd torn out all the seats and rattling like the inside of a concrete mixer. Kreutzer already had the Super-D's tandem rotors spun up to speed and he was ready to get airborne. He had protested, of course, when we asked him to fly us out to Central Park but Jack had certain powers of persuasion. Namely he told Kreutzer that if he didn't volunteer for the job we would just leave him on Governors Island to starve. When Jack says something like that people tend to assume he's not bluffing.

As soon as I reached the cockpit Kreutzer took us straight up a hundred feet and then pushed forward so hard I toppled backward and landed on my ass. He looked down at me from his pilot's seat as if he might start laughing.

"How many flight hours do you have on this thing?" I shouted over the roar of the engines.

Kreutzer snarled back, "More than you, asshole." Fair enough.

Carefully I climbed up into the navigator's seat. Jack, in the copilot's seat, handed me a stick of gum to help pop my ears.

We streaked across the harbor and into Brooklyn airspace, keeping low and moving fast. We were taking the first of many dumb risks this mission would require. While we were certain that Brooklyn was swarming with the dead and that some of them would see us, we could only hope that Gary's ability to use the dead as spies didn't extend to that kind of range—or, perhaps, that he wouldn't be paying attention to the outlying boroughs.

The position of my seat kept me from seeing down to street level so I was thankfully spared the sight of any surprised-looking dead who might have spotted us. All I saw was the occasional building flashing by right outside my window—the courthouse, the Williamsburg Savings Bank clock tower, the Jehovah's Witnesses headquarters. As we passed into Queens Kreutzer brought us up another hundred feet and banked toward the river. "Last chance," he said.

I frowned in confusion—then looked out the canopy at the ground below. We were even with the UN complex, the Secretariat Building as white and shiny as a tombstone where it towered over the corpse-choked East River. My brain did a reversal of perspectives and I realized what he was saying. We could just fly over there right now and get the drugs and leave. I could call Ayaan and abort this suicide mission. I didn't see any pigeons—maybe Gary had actually kept his word and cleared the way for us.

So close. It was right there. Right there!

Jack put a hand on my shoulder and squeezed. He wasn't threatening me, or even reminding me of my responsibilities. Just emotional support, from a guy who I would have thought incapable of such. I turned to nod at him and sank back into my seat.

It wasn't long before Kreutzer had us hovering over the Queensboro Bridge where it crossed Roosevelt Island. That was as close as we dared to get to Manhattan in our noisy conveyance. I got up from my seat and looked down through the chin bubbles. I could see the dead far below, crowding around the bridge pylons, their heads craning upwards and their hands reaching for us.

Kreutzer turned sideways in his seat. "I don't know if either of you has accepted Jesus Christ as your personal savior, but now might be the time."

We ignored him and headed aft to the cabin. Jack and I took turns sealing one another into hazmat suits, just like the ones Ayaan and I used when we first came to Times Square a few days—or a lifetime—ago. These were Coast Guard issue, meant for use during toxic-spill cleanups, so they were thicker and more unwieldy, but I had tested mine out and knew I could still walk in it. When we were suited up Jack ran me through the basics of fast-roping. He fitted me with a nylon harness that looped over my thighs then attached a descender—an aluminum figure eight—to my crotch with carabiners. When he was done he opened a hatch in the belly of the Chinook with a burst of white light and hooked up a winch for our lines. One end of the line went through my descender in a complicated loop. Jack attached a safety line to the back of my harness, and I was good to go. "See you downstairs," I said, trying to sound tough. Jack didn't respond so I held my breath and stepped out through the hatch.

They call it fast-roping because "falling like a rock" doesn't sound like proper military jargon. I could slow myself down if I didn't mind burning my gloves—the friction from the ropes got intense—but I spent most of the descent in free fall, just like Jack had taught me. Falling objects all descend at the same speed—Galileo proved it—but when you're carrying a fifty-pound pack, it sure feels like you're dropping even faster. I slowed as I neared the ground, grabbing hard at my line until my gloves literally began to smoke and then flexed my knees just as I touched the concrete roadbed, rolling away from the impact so I didn't break my ankles.

In a second I was up and holding the rope while Jack followed me down. We unclipped the various lines and harnesses and waved at Kreutzer, but he was already slipping sideways in a wide turn that would take him well out of sight of Manhattan. In a few seconds he was hidden behind a row of buildings and the world was suddenly silent, with only my breath and the creaking of my suit to keep me company. Jack had expressly forbidden speaking during this part of the mission, just in case. All it would take was one dead man to notice us and we would fail, and our lives would be forfeit.

The bridge rose away from us on either side, a tendril of concrete flanked by high iron towers. To the east lay Manhattan, the Upper East Side, and then Central Park. We had a long walk ahead of us. We got started without a word.

Chapter Twelve

Our walk through the Upper East Side made my bones ache and sweat pool in the small of my back, but we weren't spotted, which was the main thing. The streets were deserted—presumably Gary had pulled all of the dead away from this area to join the ranks of his army. That didn't mean we took a lot of chances. We moved through the streets of Manhattan using a cover strategy that Jack called "bounding overwatch," which meant I would hide in a shadowy doorway, my eyes scanning a street corner while Jack crossed the open space as fast as he could. Then he would take up position behind some kind of cover and I would do what he had just done, though far more clumsily.

We saw a number of buildings that had been pulled down by brute force—presumably for the bricks that built Gary's tower. Hands and feet stuck out of the resulting rubble piles. Clearly Gary hadn't worried much about job-site safety when he sent his troops out for building materials. We saw only one active dead man, which was just enough to give me heart palpitations. If Gary had been using his eyes at that moment, we would have been screwed—and there was no way we would know, not until we got to the park and found Gary waiting for us. Thinking about it made me want to panic, so I tried not thinking about it. Which didn't work.

The dead guy was standing in the middle of Madison Avenue, a stretch mostly bare of cars. He had his back to us, staring at a storefront covered up by a hoarding that had been turned into one giant billboard. COMING 2005: LA PERLA, the ad assured us. Beneath was a blow-up of a woman wearing nothing but bra and panties, her back arched, her face turned to the camera with a look of disinterest. Even enlarged ten times her normal size her skin looked flawless, poreless.

His skin was discolored and blotchy, riddled with sores and sloughing away from wounds on his hands and his back. His head moved back and forth, his neck making a wet click every time. What could he possibly be looking for in the advertisement? Did he think the giant woman was some kind of food? I had never seen any evidence that the dead were interested in sex.

Jack and I waited for fifteen minutes behind the side of a building, waiting for the corpse to move on, but it became apparent he wasn't going anywhere. Finally I looked over at Jack and took a combat knife from my pack. He nodded. I had intended to hand him the weapon but apparently it was my turn. He lifted a finger to his faceshield—be quiet about it, he was telling me.

I figured it was better to be fast. I ran up to the ghoul as fast as I could in my bulky suit, the knife held high so I could stab it right down into the top of his head. I stopped cold, though, when the dead man spun on one unsteady ankle and turned to face me head-on. His eyes were so obscured with white sclera that his pupils were completely hidden. He must have been nearly blind. His jaw hung loose under his skin, unconnected to the rest of his skull. I had never seen a dead man in such lousy shape. Pity welled up inside of me, but not before I had brought the knife down, skewering his head. He dropped to the pavement in an ungainly heap.

We reached the edge of Central Park less than an hour later. We scoped out the devastated landscape—dried mud, lots of it, and plenty of denuded trees which offered some cover. We could see a few of the dead milling around but they were far enough away not to spot us. We hoped. Jack led me into one of the transverses, the streets which run crosstown through the park. We headed down between the stone walls that turned the transverse into an artificial box canyon and soon we were up to our ankles in brown water. When the dead ate the grass and the plants of Central Park they removed the only thing standing between the manicured public gardens and erosion. The first good rain had turned Central Park into a series of arroyos, prone to flash flooding and the weathering effects of white water. Now the transverses were shallow rivers and the old water catch basins of the park—the ponds, the lakes, the Jacqueline Kennedy Onassis Reservoir—were reduced to oily puddles. It's impossible to walk silently through standing water but luckily we didn't have far to go. About a hundred and fifty feet into the transverse, we came across a pair of tall iron gates set into the retaining wall. Beyond lay darkness—a lot of it.

Jack took his police lockpick out of his bulging pack. The lock on the gates looked simple enough but it took quite a bit of straining and twisting to get it open. At one point Jack took out a metal file and scraped noisily at the face of the lock. Perhaps it had rusted shut. I was busy keeping an eye out for the dead, so I couldn't tell you. Finally the lock popped open with a clang and we were inside.

The tunnel beyond the gate had a sandy floor (now submerged under a few inches of water—I could see the sand at my feet, glittering here and there with flecks of mica, the sand erupting in billowing clouds every time I shifted my weight) and a vaulted ceiling of white brick. There were lights up there but they weren't working. A fine mist of water filled the air of the tunnel, obscuring visibility past about ten feet ahead of us. Our own shadows loomed before us in that mist, floating on vapor. Every movement I made seemed magnified, enlarged beyond all significance. The shadows multiplied as we moved into the darkness, their swirling shapes looming toward me or racing away on the reflections of our lights in the water. There could have been anything in that tunnel—an army of the dead could have been coming straight at us and we would never have known. The close walls and round ceiling of the tunnel seemed to stretch out, threatening at any moment to disappear and drop us into infinite darkness without warning.

Eventually we came to a room full of turbine equipment—long dormant, thankfully, or we would have been electrocuted. The big round machines lay in a row like eggs or sleeping forms between us and a wrought-iron spiral staircase that led upward into misty darkness. Our rubberized boots didn't clang so badly on the steps but the water that poured out of the folds of our suits as we ascended made for a sloshing, dripping, noisy climb. At the top of the staircase sat a room made of brick, containing only a few sticks of broken furniture and a stained mattress in one corner. There were windows but they showed nothing but sloppily joined bricks. There was one door—a big locked steel fire door that was our next destination. Assuming it led anywhere.

Gary had built his tower across a big patch of Central Park without, apparently, thinking much about what was in the way. He had torn down many of the park's buildings for bricks but others—those near the Great Lawn—had simply been incorporated whole into the structure. Belvedere Castle, one of my favorite places in New York City, had become little more than a buttress for one enormous curtain wall. On the uptown side of the tower the southern reservoir gatehouse had found a similar purpose. It had been built right into the tower, something Jack had seen in the video product we took from the Predator. What Gary didn't know, we hoped, was that there was a tunnel leading from the south gatehouse to one of the transverses. The tunnel we had just come through.

It was possible that the door we faced now could have been sealed off during construction. It was also possible that it opened directly into Gary's personal apartments. Or into a guard room full of violent corpses. There was no way of knowing without trying it.

This was our plan, then. Ayaan would distract the dead—drawing as many of Gary's thousands of soldiers to her as she could, holding out as long as she might on top of the Museum of Natural History. Simultaneously, Jack and I would break into Gary's fortress, kill any of the living dead we found inside (including Gary) and get the survivors to a place where Kreutzer could come pick them up in the Chinook. It was the best idea we'd come up with. I was committed to it, ready to give my life for its success. We both were.

Jack didn't waste any time. He grabbed the doorknob and turned. The door swung open on well-oiled hinges, revealing a dark brick-lined corridor beyond. None of the dead appeared to attack us. Dry air blew across us, blowing away all but a few tendrils of mist rising from the spiral staircase. He closed the door again—we weren't quite ready to stage our raid.

Jack shrugged out of his heavy pack and dropped it to the floor, then helped me do the same. He unzipped my pack and started drawing out long silver cylinders with nozzles on their ends, the kind you would use to store compressed gas.

I had never seen them before. "What are those?" I whispered, my voice sounding inaudible even to me inside my faceshield.

Jack looked up, his calm face framed perfectly by the square window of transparent plastic. "There's been a change of plan," he said.

Chapter Thirteen

The bodies arched and heaved, backs curling, heads pushed down by feet looking for purchase. A thousand moving corpses strained with their arms and legs, pushing each other upward, the limbs of the ones on the bottom snapping like dry sticks. The one on top, an Asian girl in a pair of bloodstained pink Sanryo overalls, reached up with one hand and touched the coping of the planetarium's roof. A Somali girl with a bayonet on the end of her rifle lunged forward and impaled the dead girl's head like a pineapple. When the bayonet retracted the Asian girl rolled down the side of the undead human pyramid to smack the asphalt of Central Park West. A man in an Armani suit with one leg hanging in tatters slumped forward to take her place. One of the Somalis opened up with a .50 caliber machine gun mounted on a tripod and his body erupted in chunks of rotten meat that pelted the bodies below like foul rain.

The inhuman pyramid wasn't going to work. Instead Gary turned to his original plan and looked through the eyes of a dead man deep within the ruins of the Museum of Natural History. A small squad requiring constant attention had found its way through some of the rubble, climbing clumsily over fallen statuary and through gaps in collapsed piles of shattered brick. Stained with red dust, their eyes drying up in their sockets, three of them had clambered up a length of twisted and broken track lighting to reach the fourth floor. Gary had left them to their own devices for only a minute or two while he tried to assemble the pyramid, but in that time two of his dead scouts had managed to walk right off of a balcony and fall back to the floor below. One had a pair of broken legs and was useless—Gary snuffed the life out of it on principle. The other didn't need his attention. She had impaled her own head on an exposed shaft of rebar. The third, still-functioning corpse had come up short, unable to proceed. He was standing quite motionless, his arms at his sides, his head moving back and forth. He was trying to process what lay before him, a shadow looming out of the cool darkness of the museum—a skull big enough for him to climb inside with teeth like combat knives and eye sockets bigger than his head.

It was a Tyrannosaurus rex skull. The dead man was trying to decide if it was food or an enemy or both. It was neither, of course—there wasn't even any marrow to suck out of the bone, since the skull was merely a replica made out of polymer resin. Gary snarled and seized direct control of the ghoul's arms and legs. His soldiers had always been stupid, of course, but they also hadn't been fed since the day Mael took control of them. As a result they were losing ground against the more insidious kinds of bodily decay. Their eyes were white with corruption, their fingers gnarled and contorted. By forcing the dead man to march at a brisk pace Gary was damaging his vital tissues beyond repair. In a matter of hours this particular vessel of his attention would fall apart completely. Irrelevant, he told himself. He only needed a few more minutes out of this one. According to the museum directory the hall of saurischian dinosaurs butted up against the top level of the planetarium. If there was a way to reach the roof it would be nearby.

Gloom hunched over the dinosaur exhibit but not total darkness. Gary tried to relax the corpse's failing eyes and perceive where light was coming in. By trial and error he eventually managed to steer the dead man in the right direction—to a sizable gap in the wall, a place where bricks had fallen away and plaster had crumbled until sunlight could thrust inside in a whorl of fresh air. Gary shoved his distant body into the hole and pushed. The dead man's flesh snagged on broken pipes and wooden beams—snagged and tore away—but he moved, inch by inch, closer to the outside. Finally his face emerged into the light, and for a moment Gary could see nothing but white as his avatar's degraded pupils tried desperately to constrict. When his vision finally cleared he looked down and saw just what he wanted to see—the roof of the planetarium, not three feet below, tar paper and ventilation fans and Somali child soldiers. He had a way through! Gary immediately switched his attention to call up hundreds of his troops—no, thousands—and head them toward the Museum of Natural History. He intended to exploit this weakness fully.

Then he dropped back into his scout's damaged brain again, just to scope out the situation—and found himself staring into the face of a smiling teenaged girl. She had a small spherical green hand grenade in one hand. Gary tried to make the dead man snap at her fingers with his teeth but he couldn't stop her from pushing her grenade into the dead man's mouth. He could feel the roundness of it, the uncomfortable weight in his mouth. He could taste the metal.

He hardly needed to stick around for what came next. The gap in the wall would be useless, then—the girls would be aware of it and could easily cover any troops he tried to send through.

"Fuck!" he shouted, and turned away from the ramparts of the broch. Back in his own body for the first time since the siege had begun he stamped down the stairs, the mummies following close behind him. He left Noseless on the top level to watch the ongoing battle. In a sort of halfhearted way he continued to pay attention to the struggle to the west where his troops were being picked off one by one, but he wasn't immediately interested in the details. Ayaan wasn't going anywhere and neither was he. He just needed a little time to regroup, rethink.

He reached the main floor of the tower and slumped gratefully into his formalin bath. It was getting harder to move around on his own these days—perhaps he was spending so much time in the eididh that his muscles were atrophying. Something to worry about when he had a chance. When this was over and he could—

PHWHAM. PHHHWHAM. PHHWHAM.

Brick dust sifted down from the galleries above and sprinkled across his bath like paprika. Gary sat up with a great sloshing and grabbed for information. The west side of the broch was wreathed in smoke that hung motionless in great wreaths in the air. Noseless had fallen to the wooden planking of the top gallery, knocked clean off his feet by the impacts. Gary forced him to stand up again and take a look.

One of the girls had a rocket-propelled grenade launcher—the same weapon Dekalb had used on the dead riot cops. She was firing directly at the broch, the rocket grenades coming at Gary's vision like deadly footballs spinning through the intervening air, trailing behind them perfectly straight trails of white vapor.

PHHHHHHHHHHHHWHAM.

Gary stewed in rage as he summoned up more of his troops—screw it, all of them!—and hurled them toward the museum. He would end this now, any way he had to. If he had to knock down the entire planetarium with the sheer brute strength of a million dead men he would do it. If he had to tear the place down himself, he would! He sent his giant striding forward through the undead tide, his long legs propelling him forward faster than the rest of them could walk. He sent Faceless out to be his eyes—she had eaten recently enough that her vision wasn't clouded by rot. This wasn't going to stand, goddamn it!

The army of the dead was surrounding the planetarium in ranks a hundred deep, their shoulders bent to pushing at the frame of the building until they were trampling one another, when Gary heard the gunshot. With his own, physical ears. His attention snapped back to his own senses at once.

That sound had come from inside the broch.

Chapter Fourteen

Jack got to work by the illumination of a handful of chemical lights. We took off our hazmat suits to make it easier to work and I waited patiently for Jack's instructions. He unzipped the big pack I had carried into Gary's fortress and took out a couple of foil packets covered in warning stickers and small-print type. I peered into the pack myself and had no idea what I was looking at. Other than the metal gas cylinders there were neat stacks of electronic components and bricks of something soft-looking and off-white. I did notice what was missing: guns. There weren't any firearms in there at all. No pistols, no assault rifles, no shotguns. No rocket launchers or sniper rifles or machine guns.

No knives, either. The combat knife strapped to my suit's leg was the only weapon I could find. I unzipped Jack's pack, thinking maybe he had carried all the armaments because he didn't trust me not to accidentally shoot off my foot (a fair-enough assertion, if that was what he had actually been thinking. It wasn't). He reached over and stopped my hand. "I'll unload that one," he said.

"Are you ready to tell me what we're doing?" I asked, cautiously.

"No," he said.

Pure Jack style. Just no, negative, unh-uh. He took the Iridium cell phone out of my pack and laid it on the floor after checking for probably the third time that it was set to vibrate and not to ring. It almost certainly couldn't get a signal through all those stone walls but he wouldn't take the chance. "One at a time, and very slowly, start handing me those bricks," he said, pointing to my pack.

I took one out. It felt slightly powdery, like a crumbling bar of soap, and it came wrapped in a thin sheet of plastic like Saran Wrap. I left a depression in the brick where I held it with my thumb but Jack didn't seem to mind. He stripped off the plastic and then picked up one of the compressed gas cylinders and wrapped the puttylike substance around the cylinder, smoothing it quite carefully. As he worked with it the stuff lost its powdery consistency and became rubbery and malleable.

I had seen the stuff before. It's common enough and cheap enough that it regularly shows up in the arsenals of most developing countries. Not to mention terrorist training camps. "That's Semtex, right?"

Jack glared at me.

Foolish me, I thought he was angry because I had used the European name for it. "Sorry. C-4. Plastic explosive. You're going to blow Gary up."

"Something like that." He returned to his work, fashioning a charge around the end of a second cylinder.

I had to know. I picked up one of the cylinders. It had a faded sticker near the nozzle showing two symbols. One was a triangle containing a broken test tube. Cartoon fumes rose from the point of breakage. The other symbol was a skull and crossbones.

The foil packets contained two piece atropine autoinjectors. First aid in the event of a chemical weapons spill. "What is it in those cylinders, sarin?" I asked, very, very calmly.

"VX." He sniffed, as if I had offended his professional pride. "It's got an LD50 of ten milligrams, either inhaled or cutaneous."

A lethal dose of one thirty-thousandth of an ounce. One little droplet is all it takes. I knew a hell of a lot more about LD50s and cutaneous versus ocular exposure rates than I had ever wanted to. This stuff was my worst nightmare back when I was working as a weapons inspector. It would have been everybody's worst nightmare if anybody had ever been crazy enough to use it. Even Saddam Hussein, when he tried to wipe out the Kurds, had used less dangerous nerve agents than VX. The British invented it. They traded it to the United States in exchange for the plans for the atomic bomb. It was that lethal.

"The military tried everything they had when the Epidemic broke out," Jack told me. "There was a rumor they were going to nuke Manhattan but I guess they couldn't make it happen in time. They did try gassing Spanish Harlem. This is all that's left of the assets they brought down for that project."

"They used nerve gas against the living dead?" I asked, incredulous. I suppose if I was put in the same position, I might have grasped at straws, too, but surely that was overkill. "Did it. . . did it work?"

"It should have. A dead guy is pretty much just a nervous system that can walk around and VX is a nerve agent. It short-circuits the acetylcholine cycle. It should have worked."

Obviously it hadn't. If anything, the military had probably succeeded only at wiping out any survivors holed up in the neighborhood while leaving the undead untouched. The things we do with the best of intentions. . . I shook my head. "Then you aren't here to kill Gary at all."

Jack reached into his own pack and pulled out a handgun, a Glock 9mm. He didn't point it at me, didn't threaten me at all. Very carefully, the barrel pointing at the wall the whole time, he placed it on the floor.

"I told you one time about my contingency plan. About how I used to think about killing them in their sleep." He continued to build the charges around the cylinders. I did nothing. I remembered quite well what he had said. It had scared me then—it scared me more now because now I knew he meant it. He went on. "There's no hope for a rescue attempt, Dekalb. It just can't be done. I ran through a million scenarios in my head and there's no way the two of us come out alive."

"You don't know that," I countered.

He blinked and looked away from me. "Dekalb," he said, "what's the crew-carrying capacity of a Chinook helicopter with the seats taken out?"

My jaw opened and closed spasmodically. "You don't—" But he did. He knew the answer. So did I. Maybe a hundred people if you're not going very far. We could rescue only half the survivors.

Jack clearly didn't want to have to choose which ones to leave behind.

"There's nothing to be gained by us dying like that. Still, we can do something for the survivors. We can keep them from being his lunch. Or rather I can."

He tossed me one of the atropine injector kits. If I was exposed to nerve gas the only thing that could save me— the only thing—was jabbing the enclosed hypodermics into my buttocks or thigh. If I hadn't been exposed to nerve gas but jabbed myself anyway, the atropine would kill me instead.

"You can get out of here. Go back the way we came. Meet up with Kreutzer and have him take you to the UN. Get the girls off of that rooftop. You can still complete your mission. You just have to let me complete mine."

Which meant consigning two hundred men, women, and children to their deaths.

"Dekalb—I needed you to come this far only because I couldn't carry all of this gear on my own. Now let me do you a favor. Just turn around and go."

I didn't know what to say. I definitely didn't know what to do. I most certainly had no idea what my next reaction was going to be. If I could have stepped out of my body and spoken with myself I would have advised against it.

It was a kind of spur-of-the-moment thing.

The Iridium cell phone buzzed with a small, unobtrusive sound. It vibrated against the flagstone floor, wobbling and dancing. It slid a few inches across the floor and stopped. It started up again a second later. This was Ayaan's signal to us, the message that she had drawn Gary's undead army to her position. Away from us. Jack and I both stared at the phone.

We looked up at the same moment. I had my combat knife in my hand, pointed at his stomach. He had the Glock in his hand, pointed at my heart.

I lunged.

He fired.

Chapter Fifteen

Jack's best plan—the one he'd spent days dreaming up, planning for, imagining ways it could be implemented— was to kill every living person in Gary's fortress. He would build eight bombs, each of them containing enough VX nerve gas to wipe out a city neighborhood. He would strap these bombs to his body. Then he would run through the fortress with a detonator in his hand. Either he would make it outside and into Gary's farm, where the survivors were held—and perhaps in the process get one last look at Marisol—or he would be stopped by attacking ghouls along the route. Either way, he would trigger the detonator. The resulting cloud of poison gas would spread throughout this part of the city. It would take hours to dissipate. Anyone who was exposed to it, even for just a few minutes, would die. There was no immunity to VX. You couldn't even hold your breath and hope it would go away. Once it got on your skin you were dead. There would be no time to wash it off.

He believed that by using a nerve gas he would insure that the dead would not rise again. VX worked by short-circuiting the entire nervous system, making it impossible for the body to function. Maybe it would have prevented

Marisol and the survivors from Times Square from reanimating. We'll never know.

We tried to kill each other in that last ugly second, with everything we had. I stabbed him with a combat knife, throwing myself on top of him. He used every bit of skill he had with a firearm and tried to shoot me in the heart. Shooting a human is different from shooting a ghoul. When you are shooting a living, and especially a moving, human being then head shots, Jack could have told me, are difficult to make even at point blank range when you're shooting from the hip with a pistol. Even if you connect you're firing into the most bony part of the human anatomy, the part most likely to deflect a shot. You might just graze your target's scalp, which is just going to make him angry. You might hit him in the jaw, which makes for an ugly wound but in the shock of impact most people won't even feel it. A shot to the chest, however, will puncture a lung at the very least. In terms of stopping power you want to always aim for the torso.

I had no training in knife fighting. I didn't know any special moves. I certainly didn't know how to effectively kill a living human being with a knife. I just jumped and stuck my knife out and hoped for the best.

He missed. It's possible, I suppose, that he didn't really want to shoot me, that he was just warning me off. This is Jack we're talking about, though, so I think that we can safely discard that possibility. It's much more likely that he couldn't really see me. All this happened, remember, in the glow of four chemical lights. Glowsticks. I was a shadow coming toward him in a room full of shadows. He missed.

I didn't.

There was blood—so much blood—on both of us that I didn't realize what had happened until later when I had a chance to examine myself and didn't find any smoking holes. I had managed to gut him through several arteries and major veins. His blood didn't just leak out, it erupted from his belly. The savagery of my cut was such that I lodged the knife inside him and just left it there. It was like digging into a perfectly cooked porterhouse with a steak knife. It was like gutting a fish.

I would think about that for a long time afterwards. In that moment I just lay on top of him, breathing hard, totally unaware of what was happening around me—just knowing that I was still alive, pretty sure that wasn't going to last.

The gunshot was heard throughout the fortress. A dead giveaway.

When the door flew open I didn't hear it though it must have slammed pretty hard. When the dead hands reached down and grabbed at me I was barely aware of them. I was more conscious of how my weight made me slip out of their grasp time and again. I felt like the original immovable object. I felt as if no force in space or time could move me.

Eventually the dead just grabbed me by the ankles and dragged me out of the pumphouse. They dragged Jack out, too, in the same way. He was still alive. Sort of. His eyes were open and bright. He looked at me without any emotion in his face at all as we were pulled down a long hallway, our pants riding down as our asses were dragged over bumps in the floor, my body burning with friction where it touched the flagstones.

Then time started up again and I tried to fight back. I

lunged forward, my hands grabbing at the rotten fingers that dug into my ankles. The dead men dropped me and I rolled up to a sitting position before they could kick me to death. Believe me, they tried. I managed to get my legs underneath me, to stand up. Then five of them just sort of leaned into me, their shoulders connecting with my chest and back. They slammed me up against a wall with just the weight of their decaying bodies. The smell was horrifying, especially mixed with the oily stink of Jack's blood all over my shirt.

They didn't tie my hands—they lacked the coordination to do so. Instead they just pushed me ahead of them with their hands and feet like kids playing kick the can. Every time I turned to attack them they would just thrust me up against a wall again until I settled down.

They had all the time in the world. They weren't about to get tired. Eventually I just let them herd me on. We came to a place where the corridor opened up into a larger room, and then they knocked me down onto my hands and knees. I looked up.

Six dead men stood in a ring along the walls of the chamber. Circular and tall, the room was not as big as I might have expected. It was made smaller by the fact that most of its floor had been hollowed out and turned into an enormous basin, a tub. A bathtub. This depression was full of some kind of foul-smelling liquid. I recognized the stench of formalin—it's a precursor chemical, an ingredient in a number of chemical weapons. I had been trained to know that smell. Something the size of a large cabbage floated on the surface but I couldn't see it so well—actual daylight was streaming down through the open ceiling and I was blinded by real illumination after spending so long in the tunnel and the pumphouse.

A mummy—an actual Egyptian mummy, with filthy bandages dangling from its limbs—picked up Jack by one foot and wrapped a pair of police handcuffs around his ankle while he hung in midair. I made a mental note—mummies were very, very strong. Not that I expected to live long enough to use that information. The other end of the handcuffs was attached to a hook hanging from a chain that stretched away up into the light. The chain was retracted a few feet and Jack was left dangling like a side of beef on a meat hook. He wasn't moving at all. Blood fell from him in a thick rivulet that ran down his left arm and splashed on the floor. I couldn't look at him. If he was still alive he must be in agony. If he was dead he wouldn't be for long.

I looked back down at the cabbage-sized thing in the pool. It opened up a pair of very bloodshot eyes. It smiled at me. It was Gary's head. "Hi," he said.

I looked to my left and my right. The dead had stepped back away from me—as if they were presenting a meal to their master. I pitched myself forward, my hands like claws, intending to dig out Gary's eyes or something. Just hurt him, any way I could. I had come a long way from the peace-loving civil servant he'd met in Union Square. He was about to find out just how far.

Gary stood up in his bathtub with a noise like breakers on the beach and reached out one hand to slap me to the floor. My breath exploded out of my lungs and spots swam before my eyes. I looked up and saw the hand that brought me down. It was like one of those oversized foam hands you get at sporting events. It was enormous, the individual fingers as thick as saplings. Gary was naked, his body a rippling mass of fat and dead veins. Corpse-flavored gelatin stuffed into lumpy sausage casings that threatened to split open at any moment.

He was seven and a half feet tall. He was six feet wide. He must have weighed a thousand pounds. His head hadn't grown at all. It looked tiny, a wart growing out of his shoulders, his neck submerged under rolls of fat. He glanced down at himself.

"Between-meal snacks," he explained.

Chapter Sixteen

The infamous Jack hung from the galleries, his motionless body twisting now this way, now that. The blood that had spurted from his arteries was barely trickling out now. In his mind's eye Gary could see the golden energy of his life, once fierce and self-contained, turning to wisps of wan smoke, his body barely warmer than the air around him.

A drop of blood fell from his dangling left hand and struck the flagstones with a soft spattering sound.

"So. . . I win," Gary said, not really sure what that meant. He sloshed backward into the welcoming embrace of his bath. His weight had become an issue of late—his bones complained when he stood up and forced them to accommodate all that extra fat tissue. It felt far better to just lie back in the formalin and let his natural buoyancy hold him up. "It's over." It had been fifteen minutes since the last rocket-propelled grenade struck the broch. Ayaan must be out of ammunition. Dekalb and Jack were accounted for. The prisoners, according to Noseless, were scared but calm. In the entirety of New York City no one remained to challenge him. "I win," he said again. He wanted to hear it, though. He wanted Dekalb to believe it, too.

Another drop of blood fell. Drip.

Dekalb's jaw shook as he opened his mouth to speak. He visibly forced the words out. "I suppose you do. So just finish me already. Eat me now and put me out of my misery."

Gary grinned and rested his hands across his swollen belly. "No," he said.

". . . no?"

"No." Gary nodded at Jack where the Army Ranger had turned as pale as a sheet. Drip. Drip. "He's about to die. When he does he'll come back—as one of mine. Then I'm going to let him eat you." Gary smiled happily. "It'll be awesome."

Drip.

Dekalb's stomach quaked, the muscles under his blood-soaked shirt moving violently as his chest heaved with fear. He would be having trouble controlling his bowels, Gary thought. He might shit himself. That would be amusing. This was the man who wouldn't so much as speak up when Ayaan had shot Gary in the head. He was going to suffer a lot.

Dekalb ran his hands down his front, trying to smooth away the shaking. Or perhaps he was trying to wipe the sweat off his palms. He pushed his hands across his pockets and seemed to find something there. His wallet? His house keys? Something safe, comfortable, reassuring. Some false hope. His eyes were slits, though, hurt, lost and impotent. "You. . . you don't have to do that. You didn't have to do any of this—Gary, there's still a chance. You can turn this around. Save the day."

"Oh, really?" Gary sneered.

"Yeah." Dekalb sat down cross-legged on the lip of Gary's tub and rubbed at his face. "You could. . . you control the dead. You could march them all into the ocean if you wanted. You could save us. You could save the human race."

Drip.

Gary drew his head under the preserving fluid for a moment. Felt it fill his mouth, his nose, the labyrinth of his sinus cavity. He reared upward again and let the liquid drip out of his face before he went on. "The human race. The living, you mean—the people who hate me. Who can't stand to look at me. Why is that, Dekalb? Why do I disgust you so much? Give me an honest answer to that, at least."

At least the enemy thought before answering. "Because you're just like us. You can talk, you can think—the restless dead out there, your army, we can look at them and think they're just monsters. They don't know what they're doing. But you chose this."

"I chose it," Gary repeated. He hadn't considered that— he'd always seen himself as a victim of circumstance. Pushed along by events until he ended up on top of them.

"You're human—you might as well be human. And you eat other humans. There's nothing complex about it. It's the oldest taboo in the book. You're a cannibal."

Gary's stomach roiled at the thought. A dozen defenses for his actions sprung to his mind but he abandoned them at once—they were false. Dekalb was right; He had chosen to be who he was. It changed nothing. Anger clawed its way out of Gary's chest and into his mouth. He felt like spitting. "You still don't get it, Dekalb. I'm not the villain

345

here. I'm not a fucking monster. People have been trying to kill me almost since the day I was reborn—Ayaan and her Girl Scout troop from hell. Marisol, and because of Marisol, Jack over there. You came here to kill me today. There were others you don't even know about—one guy I thought was my friend, or at least my teacher. He tried to kill me, yeah. But why? Because I'm unclean, unnatural? Because I'm evil? I'm not any of those things. I'm just hungry," Gary roared. "I have a right to exist, a right to stay alive as long as I can and that means I have to eat. That means I have a right to eat."

Drip.

"You can judge me all you want but here we are. I win. I'm going to live forever—and you're going to die."

Drip.

Jack's body began to convulse, the muscles staging a final protest. He quivered on his line, his shoulder smacking against the wall and sending him spinning. His mouth opened and a liquid cry of horror came out, a raw, wet animal sound that trailed off into a rattle. Partly the symphony of the damned and partly the wail of a newborn baby.

Vomit flowed out of his nose and mouth. His chest gave one last spasmodic heave and then he just stopped. His systems shut down. He died.

"You have about a minute before he reanimates," Gary suggested, both of them staring at the brand-new corpse. "Any last requests?"

Dekalb laughed, a bitter explosive sound. He reached into his pocket and grabbed something there. Gary stirred but relaxed when he saw what Dekalb had found—a hand-rolled cigarette and a pack of matches.

"I didn't know you smoked," Gary giggled.

"If I'm going to start now I'd better hurry." He tucked the cigarette between his lips and opened the matchbook. "Osman—you never met him—gave this to me before I left Governors Island. He said it would relax me. Maybe it'll make it less painful to be eaten alive. But that would ruin your fun, wouldn't it?"

Gary lifted one dripping arm in a dismissive gesture. "I'm not a complete asshole. Go for it. A last act of mercy."

"Thanks." Dekalb tore one of the paper matches free and put the head against the striking strip on the matchbook cover. "By the way, somebody owes you an apology."

"Oh?"

Dekalb nodded, his absurd joint bobbing in his mouth. "Yeah. Your teachers in med school. They forgot to tell you that formalin is highly flammable." The match struck and lit with a tiny hiss. Dekalb snapped it away from himself in a fluttering arc that dropped it right into Gary's bathtub.

Chapter Seventeen

The flammable liquid ignited all at once with a great FFFHWOOMPing noise as all the air in the room was sucked into the conflagration. A fireball of incredible light and heat shot upward through the open ceiling while everything in the room tried to catch fire at once. I raised my arms to protect my face as fire roared out at me even as I tried to catch my breath. My feet left the floor and everything turned over on me and I could feel the hair on my forearms curl and singe. I lowered my arms and found myself on my back.

Painfully I sat up until I could see Gary again. He had become a pillar of molten flame. His enormous overstuffed body shook convulsively as burning fat seeped from his broken skin and dribbled down his limbs like candle wax.

As I stared—and believe me, I was staring, there was a brutal hypnotic quality about the horror before me that would not let me go—he struggled to recover himself, to regain control of his body. The pain. . . I can't describe the pain he felt. No one could, no one living. Human beings don't ever experience being burned to death, not the same way Gary did. Even when we're burned at the stake we are spared the worst. We inhale a little smoke and pass out from asphyxiation.

The dead don't breathe. They don't faint, either. Gary was dying in the most excruciating way possible but he was not allowed the mercy of unconsciousness. I could see him trying to regain control of his rebel body, to fight through the pain. His hands flexed, his arms came down. He was trying to grab something. Anything. Me.

I barely rolled out of the way as a massive burning arm slammed down on the flagstones beside me. I could feel the hot wind coming from Gary; I could feel the superheated air displaced by his strike. My feet pushed hard to get underneath me; my arms flexed to lift me off the ground. If I didn't get up to a standing posture in the next second I was doomed.

Gary swung around, his arms extended like clubs, the light they gave off dazzling me as I slipped just under his grasp and came up with my back against the wall. He pulled back an arm and tried to punch me with an enormous burning fist but I managed to dodge. The punch collided with the wall and shattered the bricks there.

I had a moment of safety. Gary was blind—the fire had turned his eyeballs to cooked blobs of jelly. He cast about this way and that trying to find me in his personal darkness. I decided not to give him the chance.

I turned and ran and slipped into a corridor leading out of the tub room—and found myself face to face with a dead man in scorched denim overalls. I had forgotten about Gary's personal guards. This one didn't seem pleased at all by what I'd done to his master. His broken hands grabbed at my shirt and his mouth came open, his teeth angling for my shoulder. I reared back, trying to break his grip but it was no use—he'd gotten his index finger tangled in one of my belt loops. The best strategy I could think of was to knock him into Gary's bathtub, hopefully setting him alight. But if I had tried that I would have been pulled in right after him.

The dead man's jaw stretched open wide, preparing for the bite, when something truly surprising happened. Whatever animating spark, whatever life force I could find in Overalls' eyes (and there wasn't much) drained out of him. His eyes rolled back in his head and his knees buckled. Lifeless, twice dead, he slid down beside me and nearly yanked me off my feet.

A dead woman with cornrows in her hair appeared to replace him, but she dropped dead before she could even touch me. Good thing. I was still busy trying to untangle Overalls from my belt loop.

I got free and ran—just ran as fast as I could, with no idea where I was going. I came to the bottom of a flight of stairs and tried to remember whether the dead had dragged me down or up when they took me out of the pumphouse. I was still standing there in indecision, desperate to get out of the dark fortress, when I heard footsteps from above coming toward me. Two sets of footsteps. One slow, measured, rhythmic, the other jumbled and chaotic as if someone with no coordination at all was trying to keep pace. I'd heard footsteps like that before, in the hospital in the Meatpacking District. That had not ended well.

There was no place to hide and I had no weapons. I would have died, no question, if the creatures coming down the stairs had wanted to take my life. Lucky for me they didn't.

A mummy with a blue ceramic pendant dangling from

her neck appeared out of the gloom. She—I could see rough angular shapes like breasts and hips under her tangled linen wrappings—led one of the dead behind her, a man with no nose. Just a gaping red hole in the middle of his face.

Three steps above me they stopped in unison, in a way that suggested they were in close communication. She placed her hands on opposite sides of his head and pressed hard as she leaned her forehead against his. The dead man made a strange dry sucking noise, raspy and painful-sounding, that had to be him drawing breath in through his wound. When he spoke it was clear to me somehow that it was not his own voice I heard, but that of someone else, speaking through him.

"He's not so much in his right mind anymore, our Gary. He can't hold his end up, if you catch me right. This place'll be crawling with the dead anytime now. I'm guessing you don't want to be here then."

I licked my lips. "Well, yeah," I said.

"Come with me then, lad. There's work to be done," he said. The mummy stepped past me, dragging her pet dead man behind her. When he couldn't keep up she picked him up and carried him in her arms, his dead limbs dangling, his mouth slack and open and toothless. She moved quickly, far more quickly than any of the dead I'd seen so far, and it was difficult to keep up in some of the narrower passages we had to crawl through. I must have run in exactly the wrong direction when I left Gary's tub room. If it wasn't for my Egyptian guide, I would never have found my way out.

Eventually we emerged into bright daylight and fresh air. I didn't realize until I got some clean air into my lungs just how much soot I had inhaled. Gary's fortress was burning—the plume of smoke trailing from the top of his tower was shot through with sparks. I didn't care too much about that. There was no point in going back inside.

I did care about the fact that the mummy had brought me out onto a lawn of scruffy-looking plants surrounded by quaint brick houses. Gary's stockyards, where the prisoners lived. I called out Marisol's name until I started coughing, my scorched esophagus protesting vigorously against any further speech.

Doors and windows opened in the houses and terrified faces looked out at me. As I stood there wondering what to say to these people Marisol came running up to me with a chipped teacup. It was full of water that I gulped down with gratitude.

Marisol gave the mummy one quick glance and got over any surprise she might have felt at the Egyptian woman's presence. I suppose she must have seen lots of dead people during her time of imprisonment.

"Where's Jack?" Marisol asked.

Jack. Sure. Jack, who as far as I knew was at that moment hanging upside down by one foot in Gary's tub room. Dead. Hungry. Unable to get down. "He didn't make it," I told her. No point in going into the details.

She slapped me hard across my cheek.

"Okay." I sat down hard on the patchy grass.

"That's for getting him killed. Now. What the hell is going on? Is Gary dead? Please tell me that Gary is dead."

I nodded. No point in telling her I wasn't sure. I mean, I didn't want to get slapped again. "Yeah, he burned to death."

"Good. What's the plan?"

I thought about that for a while before answering. There had been a plan—then the plan fell apart. Except now maybe it might still work. "We have a helicopter coming. That fire should be all the signal our pilot needs. He'll be here in maybe ten minutes. Then we'll get you out of here. There's one problem, though."

"One problem? There's only one problem?" Marisol asked. "That makes this the best day ever!"

"Calm down, alright?" I stood up and handed the tea cup back to her, having caught my breath for the moment. "There's not enough room in the helicopter for all of us to go at once. But look—we're protected by this wall." I pointed at the fifteen-foot-tall brick wall that ran all the way around the stockyards. It butted up securely against the side of the fortress and was clearly designed to protect against undead attack. "We'll take the women and children first, then come back and make a second trip for the men."

Marisol bit her lip so hard it bled. I could see the blood. Then she nodded and grabbed me by one ear. She pulled hard and I could do nothing but follow her, protesting madly.

She took me all the way past one of the houses before releasing me. I stared at her, truly pissed off—I'd just risked everything to save her from Gary, after all. Then I looked up and saw what she was trying to communicate to me.

There was a fifteen-foot-wide gap in the wall—a place where Gary hadn't quite finished his construction job. There were tidy piles of bricks lying around, ready to be put in place, but no work crew around to finish the task.

Meanwhile, on the other side of that wall were perhaps a million dead people. A million dead people who hadn't eaten in days.

Chapter Eighteen

The dead don't run. They hobble. They limp. Some of them crawl. The faster ones trample those with fractured or missing legs. The stronger amongst them push the weaker to the side.

They make no noise when they walk, no noise at all.

They came at us like a wave, a wave of limbs and contorted faces, eyes wide, clouded and vacant, hands, fingers coming at us like the foam on the top of a breaker, fingers, claws, nails. Visually they were hard to look at, their details hard to discern, one dead thing difficult to tell from another. Their mouths were open, every one of them. They were too human and dispassionate to see as a herd of panicked animals, too animalistic and insatiable to think of as a crowd of people. They all wanted one thing: us.

When a mob is coming for you, there is no emotion except fear.

There was one of them—a woman in a dress that had been soiled and stained with blood and even burned, it looked like—a woman who was faster than the others. She strode boldly ahead of them and as she got close we saw there was no skin on her face or neck, just the twanging elastic bands of her facial muscles that snagged on her vicious-looking exposed teeth. Her eyes were dark pits under a thick gel of clotted blood like cold spaghetti sauce. Her hands reached for us, the fingers clenching again and again, her hair flowed out behind her in great tangled ropes.

Marisol picked up a broken brick. She squeezed it in her hand a couple of times and then with a little yell, "Hyah!" she flung it as hard as she could at the dead woman's face. It struck her square in the forehead, in the exposed skull. The dead woman collapsed into a heap, her head like broken pottery.

It broke the fear, a little. Enough.

Marisol and I began to grab bricks and shove them down in the dirt, trying to close the hole in the few minutes we had before the dead arrived. It was pointless busywork, of course, but it was better than panicking. "Marisol—go get—the rest—to help," I gasped, between bricks. She nodded at me and turned around to head to the houses behind us. She didn't get any further than a step or two, though. When I saw why I dropped the brick I was holding.

The mummy was there—the one who led me out of the fortress. She held the dead man with no nose on her lap like a mother tending a sick child.

"What do you want?" I demanded. "What are you?"

The voice that spoke to me gurgled out of the dead man's throat, an affectless growl that belonged to neither him nor the mummy who clutched him. It belonged to Mael, of course, Gary's teacher, but I had no way of knowing that at the time. He hardly bothered to introduce himself. "What am I? Just bits and pieces, is all, odds and orts and not enough of them to add up. I'm no harm to you. Quite powerless on my own. Then again, I might be a help."

I stared into the dead man's eyes. "Listen, I don't have time for this." I gestured for Marisol to get the others, to keep filling in the hole. She ignored my waving hand and stared at the mummy.

"I do. I've all the time in the world, lad. More time than I want, to be frank. I have a certain accommodation with the fine lady of Egypt you see here. Her and her mates. Now I can't lift a finger to aid you, seeing as I haven't any. I'm fully bodiless right now, to the extent I had to borrow this poor bloke's mouth. Milady has a real talent for knocking heads, though. Are you interested in hearing more, lad, or should I piss off and leave you to your bricklaying?"

I had seen how strong the mummies were. How many of them could there be, though? Hardly enough to take on the crowd of dead people outside the wall. They might slow the walking corpses down. It might help.

Still. I'd come this far by knowing not to trust the dead. "You obviously want something in return. Help us and we'll talk about it."

Marisol kicked me in the shin. "He means he'll do whatever you ask." She stared at me and mouthed the words "Hey, asshole." Then she jerked her head in the direction of the dead mob, maybe five minutes away from us at their current speed.

I guess she had a point.

The dead man smiled. "It's nothing you'll mind doing. It's just finishing what you started. I'm a two-time loser, friend. I sacrificed myself to save the world, and I failed at dying. I tried to oversee the end of the world, but I was no good at being dead. What comes after that? What's more important than the end of the world, I'd like to know? There's got to be something for me still, because I'm not allowed to just die. Do you ken it now? I've been shivered down to fragments of what I was. I can't rest until they're reunited. And I think you know who's holding the best of me."

"No—I have no idea what you're talking about," I confessed.

The dead man's eyes rolled in their sockets. One of them got stuck showing only white. "Gary, you oaf! Finish him off! Until he's well and truly dead I'll never sleep easy! He ate me—bit into my head like a melon, and now he's got half my soul in his belly. Free me and I'll save all your friends."

"Gary's still alive?" I asked.

"You said he was dead," Marisol insisted. Well, I had said that. I'd believed it, too, mostly. I shrugged.

I'd set him on fire. Burned him alive, or undead, or whatever. Then again, I'd also seen him take a bullet in the head and he'd come back from that.

I glanced over at Gary's fortress. It was still smoking, though I couldn't see any more sparks shooting out of its top. I was unarmed and already exhausted. If I didn't do this, though, he would just come back. Over and over again, forever, until everyone I knew and loved and cared about was dead. Including myself.

"Don't wait for me if I don't come back out in time," I told Marisol.

"Okay." She nodded enthusiastically.

Just as I began to move the mummy punched the dead man so hard in the face that his head collapsed. I might have shrieked a little to see that. The mummy ignored me. I guess my conversation with the ghost was over. She climbed over our pathetic attempts to fill the hole in the wall to stand outside, her arms crossed, waiting for the dead to come. From inside the fortress other mummies emerged—maybe a dozen of them in total. They moved far more quickly than the dead ought to. I gave them a wide berth on my way back inside.

Once inside the fortress it wasn't hard to find Gary's tub room. I just followed the smell of overdone bacon. Smoke filled the open space at the center of the tower, an oily, nasty fuming smoke that smudged my clothes where it touched me. Everything in the big room was covered in a thin film of fatty soot. Human beings didn't belong in a place like that but I did. I had to be there. I stepped closer and peered into the gloom of the empty bathtub. The bricks were spalled by the intense heat of the fire, some of them pulverized by the blast. A pool of molten fat in the center of the tub still bubbled and flickered with tiny flames.

What was left of Gary leaned up against the rim, one sagging shoulder pressed hard against the bricks. Gary's legs were nothing but scorched sticks of bone that stuck out from the charred mass of his abdomen. They looked like the legs of a stork, perhaps. Something of his torso remained and his arms, clublike appendages that were curled across his chest. His head was still smoldering. It had sustained less damage than the rest of him—the one part of his body that hadn't been made mostly of combustible fat. His eyes were gone, as well as his ears and nose, but I could sense somehow he was still in there.

"Dekalb," he coughed. "Come to gloat?" His voice was

nothing but a dry rasp.

"Not exactly."

"Come closer. I'm glad for the company in my last couple of minutes, I guess. Come on. I don't bite. Not anymore."

I figured I could handle him now by myself. The voice—the ghost, or whatever it had been—had told me Gary could no longer control the undead. It would just be the two of us. At least, that's what I was thinking when I stepped closer to the tub. Then I heard a rattling noise like a length of chain being dropped from a height. Exactly like that, in fact. Jack must have climbed up his own chain—then laid in wait, in ambush, for somebody, anybody, to walk directly underneath him.

He was on my back, his legs wrapped around my waist, his teeth in my neck. His fingers grabbed at my face, one of them sinking into my left nostril and tearing, ripping at the flesh there. I shook back and forth, desperately trying to dislodge him as warm blood ran down my already-stained shirt. I heaved backward, unable to catch my breath, my body still stunned by the force of impact. No, I thought. No. I'd come so far, so far without getting badly injured, without being killed—

"Sucker!" Gary chortled, without lifting his head.

Chapter Nineteen

I threw myself backward, knocking Jack against the wall, trying to crack his spine, trying to break his hold on my face. It only made him more determined. Jack had been a lot stronger than me in life. In death he was strong and relentless. He wrapped a forearm around my throat and pulled, trying to break my neck. He succeeded in pinching my windpipe shut.

I swung around wildly, my hands pulling at the legs he had wrapped around my waist. I might as well have tried to bend iron. The little air in my lungs turned to carbon dioxide but I couldn't exhale. Suddenly dark stars were spinning in my vision, sparkles of light like signal fires, one each for the neurons dying in my head as I asphyxiated. I lost it, lost all reason at that point and just panicked. Without a thought in my head I dashed forward, away from the thing on my back, my subconscious mind unable to realize that it was still attached. Jack's grip on me merely tightened as my feet dug for purchase in the brick floor. Like a mule pulling a plow I tried to pull away from him.

Anoxia distorted my hearing—the sound of my heart beating was a lot louder than the noise of Jack's vertebrae cracking inside his neck. He let go of me in a sudden and unexpected way and I slumped forward, catching myself on my hands, saliva streaming from my mouth as my body heaved for air. Not so much breathing as swallowing oxygen, gulping it down. I tried very hard not to throw up. If I had I would surely have aspirated something and drowned in my own vomit.

My eyes hurt, the tiny blood vessels inside them burst open by the fury of Jack's assault. I blinked them madly to get some tears going and then turned to sit down and touch my throat tenderly, trying to soothe the burning flesh there. I looked up.

I did a double take when I saw what had saved me. Jack hung from his chain, the links wrapped tight around his throat. Tight enough to be buried in his deliquescent flesh. Somehow while waiting to ambush me he'd gotten tangled up in the chain. It probably hadn't bothered him—he had no need to breathe—until the constricting pressure had shattered the bones in his neck. His body dangled limply in the coils of the chain like so much cast-off clothing.

His head remained animate. His eyes stared hard at me. His lips moved in anticipation of one more bite of my flesh. I looked away.

Then I realized I was bleeding to death. I looked down at my chest and the fresh blood that covered me. I reached up two trembling fingers and felt out the contours of my wound. Jack had bitten me very close to a major artery. He'd taken a chunk out of my body, out of the back of my neck. I could stick two fingers in the wound. I tore a strip off of my shirt and jammed it into the gaping hole—anything to stop the flow of blood.

"Oh, man, that was too good," Gary laughed as I

clutched the bandage to my neck. "Do you get it now, Dekalb? The human race is over and you living guys came in last place! You can't compete, man. You don't even qualify."

I lurched to my feet, one hand on the rough brick wall to steady myself. I got a pretty bad head rush just standing up. A definite bad sign. I walked over to the tub and stepped down onto the cracked floor.

"You can't destroy me, asshole. You can shoot me in the head and you can burn me to the ground but it doesn't matter. I can repair myself—rebuild myself!" Gary's mutilated head rocked against the bricks as he spoke. "I'm invincible!"

I kicked at his neck until his head came away from his body and rolled away on the floor.

I wasn't quite done. It took me a while to find the pumphouse again but it was necessary. I needed a bag and I needed to make sure the VX cylinders weren't going to go off on their own. In the fading light of the glowsticks I peeled the plastic explosives off the canisters. I disassembled the detonator and broke the parts, scattering them around the room. I buried the cylinders under some loose bricks. There wasn't much else I could do—you can't just dump nerve agents into the sewer system or throw them in a landfill but at least this way no wandering dead guy would unleash the chemical weapons by accident.

There was another weapon of mass destruction to consider. I didn't like it but I would have to take it with me. I emptied out one of the heavy packs that Jack and I had brought to the fortress and stuffed Gary's head inside. I believed him when he said he could eventually regenerate himself, that he could survive anything. I could crush the head to a fine paste but even that might not be enough—after all, he had survived being shot in the brain. By keeping the head with me I knew I would be able to kill him again if he came back. As many times as it took.

Jack's Glock 9mm went into my pocket. It wasn't much but it was a weapon and obscenely enough its presence made me feel safe. That was something I needed. My injuries made me feel as if any second I might just collapse.

By the time I was ready to leave the fortress my breathing had become labored and my vision was shot. When I staggered out into the daylight I was momentarily blinded. What I finally saw cheered me up a lot. An orange and white blur hovering in the air. Coast Guard colors—that would be Kreutzer. Oh, thank God. He had come. I had half-expected him to take the Chinook to Canada. Something yellow hung beneath the helicopter but I couldn't quite focus enough to make it out.

By the time I reached the lawn between the houses Marisol already had the survivors lining up to get on board the chopper. Rotor wash from the Chinook cleared the blur out of my eyes and I saw the look on her face. It was one of total disbelief—and hope. I'd never seen her look like that before.

I ran to the hole in the wall and saw thousands of dead men just outside, impatient in their lust for food, being held back by six mummies. Just six. The Egyptians had their arms linked where they stood side by side in the gap, their backs to me. The collective weight of hundreds of dead men and women pressed against them but they held fast, kicking back those who tried to climb between their legs. I saw the female mummy—the one I'd spoken to—head-butt a dead boy and send him flying.

Out there in the midst of the dead, though—one of them stood head and shoulders above the rest. Literally. A giant making his way toward the line of mummies. He batted the other ghouls away from him like flies as he approached. Whether the mummies could stand against his onslaught was still an open question.

Enough—I didn't have any time left to worry. That line would hold. It had to. I turned around and saw the helicopter with clear vision as it made its descent. The yellow blur beneath it turned out to be a school bus attached to the Chinook's undercarriage by three steel cables. Kreutzer put the bus down gently—well, it rocked badly as its tires popped one by one, but at least it didn't turn over—and then dropped in for a landing twenty feet to the right, the cables draped along the ground. He popped the ramp at the rear of the chopper and living people stormed on board, Marisol screaming at them to keep the line orderly and neat. "Women and children first!" she screamed, "and no fucking shoving!" Other people clambered into the bus through the back emergency door. The line of survivors waiting to get seats never seemed to end but without really thinking about what I was doing I found myself bringing up the tail of the line, calling out to Marisol to see if she'd done a head count.

"That's all of them," she screamed back over the noise of the helicopter. "Every last one!"

(I would speak with Kreutzer later about how he knew to go and fetch the bus, how he knew that there wasn't going to be enough room in the helicopter for everybody. "I was in the systems motherfucking directorate of the USCG, you know?" he swore at me, as if that should explain everything. "The computer techs. We're good at math!" He had figured out how many people could fit in an empty Chinook and decided that we would come up short. I never really liked the guy but I have to admit that was some excellent thinking on his part.)

I watched Marisol climb into the back of the helicopter and then I clambered into the bus, using the front entrance. There was barely room for me to stand on the steps. A truly nice couple of survivors offered to give up their space for me in the aisle but I declined. As the bus lifted into the air, its metal frame creaking alarmingly and its suspension falling apart and dropping from the undercarriage as if the floor might give way at any minute I wanted to be able to look outside.

I wanted one last look at the city, that's all. I barely glanced at the mob of dead people below us as the mummies gave way and they surged into the fortress, two million hands raising to try to grab at us as we flew away. That wasn't what I was looking for. I wanted the water towers. I wanted the fire escapes and the overgrown rooftop gardens and the dovecotes and the ventilation hoods like spinning chef's toques. I wanted the buildings, the great square solidity of them, their countless empty cubical rooms where no one would ever go again and I wanted the streets too, the streets clogged with cars with abandoned taxis sprouting everywhere like bright fungi. I wanted one long, meaningful look at New York City. My hometown.

I knew it would be my last chance to get a good look. My body was already burning with fever, my forehead slick with sweat though chills kept running down my back like ice cubes falling. My head was light, my tongue coated.

I was dying.

Chapter Twenty

Dear Sarah,

I guess I'm not coming back to you.

I guess I'll never see you again. The thought is too big to deal with right now.

I may not have enough time left to finish this letter.

Yesterday Ayaan hugged me on the roof of the Museum of Natural History, but I could feel the hesitation in her embrace. She could see in my eyes what was going to happen.

No matter, I told her. We were almost done.

My fever had abated. It came and went in waves, and I was feeling pretty lucid. I had developed a new symptom, a kind of queasy rumbling in my guts but I could keep that to myself. I asked her what it had been like, up there on top of the planetarium, and she showed me.

In the last minutes of the siege, just before Jack shot at me and Gary realized that he was being set up, the Museum of Natural History had been attacked by a million corpses with their bare hands. Many, many of them had been crushed as they put their shoulders to the metal frame of the building, their weight added to the pile. I didn't bother to look over the side and thus see what trampled ghouls looked like. The dead had wreaked so much damage on the planetarium that the roof we stood on slanted to one side and Kreutzer could barely keep the Chinook from rolling over the edge. We wasted no time getting the girls on board and getting out of there, even abandoning some of the heavier weapons and supplies. We were airborne in five minutes and headed straight for the United Nations complex on the far side of the city.

"Gary's dead." I filled Ayaan in on what had happened in her absence, shouting over the Chinook's engines. I left out most of the grisly details. "I still don't know if the mummies were leading me into Gary's trap or if they were being sincere. Either way, they saved the day. We took the survivors back to Governors Island—Marisol's going to build something there, something safe and meaningful." Ayaan nodded, not terribly interested in my story, and stared out one of the porthole-like windows. I wrapped my hand through a nylon loop sewn into the ceiling of the cabin to steady myself and moved closer so I didn't have to yell. "So I'm sorry."

"Why is that?" she asked. Her thoughts were elsewhere.

"You didn't get to martyr yourself."

That got a bright little grin out of her. "There are many ways to serve Allah," she said. I'd like to remember Ayaan that way. The light from the porthole blasting across her shoulder. Sitting with her hands in her lap, one knee bouncing up and down in anticipation. When Ayaan got truly excited she couldn't sit still. She thought it a weakness but to me it meant so much. It meant she was human, not a monster.

We set down in the North Garden of the UN, a patch

of green just off First Avenue that had been closed to the public since September Eleventh. The girls deployed from the Chinook's rear ramp in standard battle order but it looked as if Gary had been true to his word, which surprised me a little. There weren't even any undead pigeons to bother us. I led the girls to the white security tent at the visitor's entrance, past the "NonViolence" sculpture which takes the form of an enormous pistol with its barrel tied in a knot. They didn't know what to make of it. A world without guns to them is a world that can't protect itself. Before the Epidemic began I used to fight that attitude.

Oh God—there's a pain, shit! Motherfucker! A pain in my head and I—

Sorry—I'm back. It took an hour to get the power going—I'm not an electrical engineer. Sweaty, bruised and half blind in the dimness of a bunker under the security tent, I got the emergency generators going and the whole complex came to life, a random pattern of lights appearing on the surface of the Secretariat Building, the fountain out front spitting out a ten-foot plume of greenish scum. Thank God there was still fuel in the reservoir. I had dreaded the idea of searching for the drugs in pitch darkness the way I had done at St. Vincent.

Inside the General Assembly Building I stopped and had to take a breath. It was strange to be back in a place where I used to have an office—that life was removed from me not only in space and time, but also by a psychological breadth I don't think I could measure. The soaring Jet Age architecture of the lobby with its terraced balconies and—how pointlessly heartbreaking now—its model of Sputnik, hanging by wires from the ceiling, spoke of not just a different era, but a different kind of humanity, one that had actually thought we could all get along, that the world could be as one.

Of course, the UN of my experience had been riddled with corruption and class snobbery but it still managed to do some good. It fed some of the hungry, tried to keep the lid on genocide. It at least felt guilty when it failed in Rwanda. All that was gone now. We were back to the state of nature, red in tooth and claw.

We passed the personalized stamp shop on our way to the Secretariat Building, a place where tourists used to be able to get their picture put on a sheet of legal, usable stamps. I barely gave it a glance but Fathia called out a sharp warning and suddenly the cold air of the lobby exploded with noise and light. I dove behind a leather-upholstered bench. When I looked up I saw what had happened. The shop's camera was set up to display a video picture of everyone who walked past as an enticement to the public. When the girls walked past they had seen their own images reversed on the screen, seeming to move toward them. Naturally they had assumed the worst: active ghouls. The video monitor was a heap of sparking shards by the time they were done.

Sarah—will you even remember television when you're grown? I would have let you watch more American sitcoms if I knew it wasn't going to become a habit.

My hand is shaking almost spastically and I'm not sure you'll be able to read my handwriting. I know you'll never see this, anyway. I'm writing for myself, not my far-flung daughter. Pretending this is a letter to you helps me keep you in my mind's eye, that's all. It gives me a reason to keep going.

Please. Let me live long enough to finish this letter.

Anyway. There isn't much more to tell.

On the fifth floor of the Secretariat Building we found the drugs exactly where I'd thought they would be. There was a complete dispensary up there, as well as a miniature surgical theater and a fully functional doctor's office. The pills we needed were lined up carefully on a shelf in a row of plastic jug after plastic jug. Epivir. Ziagen. Retrovir. There were so many that the girls had to take them out fire-brigade style. One by one they filed into the elevators and out of the building. Fathia took the last four jugs in her arms and turned to address Ayaan, who hadn't lifted a finger.

"*Kaalay*!"

"*Dhaqso.*"

"*Deg-deg*!" Fathia implored and then she, too, was gone. Ayaan and I were alone.

I could hear my labored breath in the cramped dispensary. "I hope it won't sound condescending if I tell you how proud I am of—" I stopped as she unlimbered her weapon.

One of her eyes was open quite wide. The other one was hidden behind the leaf sights of her AK-47. The barrel was lined up with my forehead. I could see every tiny dent and shiny scratch on the muzzle. I watched it wobble back and forth as she switched the rifle from SAFE to SINGLE SHOT.

"Please put that away," I said. I'd kind of been expecting this.

"Be a man, Dekalb. Order me to shoot. You know it is the only way."

I shook my head. "There are drugs here—antibiotics—

that might help me. Even just sterile bandages and iodine could make a difference. You have to give me a chance."

"Give me the order!" she shouted.

I couldn't let it happen like that. I couldn't bear it, to go out like that. Like one of them. Her weapon should be used for putting down the undead, not for taking a human life.

No, that wasn't it. I'll be honest. I just didn't want to die. Gary had told Marisol once about his days as a doctor, about the dying people he'd seen who would beg and plead for just one more minute of life. I understood those people in a way I could not understand Ayaan or Mael and their willingness to sacrifice everything for what they believed in. The only thing I believed in at that moment with that rifle pointed at me was myself.

My generation was like that, Sarah. Selfish and scared. We convinced ourselves that the world was kind of safe and it made us make bad choices. I'm not so worried about you anymore, or your generation. You will be warriors, strong and fierce.

I reached up and touched the barrel with one finger. She roared at me, literally roared at me like a lion, summoning up the courage to kill me regardless of my wishes. I held the barrel in my hand and I swung it away from me.

When I looked at her eyes again she was weeping. She left without another word.

I didn't follow her, of course. I wouldn't be going back to Somalia. I wasn't going anywhere. It was too late for antibiotics, too late for anything. Still. I wasn't ready to just give up. I sat down on the floor and rubbed my face with my hands and thought about what had happened, and what was going to happen, for a long time.

At one point my leg went numb, and I struggled up to a standing posture with much cursing and falling down and a little bit of crying. I kept hoping to shake off the numbness. I fully expected the pins-and-needles feeling you get when your circulation comes back. It didn't come.

Just to have something to do I found a yellow legal pad and a pen and started writing this down. I wrote down everything that has happened, as it happened, since I left you behind, Sarah. It took me hours. My leg is still numb. The lights flickered every once in a while, and I worried I would be cast into darkness for my last hours. So far I'm good, but, ugh, hold on—

I threw up blood just now. My body is breaking down.

Please, doctor. Just one more hour. Just one more minute.

Just. . .

Okay, I'm back, Sarah. I needed to black out there for a while. Now I'm back and I'm feeling a lot better, a little light-headed and forgetful, perhaps. Kind of hungry. Better enough that I can finish this letter even though I'm having a lot of trouble holding the pen now. I have Gary's head on the table in front of me, watching me as I write. It doesn't move or anything, but it doesn't need to. He's in there hating me, hating Ayaan, hating Mael. Blaming everybody for his downfall except himself. He's just like me, Sarah. Both of us looked death in the face, comforting, appropriate, timely death and both of us said no because we were scared.

You're probably wondering something, or you would be if you were actually reading this. You're probably wondering how I can know what he's thinking. How I could write all those passages from his point of view, describing things I never saw or experienced.

Maybe you think I made it all up.

Or maybe you already know. Maybe you know that the room next door to the dispensary is an emergency-care ward. A room full of hospital beds and all the emergency medical equipment necessary to keep someone alive until they can be moved to a real hospital.

Equipment like ventilators and dialysis machines.

Please. Give me just one more minute.

Coming Summer 2007

MONSTER NATION

Learn how it all began...

Turn the page for an
exclusive preview.

From Monster Nation...

Here's what she had:

She was dressed all in white. Drawstring pants, halter top, linen jacket. Sandals and sunglasses, with her short blonde hair pulled back in a tight bun. A niobium stud in her nose and a tribal tattoo around her belly button, a sun with wavy triangular rays that flashed every so often as her top rode up and down with the rhythm of her walking.

She felt good: she was smiling, swaying her hips a little more than she needed to. She remembered wanting to slip her sandals off and feel the rough rasp of the sidewalk with her feet.

How much of this recollection could she trust? It was pretty threadbare and frayed around the edges. All the sounds she heard when she went back to this place were low and distorted. Oceanic vibrations. She couldn't smell anything. The light seemed to hang in the air in individual packets, stray photons pinned in place.

Worst of all there were no words. No names or signs. She bopped right past a stop sign but in this sunny space it was just a blank red octagon. Stop, she thought to herself. Stop, stop stop! The word wouldn't manifest.

Palm trees. Rollerbladers and homeless people

competing for sidewalk space. This was California, unless a million movies had steered her wrong. No place famous, just seedy and a little run-down in a charming multi-cultural way. A four way intersection with a food market selling Goya products, a free clinic, a boarded up storefront with no sign and some kind of bar. What she might be doing there she had no idea.

Time started up and the light moved again: with the scene set the action was ready to begin. At the intersection a Jeep Cherokee slurped up onto the curb and smacked into a stone bench with the sound of tin foil tearing and rattling. The car rocked on its tires, its windows the color of oil on water. Time hovered and danced around the scene like a bumblebee in search of nectar. Cubes of broken glass spun languorously in the air while clouds raced overhead in a fractured time lapse. She was frozen in place, in shock, in mid-stride. How much time passed? A minute? Fifteen seconds? The driver's door opened and a man in a blue western-style shirt tumbled out.

The look on his face made no sense at all.

He staggered a bit. Grabbed at the bench, at the hood of his car. He was having trouble walking, standing upright.

Of course she went to help him. She was supposed to—why? What was she? A doctor? A nurse? The belly tattoo and the nose ring made her think otherwise. Massage therapist? The look on his face: slack. His jaw didn't seem to close properly and his eyes weren't tracking. Stroke? Seizure? Heart attack? She had to help. It was an obligation, part of the social contract.

He was dead when she got to him.

The man was dead but he was still moving. An

impossibility, a singularity of biology. The point where normal rules no longer apply. The recollection began to break down at this point into raw sense-data. The synthetic fabric of his shirt where she touched it, the oils of his skin, the pure and unadulterated comfort of his arm as it crossed her back, holding her to him, hugging her—brother—father—boyfriend—husband—priest— something, some male presence, still welcome and good and wanted because she didn't know what was going on, just glad for the human contact in a scary moment when nothing quite worked the way it should.

The pain, intense and real, far more real than anything else in her memory, as thirty-two needles sank into her shoulder, into her skin, his teeth.

That's what she had. Everything else was torn away leaving ragged edges, bloody sockets. Her head was full of grimy windows she couldn't see through everywhere else she looked. Her memory was dead and rotting and it had left her only these few scant impressions. Everything else was gone.

For instance: she couldn't remember her name.

UNEXPECTED ENCOUNTERS

By

E. H. Clark

ISBN: 1-4140-5486-6 (e-book)
ISBN: 1-4140-5487-4 (Paperback)
ISBN: 1-4140-5488-2 (Hardcover)

Library of Congress Control Number: 2003099575

This book is printed on acid free paper.

Printed in the United States of America
Bloomington, IN

1stBooks - rev. 03/09/04